I0622415

Dedicated to my family.

Especially for Wayne,
Creator of Imaginary Places.

GIRL IN TWO WORLDS

PAMELA WAYNE

Pamela Wayne
Author

With the vision of inspiring young women to
discover their feminine mystique, Pamela's story
takes you into the two worlds of Julia Wainright,
a magical journey of empowerment and self-discovery.

www.PamelaWayne.com

www.MillenniumAdventures.com

www.Planet-Millennium.com

www.FreedomWithinFoundation.org

Deluxe Color Edition available!

Visit Pamela Wayne on:

YouTube   Facebook   Twitter

Cataloging In Publication Information

Wayne, Pamela.

Girl In Two Worlds / by Pamela Wayne.

ISBN B&W Edition: 13: 978-0-6159120-5-9   10: 0-6159120-5-2
ISBN Deluxe Edition: 13: 978-0-6159120-7-3   10: 0-6159120-7-9
ISBN Ebook Edition: 13: 978-0-9642022-5-2

1. Philosophy. 2. Fantasy / Science Fiction. 3. Spirituality.
4. Self-Actualization. 5. Esteem. I. Title.

Edited by Mel Wayne, Creator of Imaginary Places
A special thank you to our Creative Director, Clifford Robbins.

Illustrations and maps by Peka, Ignacio Abad Donado & Mel Wayne

∞ The characters and events in this book are fictitious. Any similarity to
real persons, living or dead, is coincidental and not intended by the author.

∞ No part of this publication may be reproduced or transmitted,
in any form or by any means, electronic, mechanical, or digital,
including photocopying, recording, digital download, or by any
known information system, without prior written permission
of the copyright owner.

Second Edition: Printed in the United States of America

Copyright ©2015 by Millennium Adventures™. All Rights Reserved

Table of Contents

Daynight of the Raven

Chapter I
Two Bodies

Ever since my twin brother fell into a coma, my world has been turned inside out and upside down, actually, *both* my worlds. I'm on another planet right now. I'm also living on Earth. Alive in two bodies.

My rebellious brother, Hunter, took my father's Triamulet and wore the gold necklace to bed, went to sleep, fell into a coma, and then he traveled to Millennium.

Before I get ahead of myself, I need to tell my story from the very beginning. Before my family had been torn apart. Before my world had been split in two.

My mother and father named me Julia.

Julia Rose.

We are the Wainright family, all thirteen of us. That's right, my parents decided to have eleven children.

Eleven!

I don't know what they were thinking.

As their oldest daughter, I became the *chosen one*. What that means is, my waking moments were spent helping Momma raise her house full of "rug rats", as Daddy often called them. My twin brother, Hunter, always got a pass when it came to helping with the chores.

Momma babied him.

Before you hear any more about my complicated family, you need to know that right now I'm on a planet called Millennium, a spectacular Earth-like planet within a binary star system located in the Andromeda Galaxy.

Just imagine, two suns. And six moons.

Aboard the wooden ship, *Skipbladnir*, Nyx and I are sailing the mysterious Sea of Circles toward Time Island. Nyx is a Utopian. We have just returned from an unforgettable journey in search of my brother, Hunter.

Nyx, who is a wise female sage, waits below deck with the ship's captain and crew. She has left me alone, here on the upper deck.

So I can think about my choice.

My decision.

She shouldn't be that concerned, I know what I'm doing. I've made the right decision. My thoughts are clear and purposeful as I fill my lungs with the fresh Millennium air.

While I wait for the her return, I gaze in amazement at the wonders of Millennium.

If only I had my camera to capture the spectacular scenery.

I stand on a ship, on the Sea of Circles, in a 150-mile-deep cauldron called the Discordia Crater by the native population. Its colossal falls of fire and ice descend from the heavens.

Like nothing you've ever imagined.

You wouldn't believe the atmosphere. Overhead, the sky is red. *Fiery* red. To the east, a black sky crawls toward our ship. To the west, a blue sky hugs the horizon.

Millennium is a gyro planet, with two unworldly red and black rings—cosmic dust and debris—spinning around her body every twenty-four hours. This is why the sky changes color, from blue to red to blue to black, every daynight.

Here's the weird part. For each daynight I'm here, fifty days pass me by on Earth. It's hard for me to accept that for every week on this planet, one year goes by at home.

Five daynights since my arrival.

Almost eight months away from my family.

You would think that being on another planet would be the ultimate high, the most incredible experience of a lifetime. Of course it is, but I've discovered something just as phenomenal, just as emotionally life-changing.

For the past five daynights on Millennium, I've experienced the most unbelievable dreams.

Real dreams.

Unworldly dreams that transcend time and space.

During my Dreamtime, as Nyx calls it, I find myself back on Earth, inside my comatose body observing my family. I am actually *there*.

My spirit—my soul—awakens within my body.

This might sound like a magical experience, but waking up in a coma can be frustrating because you want to move—get up and talk to your family; tell them you're okay.

Imagine you are comatose right now. Trapped inside a helpless, immobile form of yourself. It is such an enlightening, out-of-body experience. Your muscles and bones feel lifeless— but you can see, hear, smell, taste, and feel everything.

Lying in my hospital bed with the purple headboard, I watch my parents and my three brothers and six sisters live out their daily lives. Every sound, every word they say, becomes magnified. Momma's cooking smells so delicious. The fragrance of Monterey pines mixed with the ocean air is unmistakable.

Everyone likes to touch my face. Probably to see if I feel warm. You know, still alive.

Momma kisses both my cheeks and tells me how much she loves me.

Daddy sits by my bed and reads me stories from *Brothers Grimm Fairy Tales*.

My boyfriend visits me and talks to me and holds my hand.

I feel everything during my coma, both physical and non-physical.

What I mean is, I *really* feel my family's emotional pain. Their inner turmoil can be seen on their faces and heard in their voices as I observe them observing me.

Across the family room, my brother rests in his *own* coma. Lying motionless in his enamel-blue hospital bed, Hunter can't see me.

Because he is a boy. Can't see anyone because he's a boy. You see, boys don't experience Dreamtime. Only girls.

Dreamtime has been both a blessing and a curse. What I mean is, when I'm home in my comatose body, it feels great to see my family, but I can't talk or move—let them know I am all right—tell them how much they are loved.

On my third visit home, computer technology allowed me to communicate with my family while I lay in a coma. That life-changing experience became our salvation.

Before I go on and on about my dream visits to Earth, or tell you about my extraordinary journey on this amazing planet, let me keep the promise I made a few moments ago and start at the very beginning, so you understand *why* I'm in a coma on Earth and how I got here, on Millennium.

When you were little, did you ever experience a day in your life when everything changed radically? Things were never the same? If so, you'll know exactly what I'm talking about.

If you haven't, you're lucky.

Our lives changed completely when my father, Dr. Wayland Wainright, did not wake up. Momma found him unconscious and called 911. The ambulance came and rushed him to the hospital in Monterey.

Since then, I've always hated the sound of emergency sirens. You know, those high-pitched screamers that make you want to cover your ears.

"That bad day in July", as my mother called it, happened right after my seventh birthday. The trauma of that trip to the hospital burned permanent images into my memory, like freeze frames in my mind.

Ugly photographs.

Sad pictures.

The brightly lit room with all the blinking lights and equipment—the emergency room—scared me half to death. I thought I'd be trampled by the nurses running about. They treated Daddy mean, sticking tubes in his mouth and needles in his arms.

Like a movie scene I will never forget, the doctors and the nurses stood over my father while Momma sobbed frantically. The way she cried uncontrollably, I truly believed my father had died.

The hospital smelled odd—like our medicine cabinet at home. The emergency room felt cold. Ice cold.

Maybe I shivered from the shock of seeing Daddy unconscious on a gurney with plastic tubes sticking out of his nose and mouth.

That horrible day, Momma dressed me in a hurry. I wore a purple jump suit with different colored tennis shoes—one pink and one blue. I hid my feet under my chair.

Just a shy little girl, and I remember feeling embarrassed. How stupid is that?

My father's dying and I sat there worrying about my shoes—how I looked.

My mother should have left me home. Children shouldn't be in emergency rooms. I understand now why she took me with her to the hospital. She has always needed me with her, even when I was seven years old.

The doctor told her, "Your husband has lapsed into a coma. We won't know why until we conduct further tests." He asked her if he had hit his head or had been in an accident.

Shook her head, *no.*

Every time my mother burst into a crying rage, I became more and more frightened. I remember thinking, *Does a person ever run out of tears?*

My grandparents came to get me at the hospital. They had to pull me away from my mother. Or, maybe it was the other way around.

I cried all the way home, believing I'd never see my father again.

Grandma and Grandpa stayed with us at our house in Carmel.

Carmel-By-The-Sea is in Northern California. On the ocean.

We didn't see our mother all that week. Momma, pregnant at the time, kept a twenty-four-hour vigil beside my father's hospital bed.

She never came home.

At seven years old, I helped Grandma with the household chores. That included caring for my little sisters and brothers. At that age, I already knew how to change the baby's diapers.

On our eighth day in a row without our parents, Grandma answered the telephone.

She dropped the receiver and shouted, "He's okay! He's not in a coma anymore! Your father is coming home!"

Daddy had awakened.

According to the doctors, his awakening was a miracle.

No one could explain his bizarre coma.

Hunter and I hugged each other.

All I thought about was Momma. How happy she'd be when my father came home. How she'd behave normal again and not act so hysterical.

That overcast morning when Daddy returned home, the last week of July, 2004, will always be remembered as one of the worst days of my life.

Our father acted differently.

Our mother acted differently.

Everything felt different—empty.

Like a ghost or evil spirit had stolen the happiness from our home.

To my mother's chagrin, all my father talked about was the magical world he had visited. She kept telling him to hush and relax, not to worry about his vision, that he had been in a coma, that he had been dreaming.

He kept telling everyone he wasn't dreaming, that he had visited another world.

Grandma and Grandpa smirked at each other.

Momma's face turned red with embarrassment.

The day after he arrived home, Daddy locked himself in his library. His obsession with Millennium had created a rift between him and Momma.

Night after night, my mother knocked on the library doors, begging my father to stop working, to come to bed, to get some sleep, to be with her.

I'll never forget all those lonely nights my mother cried herself to sleep. Over time, she became depressed.

Lonely nights.

Depressed mother.

Like a cancer, her depression slowly ate away the love in her heart for my father.

Momma searched for her true self for years to come.

Daddy held on to his story of the strange, other world like a stubborn child.

Each year after his coma, when September rolled around, Daddy would rant and rave about the terrorists destroying the Twin Towers, saying that if we followed the teachings of the great sage, Metamorphosis, the world would be free of wars and crime and murder. "Our planet would be at peace", he'd say.

My father told us that the sage's message of unconditional love had been brought back to Earth by many famous people.

"All we had to do was listen to their wisdom," my father said, "and we can change the world."

Hunter and I asked Daddy what Metamorphosis looked like.

He told us that the Sage of the Ages, as he called him, looked like an action figure in a comic book or science fiction novel.

We laughed and said, "We want to see the sage, meet him in person."

"You will never meet Metamorphosis, he lives too far away," my father said with a distant look in his eyes.

Based on Daddy's descriptions, my brother drew pencil sketches of Metamorphosis. The illustrations depicted the sage character as having a long white beard and butterfly-like wings with four arms and a tail. He wore a medieval outfit with knee-high boots and a head band with a Triangulum on his forehead.

Drawing Metamorphosis inspired Hunter's passion for fantasy and science fiction artwork at an early age.

When my mother saw my brother's fantasy illustrations, she grew irritated with, as she put it, "Your father filling your heads with nonsense."

I made the mistake of pinning Hunter's illustrations of Metamorphosis on my bedroom wall. Momma scolded me as she tore the pictures down and threw them in the waste paper basket.

As we grew older, the stories about the bizarre sage character and the fantasy planet became a heated topic in our home.

My mother always scolded Daddy with, "Don't talk about such foolishness around the children."

He'd reply, "Honey, relax. You're about a nine on the tension scale."

She'd give him a dirty look and he'd always remain silent, in total reverence to Momma's domineering personality.

Then, he'd wink at me and Hunter when she wasn't looking.

My parents argued for hours and days and months and years about my father's dream planet. He continually talked about the amazing journey he had experienced during his coma.

Over and over and over again.

Divorce was a word I became familiar with.

An ugly word.

All I knew was, it meant that my mother and father wouldn't be together. We be separated.

I learned to live with uncertainty.

That led to biting my nails.

One thing for certain, my parents acted a lot happier before my father's coma.

Momma happened to be pregnant with her fourth daughter when Daddy was rushed to the hospital.

To me, my mother *always* looked pregnant! By my sixteenth birthday, I had four brothers and six sisters.

Let's see, after Hunter and me, Ruby was born. Then, Zachary and Alexander came along. Next, my mother had five girls in a row—Emily, Grace, Astrid, Pearl and Crystal. Momma gave birth to baby Sebastian in January, 2014.

That year turned out to be a disaster for us Wainrights; the year Hunter decided to leave us.

For better or for worse, our family would never be the same.

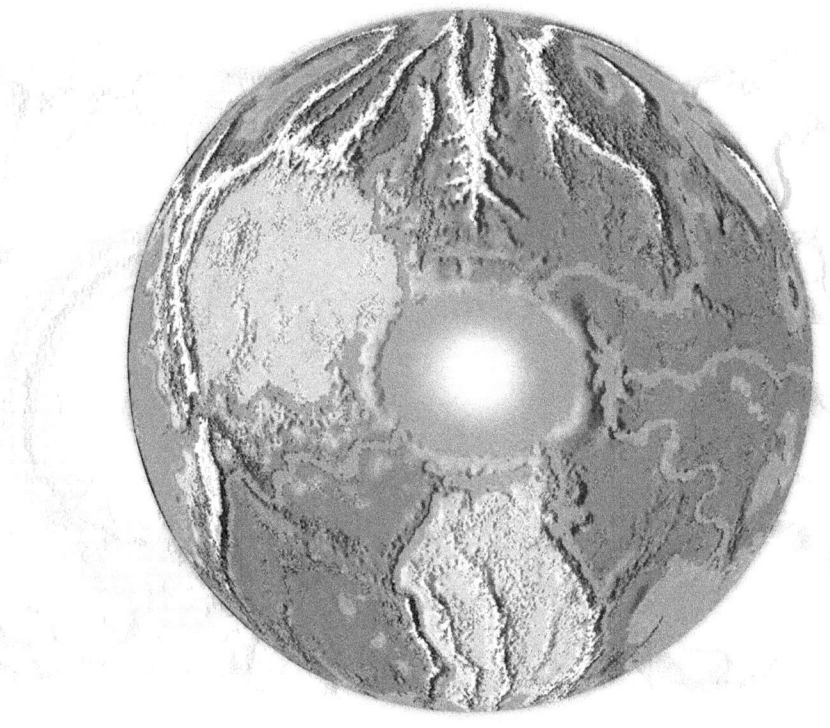

Wayland

Gloria

Prof. Josef

Elizabeth Dow

19

Chapter II
The Library

Daddy held me and Hunter in his lap. We giggled, watching the colorful fish swim back and forth. On the weekends, we were allowed to enter our father's sacred study—his library—to see his salt water aquarium.

"Sure, let the twins come in," he'd announce to my mother.

When the two of us bolted through the library doors, I always ran faster than Hunter and jumped in Daddy's arms first.

He felt so strong, so invincible.

School had just started. Hunter and I had entered the third grade together.

A year had passed since my father's hospitalization and his eight-day coma. He spent every day, his waking moments, consumed with, what my mother called, "his silly La La Land Project".

Momma hated the library. "My absentee husband's hideaway", as she referred to it.

Even if he *did* spend a lot of time in his favorite room, at least he lived with us—home with his family. It made me feel secure to have Daddy in the house.

Whenever we asked, my father grabbed a book from the shelf and read to us. We loved the leather-bound, illustrated edition of *Brothers Grimm Fairy Tales*.

For years I thought he read us all those children's stories for our enjoyment. I had no idea the fairy-tale characters and fantasy lands *really* existed, that Jacob Grimm and his brother had visited Millennium and returned to Earth to write down what they had witnessed.

"Daddy?" I asked, "Where do the fish come from?"

"The ocean, Julia," he replied.

"*That* one?" I pointed through the doors, past the hallway lined with glass, through the windows that revealed the endless Pacific Ocean.

My father nodded*, yes*, while Hunter asked, "How did they get from that big sea to this fish tank?"

Daddy explained how the fish had been caught in a net at their underwater ocean home and transported to a pet store and then to *our* house. He described how the fish now lived in a different place, a new world. They needed to adapt—survive— make the best of their new home.

"Don't they miss their families?" I asked.

"Yes, but we don't always have a choice to live where we want. Life takes us on unexpected journeys."

My father always talked to us kids like we were adults.

Maybe that's why I've always acted older than my age.

"Sometimes we wish we could live somewhere else," he said, gazing out the library doors at the restless ocean.

"Mommy says you want to be somewhere else," Hunter said, not shy to repeat what he heard adults say.

Daddy patted my brother on the head, took a deep breath and pointed at the clown fish. "There's Nemo, sweetheart. Your little friend."

Giggling, I watched my favorite red and white clown fish swim in and out of the wiggling sea anemone with the pink tentacles.

I thought about the helpless creature being captured and taken from his home.

"Is he sad?" I asked.

"What do you mean?"

"Nemo's all alone," I replied. "Where is his Mommy and Daddy?"

"Far, far away," my father replied.

Gazing at the ocean, I asked, "How far?"

"So far away they might as well be on another planet."

Frowning, I replied, "That's sad. Families should be together."

Hunter tapped his chest and said, "Like us. *We're* together."

"Nemo's mommy must be really unhappy that he's gone. Not home."

"Don't worry, Julia. His mother must learn to cope with life without him around."

When I was eight, I couldn't imagine being away from home, away from my mother.

Silently, the three of us sat together and stared at the miniature world where the creatures wanted to be somewhere else—back where they came from—back home.

I wanted to catch the clown fish, go down to the cliffs and return him to the ocean.

So he could swim free. So he could find his family.

Reunite them.

Before you hear about Hunter's rebellious decision to leave us, you need to know that my brother and I were inseparable.

Although not born identical twins, Momma liked to dress us in the same clothes—matching outfits. When we looked in the mirror, he told me I looked like a boy.

Sticking out my tongue, I told him he looked like a girl.

Then, we threw our temper tantrums, hoping that our mother might change our outfits before we had to go to school.

She scolded us. "You're both overreacting. Calm down."

I don't think we were.

When we arrived at school, the kids made fun of us, calling us Tweedle Dum and Tweedle Dee.

Eventually, we got to dress normal.

Or, at least, *different* from each other.

Momma enrolled me and Hunter into modern dance lessons when we turned eight years old. My brother hated dancing. You can't blame him, the class overflowed with giggling girls.

Within a month, clever Hunter convinced "Mom", as he called her at his young age, that he should take martial arts classes instead of dance. He asked for Karate and Tae Kwon Do lessons. So, I wanted them too.

Surprisingly, my mother enrolled both of us at the same time. Hunter never acted embarrassed that his sister attended class with him. Being taller and stronger than many of the boys, I held my own and performed really well at my weekly lessons.

When my grandparents complained about me, a girl, fighting with boys, Daddy told them that the martial arts classes were good for my discipline and mental toughness, that being able to defend myself would come in handy some day.

He was *so* right.

Hunter and I loved to sneak into Daddy's library.

We told Momma we were playing Hide-And-Go-Seek.

She'd tell us, "Stay out of that room," but we'd always forget on purpose, tiptoeing into the sacred sanctuary and hiding behind the leather sofa.

When my father discovered our hiding place, he'd tickle us until we begged him to stop. Then, he'd tell us he had a lot of work to do and he'd yell to Momma, "Come and get the twins."

It didn't take long for us to figure out a new way to sneak into the forbidden library. We were smarter than my parents gave us credit for when we turned eleven years old.

We abandoned Hide-And-Go-Seek for a new game—I Spy.

Hunter and I discovered that we could hide inside the cabinets under the giant aquarium. We had plenty of room below the ten-foot-long tank that held five-hundred gallons of salt water. The cabinet doors had louvers, so we could see and hear everything in the room through the openings between the slats.

The aquarium had been built into the wall adjacent to the garage. An extra set of doors had been installed on the garage-wall side for servicing the tank equipment.

The cabinet became our perfect hiding place. We learned to sneak out our bedroom windows onto the tile roof, climb down the metal garden trellis covered with star jasmine, squeeze through Pooh's pet door into the garage, scamper past the twelve cars in Daddy's auto court, and enter the library cabinets from the back side.

Quiet as church mice, that's my Grandma's cliché, we learned to move silently. Sometimes we invited Pooh, Hunter's golden retriever, inside the cabinet with us. So he wouldn't whine and bark. He just wanted to be with Hunter.

All those times we played I Spy in the library, the clandestine games became our childhood bond—our special secret.

Whenever Daddy invited after-dinner guests into his library, Hunter and I met on the roof and quietly made our way down to our hiding place under the aquarium.

Having secrets made me feel like a detective, like the clever girl protagonist in my *Nancy Drew* mystery books who uncovered clues so she could discover unknown information.

Little did I know that Hunter and I'd uncover clues leading to amazing adventures in faraway places.

And I mean, *far* away!

By the time we turned twelve years old, we knew all about Millennium and the gold Triamulet and Coma-X.

Chapter III
Coma-X

Daddy created the controversial Wainright Foundation in November, 2004, four months after his coma. Against his friend's and family's advice, he quit his professorship at Stanford University and proudly announced that he would dedicate his life to proving the planet Millennium existed.

Are you familiar with the saying, "Put your money where your mouth is?"

Well, that's exactly what Daddy did!

My father spent his inheritance money to finance his research foundation. His father and grandfather had been really smart with real estate investments and the stock market, so Daddy ended up with a lot of money.

As I grew older, I learned he spent much of his fortune on his obsession with Millennium, mostly on his Project: Coma-X.

The Wainright Foundation staff consisted of dedicated research scientists, mythologists, clairvoyants, and philosophers who shared a common belief—that extraterrestrial life existed.

"A bunch of strange people," as my mother often said.

During my childhood, Daddy entertained many people at our home, but mostly his best friend and mentor, Professor Johan Van Campbell. Hunter and I called him Professor Johan. We loved his long, white beard. He always wore a red rose in the lapel of his coat. If it wasn't the professor dropping by unannounced, we welcomed a parade of Wainright Foundation doctors who insisted on visiting my father.

When Daddy's scientific colleagues came to see him, my mother always cooked dinner for the guests.

We ate our meals at a twice-as-long-as-normal dining room table with a view of the ocean.

Momma's cooking always tasted delicious. But there was a price to pay.

While I watched the babies and toddlers, I had to chop vegetables and peel potatoes and empty the trash, whatever it took to get the food ready.

Although she received many compliments for her gourmet meals, dinner time in the Wainright household became stressful, especially for me.

My brothers and sisters misbehaved while Daddy ignored us and focused on his guests.

My mother demanded that I help control her out-of-control kids.

How did she expect me to keep my brothers and sisters quiet so the renowned Dr. Wainright could talk for hours without interruptions?

Have you ever tried to keep little kids quiet? Good luck!

Hunter never helped me watch the kids. Sometimes, he acted as immature as Alexander and Zachary.

Many of my father's meetings took place on the weekends, after dinner. This made Friday and Saturday nights special for Hunter and me.

We would wait until after dinner, pretend we were asleep in our beds, and then we'd sneak downstairs to the library so we could hide in the cabinet under the aquarium.

When I think of all the times the two of us hid in our secret hiding place, we were lucky that Momma never checked our fake bodies made of blankets and pillows stuffed under our bedspreads.

It wasn't until I turned eleven or twelve that I understood the significance of what Daddy and his colleagues discussed during their closed-door meetings in our library.

One Friday night, Hunter dressed up in a medieval costume so he could join his friends at a renaissance faire.

Jealous, I watched him and his buddies, who all dressed like pirates, leave for the festival. I remember being fourteen years old, in junior high.

Feeling sorry for myself, I faked a stomach ache to go to my bedroom. So I could sneak down to the library.

When I think back, Hunter always got to go places and I didn't. That wasn't fair, I should have been able to...umm...sorry, you know how easy it is to get sidetracked.

Let me focus on my story.

As I was saying, my brother had been given his freedom for the evening, so I decided to sneak down to the library.

At dinner, Daddy told my mother that he had guests arriving.

While I silently lay on my stomach with my legs propped up, I peeked through the cabinet-door louvers.

Stacks of mythology books, a deluxe, leather-bound edition of *Brothers Grimm Fairy Tales*, medical journals, and hand-drawn maps laid on the library tables and the marble floor.

I heard a noise behind me and froze.

Had Daddy discovered my secret hiding place?

Holding my breath, I looked behind me.

Hunter!

My brother crawled beside me, still dressed in his pirate costume.

"What happened?" I whispered.

Visibly upset, Hunter replied, "Dad came out to the car and told everyone I was no longer allowed to go to the renaissance faires."

"What did you tell him?" I asked.

"Nothing. Nobody talked. I just walked back into the house

with Dad lecturing me on how my grades needed to improve. He put me on restriction. Sent me to my room."

"Sorry, Hunter. I know how much you love going to the faires every year."

"Dad's going to be sorry for embarrassing me in front of Kirk and all the guys."

Hearing voices and footsteps approaching the library, I put my index finger to my lips.

"Shhh."

Hunter nodded, staring through the louvers. In the dim light, I saw the anger in his eyes.

The library doors opened.

Professor Van Campbell, and a man we had never seen before, walked into the room with Daddy. The stranger was a newly hired Wainright Foundation doctor who had come to our house for his orientation. Or, as my mother called it, his "indoctrination and brain washing".

My father poured his guest a glass of scotch and offered him a cigar. Professor Johan lit their "havanas", as Daddy called them, and they puffed away while he grabbed paperwork from the top drawer of his cherrywood desk.

Clearing his throat, he began his presentation. Daddy always spoke with passion, like he was behind a podium in a grand lecture hall at Stanford University. After all, he *did* have his doctorate, his Ph.D., in philosophy and mythology.

"The Wainright Foundation's research team has initiated Project: Coma-X, consisting of two study groups. The first group is comprised of five people who remain in a comatose state. The second group, two men and one woman, have awakened from their comas."

The doctor with coal-black hair scribbled notes on his yellow pad.

"As for this group still in a coma, the people who have not awakened yet, our scientific data indicates that the five Coma-X patients possess different heart rates, abnormal brain-wave patterns, and astonishing metabolic life signs when compared to typical coma patients."

My father handed the doctor a chart. "Here are the vital statistics of our five Coma-X patients that we have researched since 2004. All five are men. One lives here, in the United States, the others are in Europe, Latin America, Asia, and Africa."

"Their numbers are right here," Professor Johan said, puffing on his Cuban cigar while he pointed to the charts. "Look at their vital signs. Notice that the data listed under all five names have the same numbers. Each patient's heart rate indicates sixty-four beats per minute. Their body temperatures all read ninety-six degrees Fahrenheit."

The doctor glanced up at my coy father. "Are these identical numbers correct?"

Daddy smiled, combing his fingers through his goatee. "Yes, Dr. Shankar, they are accurate."

"Please, call me Hari," the doctor said, half-grinning.

My father nodded and continued. "I need to share some details not on these charts. Just like the three awakened survivors, all five of our Coma-X study patients share one trait that defies scientific explanation. They are living miracles."

He stood and held up his glass of scotch like he had been invited to toast a grand event.

"They haven't aged," Daddy yelled. "Like modern-day Rip Van Winkles, they have not grown older."

The bewildered doctor remained silent, sipping on his scotch.

While my father continued to explain Coma-X, I grinned, imagining Rip Van Winkle's long white beard that hung to his knees. Daddy read that story to me and Hunter, telling us, "Rip slept for more than twenty years".

"Three people have awakened from their coma. My investigations determined that these individuals, two men and one woman, have never met or communicated among themselves. I interviewed the children and grandchildren of these Coma-X survivors. They told me the coma lasted years, sometimes decades. In one documented case, she had been unconscious for more than ninety-four years. Almost a century!"

Dr. Shankar raised his hand to ask a question.

Daddy ignored him and continued to talk.

When my father focused on a subject, it was impossible to get his attention. We kids learned that at an early age. Don't interrupt him when he's talking.

"I also spoke to the relatives and neighbors who confirmed the awakened ones had maintained their youth during their extended coma episodes. I believe these witnesses because the three Coma-X survivors have outlived their brothers and sisters by several decades. I have three birth certificates to substantiate their birthdays. They do not look anywhere near their chronological age, especially the one woman."

"She is Elizabeth Dow," Professor Johan said. "She has given us the best descriptions and the most valuable information so far. Elizabeth will be the focus of our Coma-X research, as it pertains to the awakened group."

"When I interviewed Elizabeth in London," Daddy said, "her experience matched mine perfectly. She had awakened on Millennium, met Metamorphosis, and she was given the choice between staying there to see the Eight Great Treasures and learn the Secrets of the Universe, or return to Earth.

"When you know you can never go back to Millennium, it's a difficult decision. The Triamulet's only good for one trip. Like a round-trip ticket to paradise and back."

"Don't get sidetracked, Wayland," Professor Johan said. "Stick with the coma information."

Grinning, it occurred to me that I acted a lot like my father, always getting sidetracked easily.

Daddy took a gulp of scotch and continued.

"I have more astounding information. Unlike typical coma patients, our Coma-X group does not suffer from muscle atrophy. Their muscle tissue does not waste away, no matter how long their coma lasts. Our group can breathe without a respirator. Their skin does not break down. No ulcers or wounds develop from inactivity.

"Just like in the movies, after years of coma, they wake up and can walk, talk, and function normally. The final miracle is, they never enter into a permanent vegetative state. No PVS!"

Lying on our stomachs, Hunter and I listened to Daddy explain that the Wainright Foundation doctors and scientists were convinced that the Coma-X patients could survive without requiring special coma apparatus or monitoring.

That Elizabeth Dow fell into her coma during the late 1800s, when modern medical equipment was unavailable. She survived without a feeding tube.

Hari asked, "What is the scientific evidence that confirms the Coma-X patients' decelerated aging?"

"They are not with us right now," Daddy yelled, stepping over to a color map mounted on the wall.

He loved to sit in front of that map with Hunter and me on his lap and point to the Eight Great Kingdoms and fairy tale lands and mythological places.

My mother accused him of loving the map more than her. I never thought that was true, but Daddy sure spent a lot of time looking at that map on the wall.

Pointing, he said, "They're all alive *here*, on Millennium. This is the world where one daynight equals fifty days here at home. Try to comprehend that six months on Millennium equals twenty-five years on Earth. That's why they don't age."

"How did you get the geographical information?" Hari asked.

"Hand drawn by my associate," Daddy said, pointing to Professor Johan.

Hari leaned forward, staring at the map. "Based on what?" he asked.

"Show him," my father said, gesturing to his best friend.

"I'm not in the mood to take my shirt off," Professor Johan responded.

"You owe me one," my father said, smirking.

Professor Johan sighed, putting his cigar and drink on the end table.

He unbuttoned his shirt.

What is going on, I thought, watching the professor take his white dress shirt off and turn around.

"There's our evidence," my father said, pointing at the inked artwork.

A breathtaking, colored map of Millennium had been tattooed on Professor Johan's back! It matched the one on the wall perfectly.

"Look at that tattoo," Hunter whispered in my ear.

I poked him with my elbow, placing my index finger to my lips, reminding him, *be quiet.*

"I never thought I'd have a tattoo," the professor said, "but *this* one was worth it."

While Hari stood and examined the beautiful body art, the professor explained how Andvari, a gnome on the *Skipbladnir,* had inked the Millennium map on Johan's back during their voyage on the Sea of Circles.

"So I could remember all the geography upon my return to Earth," Professor Johan said, putting his shirt back on. "I hope you're satisfied, Wayland. Now, please, tell Dr. Shankar about our Coma-X research project."

My father's face glowed with passion; the library's amber lights twinkled in his eyes.

"During my Coma-X episode, I wasn't just on Earth. My other body was alive and breathing on another planet."

Tapping his index finger on the center of the map, he said, "When I awakened on Time Island, learned of my Time Dilation and then talked to Metamorphosis, I made a rash decision and decided to return to Earth instead of beginning my journey on the Open Road for the Eight Great Treasures. Deep down, I wanted to see the red Eternal Rose. Stay on Millennium."

"Since you insist on talking about that," Van Campbell said, "it would have been beneficial if you had stayed a little longer."

"I should have stayed a *lot* longer," my father replied.

Running his fingers through his black wavy hair, Daddy looked so sad and dejected, like a child who never got to open his birthday presents.

"Because I loved Gloria and the children so much, I made the decision to return to Earth, to come home."

"It's okay, Wayland," Professor Johan said. "Don't beat yourself up all the time. You made the right decision. Like Metamorphosis told us, 'All things happen in perfect order.' We can send someone else to Millennium. We have *two* Triamulets."

He asked my father, "Can you show our new team member your sacred medallion?"

Dr. Shankar set his drink on the end table. He must have felt intimidated because he never said a word. Just nodded and acted nervous. Uptight.

"Go ahead, Wayland," the professor said, "show Hari the Triamulet."

Daddy nodded and retrieved a safe deposit box from the bottom file drawer. Setting the box on the cherrywood desk, he reached into his pants pocket and pulled out a shiny chrome key. He opened the grey metal box and pulled out a radiant gold necklace with a triangular medallion attached to the chain.

"Here she is," he said, smiling. "The Triamulet."

My heart skipped a beat.

Hunter moved his face against the louvers. I grabbed his arm, fearful he would make noise and give us away.

The gold medallion glowed brightly in the lamp light.

We watched the Triamulet sway back and forth between my father's fingers. It sound's strange, but I felt the golden charm's energy twenty feet away.

Hari jumped out of his seat, drawn to the amulet.

My father let the doctor hold the sacred medallion.

"After we finish our research and prove that Coma-X is real," Daddy said, "we will find the perfect person to visit Millennium. Once our volunteer returns, we will have the evidence that dimensional shifting exists, that teleportation is real, that extraterrestrial life exists in the universe, that mythology and myths and fairy tales are accurate and that—"

"Slow down," Professor Johan said, interrupting my father. "Let's not get ahead of ourselves. Your team has several more years of research before the *Planet Millennium Report* is finished."

Daddy returned the Triamulet to the safe deposit box, locked the lid, and pointed at the doctor. "That's why I've hired *you*, Dr. Shankar. With all your experience with brain computer interfaces, you'll help us complete our report in the next thirty-six months. Welcome to our team."

Hari grinned and nodded his head in agreement as he crushed out his cigar in an abalone shell ashtray.

We all heard Momma yelling in the hallway that the guests were making too much noise and that the children couldn't get to sleep.

My father, red with embarrassment, escorted his guests out of the library, into the corridor. He shouted down the corridor, "I'll be right there honey; the guests are leaving now."

When he turned to close the doors, he looked straight at the aquarium.

Stared straight at us!

I held my breath for a long time before Daddy finally switched off the light. Hunter whispered that he had closed his eyes. I asked him if he was scared.

He replied, "A little."

I knew spying was wrong. I couldn't help but like it. You know, the excitement of listening to adult secrets.

Making our way out the back of the cabinet and through the garage, I thought, *Three years? Hunter and I will be seventeen. We'll be seniors in high school.*

As it turned out, we *would* be seventeen when my father released the controversial *Planet Millennium Report* to the world.

Chapter IV
My Room

Wanderlust.

Don't you just love that word? Living in our isolated sea-cliff home in northern California always gave me a sense of wanderlust. When the Pacific Ocean is your backyard, you learn that the world is bigger than you, larger than life.

Whenever I had the chance to sit on the cliffs behind our house and watch the relentless waves crash onto the jagged rocks below, my thoughts drifted to other lands—Africa and Australia and Europe and the Orient and far-away places.

By the time I became a teenager, I dreamed about getting away from home and seeing the world and writing novels about distant lands—about a young girl who could fly and watched the beautiful world below unfold before her very eyes.

You'd think I would have dreamed of visiting Millennium, but Daddy's planet scared me.

Momma hated hearing about the planet, what she called his "crazy dream world".

So, I tried to put it out of my mind.

Not sure if it really existed, it made more sense for me to fantasize about far-away places on Planet Earth.

My times spent outdoors on the seaside cliffs became restrictive because my mother demanded my constant help.

The older I got, the more difficult it became to go outside and think. Find time for myself. Just be alone.

Writing a journal—a diary—became my passion when I turned fourteen.

At the end of the day, always at night, I'd write with my

purple pen by book light, putting my life on paper.

Journaling I called it. Is that a word? Writing really helped me cope with things—clear my head.

When you write things down all that noise in your head goes away.

I found a secret hiding place for my diaries. So no one would find them. So no one would ever read my private thoughts. Know how I really felt about my life.

As I mentioned, writing down your emotions and working things out on paper is good for the soul, getting away from problems.

But my *real* escape came from reading books.

Whenever I found the precious time, I'd hide in my bedroom and bury myself in great novels that carried me away from home into my dream worlds.

Do you have a favorite place to read?

Mine happened to be the window seat of my bedroom's bay window, cuddled in a nest of pillows with my cat, Maddie.

With a panoramic view of the vast Pacific Ocean, I'd listen to the soothing rhythm of the waves while I read chapter after chapter of one of my cherished books—*Island of the Blue Dolphins*, or *The Princess Bride*, or *Jane Eyre*, or *Little Women*.

Then, laying the book in my lap and gazing at the endless blue sea, I'd get lost in my make-believe world, in the world of *The Little Princess*, or *Treasure Island*, or *The Wonderful Wizard of Oz*, or *Through the Looking Glass and What Alice Found There*.

Gazing at the ocean waves, I'd lapse into an adventurous daydream.

Alone with my secret thoughts, I'd be suddenly awakened by my mother's cries, "Julia, I need your help. Get down here. Now!

"Julia Rose! Where are you? Crystal and Sebastian need their diapers changed."

Frustrated, I'd throw down *Wuthering Heights* or one of my other favorite books and run downstairs.

If you're wondering why I always read old-fashioned paper books and not an electronic e-reader, my parents believed that the less electronic devices we had, the better off we were.

Daddy told me he learned that philosophy from Metamorphosis, Sage of the Ages.

Momma told me I couldn't have a cell phone until I turned eighteen years old.

Can you believe that!

No wonder the kids at school thought I was weird. Everyone had a smart phone!

Wanted my own phone so I could practice texting and looking at the Internet and downloading apps and well, just having one like all the other *normal* kids.

Anyway, I didn't care about an electronic book reader because I loved turning the pages of my cherished novels.

Have you ever noticed the unforgettable smell of books, especially the ones with color illustrations? Hold one up to your face and you'll know what I mean.

Besides Hunter's "high-end graphics system machine", that's what *he* called it, we had one other computer in the house. It sat in Daddy's sacred library.

Momma lived in the dark ages. She didn't know the first thing about the Internet. Told me the World Wide Web was evil. Refused to own a computer or a cell phone.

Daddy bought her a new pink smart phone. She hid it in the kitchen drawer.

She'd tell him, "Why do I need that stupid thing when I have a perfectly good phone hanging on the wall."

When I asked my father why I couldn't have my own phone, he would avoid the question as best he could by reminding me, "Your mother knows best."

I had trouble believing that.

Whenever my mother was unhappy, she'd make sure we all knew it. Momma wore her misery well, like an everyday apron.

She needed to get out more. Stuck at home, she became stuck

in the past. Other than the grocery store and an occasional trip to the mall, she never experienced the world outside her door.

My non-adventurous mother was afraid to leave the house. She became agoraphobic.

Feeling sorry for her, I would tell myself, *Momma needs your help. You must never abandon her. Be strong for your mother, Julia. She's been through tremendous stress with Daddy's coma, his endless work schedule, and the gossip about his illness, that Daddy is crazy. Momma loves you with all her heart.*

From my bedroom's bay window retreat, I remember mumbling to Maddie, "The year after next I'm supposed to attend Stanford University, but there's no way I can leave. I know Emily and Grace can't take care of Momma. Zachary will help as much as he can, but he's a boy. He's got his hands full with Alexander; that kid is wild—hyperactive.

"And then, there's Ruby. She's only two years younger than me, but she's more trouble to my mother than anyone realizes. My sister is worthless. She can't clean her room or help with the dishes or anything.

"Momma babies her. Like poor Ruby's got some kind of disease or something.

"Emily's going to be fine, as long as she doesn't eat herself to death. No wonder Grace is anorexic, pudgy Emily devours her younger sister's food when Momma isn't looking.

"The youngest girls—Astrid, Pearl, and Crystal—have to be taken care of. Always together, they get into mischief, like a rebellious little trio of gremlins. Someone has to keep an eye on them.

"Baby Sebastian needs special care. Momma can't handle the way the baby looks. She thinks everyone's freaked out about him. So what if the baby had been born with *Down Syndrome*. He's a happy baby. I feel his positive energy. He loves me."

Like a faithful friend, the cat sat beside me, listening to every word.

The soothing sound of waves caressing the rocky beach

below our home inspired me. Gave me hope.

Taking a deep breath of ocean air, I'd always change my thoughts from negative to positive. From a frown to a smile.

Daddy taught me that.

Learned the wisdom from Metamorphosis.

My father told me, "Julia, your thoughts are you; they determine your destiny. Always think positive and nothing, no thing, can harm you. You are what you think. Your thoughts become your reality."

I'd hug Daddy tightly and listen to his heart beat.

He had returned to Earth for me, for his family.

He is a good man.

No matter what anyone says, my father has always tried to help the world change for the better. The harder he tries, it seems the worse the world gets. I believe he's right: the people of Earth are not ready for the truth—the Universal Truths that Metamorphosis the great sage taught the philosophers and the prophets who have returned to Earth from Millennium.

Momma has always lived in denial. Never wanted to hear about Daddy's research.

Hunter and I secretly overheard our father explain Coma-X. So, by the time we turned fourteen years old, we knew more about Millennium than our mother.

Much more.

Whether we believed Daddy's stories or not, we didn't want to upset Momma.

The decision to never discuss our father's coma or his dream world became an easy one. I learned the hard way when I brought up the taboo subject as a teenager.

My mother really freaked out and screamed at me.

I learned the cliché, "Some things are better left unsaid", made perfect sense.

Because of our secret library visits, Hunter and I talked about Millennium all the time. We loved to look at the color map of the planet on the wall. We memorized the names of the Eight

Great Kingdoms. My favorite was Nemoria.

My brother believed the planet existed.

I wanted the distant world to go away.

Afraid that Daddy might someday leave us and go back to Millennium, I had nightmares that he would never come home, or that he'd be gone so long that I'd be an old woman when he returned to Earth.

What I mean is, my father would be *my* age, or younger than me! How weird would that be? Have you seen that movie where the teenage boy travels to the past and meets his dad who is the same age? Can you imagine your parents the same age you are?

Creepy.

I wanted to believe the mysterious planet did not exist, but deep down, I knew better.

Momma told me it wasn't real.

Our relatives gossiped that my father had gone mad, that he had lost his mind during his coma. My aunts and uncles and grandparents always upset my mother with their nasty rumors. They couldn't help themselves. Talking about someone behind a person's back was their nature—gossiping was in their blood, their DNA.

Actually, I would discover later that they *all* suffered from an *Emotional Virus*. A contagious disease called the *Dark Essence* brought to Earth by the Extractor Asteroid.

Their gossip and rumors kept my mother in a constant state of quiet anxiety.

No matter how stressful things became for Momma, nothing could prepare her for my seventeenth birthday.

Chapter V
Jeremy

You're probably asking yourself, why hasn't Julia talked about her classmates at school, or her best girlfriend? I got along with a few of the girls, but I never found a *best* friend—someone I became really close with. Our stuffy neighbors were all older and childless, so I never experienced playing with children in the neighborhood. Just my brothers and sisters.

My sophomore year, I overheard some girls gossiping about how crazy Dr. Wainright was, that the "nutty professor" believed in aliens and space creatures.

The girls pointed at me and giggled while they made fun of Daddy.

After that day, I felt that everyone looked at me like I was a freak.

They mocked me and my family—made fun of me behind my back. Sometimes, to my face.

I learned to ignore them.

Girls can be really cruel.

Momma said they acted jealous because I was prettier than all of them. I knew I was taller, but not prettier.

Being alone isn't the worst thing in the world.

I've always had my books to keep me company.

Even with all the gossip about my father, I loved school.

The old buildings at Carmel High became my fortress—my medieval castle—my safe haven. The classroom environment allowed me to escape from home. Like a sanctuary from all the household chores and feeling obligated.

A few of my teachers, the ones who taught class with passion—positive energy—became my heroes.

My English literature instructor, Mrs. Smith, told me I was intelligent and creative, one of the best writers she ever had in any of her classes. Her comments made me feel good about myself. Confident about my talent as an author.

I plan to publish a novel someday. No, I will write *many* novels by the time I'm my mother's age.

And then there were boys. Actually, I mean, *no* boys.

I avoided boys at school. Just like no best girlfriend; I had no boyfriend. The immature ones made goofy faces and teased me. The good-looking ones never paid attention to me.

No wonder.

Subconscious of my height, I kept my head down and my hair in my face and I did not make eye contact with boys, especially the ones I liked.

There were a couple of cute ones I dreamed about. I remember wishing boys were like books. So I could read them.

I mean, read them better, what they were thinking.

You know, figure out why they acted the way they did.

It wouldn't have made any difference if I *did* meet someone. Momma warned me that I couldn't date until my senior year.

The older I got, the more upset I became.

No normal girl, at least, no one I knew at school, had to wait until they were seniors to have a boyfriend. My mother's *no-dating rule* seemed so unreasonable, so unfair.

Because school had always been my favorite thing to do, I hated summer break. It meant doing extra chores and helping Momma raise my brothers and sisters.

But things change.

As my father reminded me, "The only thing for certain in life is change. And whether or not we believe it at the time, things always change for the better."

I needed something exciting to happen with my boring, worthless life.

Finally, change did arrive, just as Daddy had promised.

The end of my junior year in high school began like no other.

The first Saturday of summer vacation, June 21st, 2014, I had finished making sandwiches for my brothers and sisters, all nine of them.

Momma told me to take a break, relax.

To me, relaxation meant on thing, read a book. So, I ran upstairs, closed my door, and crawled into my pillowed bay window with Maddie to read one of my favorite stories, *Anne of Green Gables*.

I hadn't read for more than ten minutes when I noticed Mr. Estrada, our landscaper, enter our backyard and give instructions to his gardening crew.

Daddy bragged about how great our estate looked, all because of Estrada's Landscape Company.

Never paid much attention to the maintenance crew, but on that warm summer day, someone caught my eye.

A boy.

A boy my age walked across the yard.

He took his green work shirt off. His arm and chest muscles gleamed in the afternoon sunshine. He looked handsome.

No, stunning.

I dropped my book and pressed my nose against the glass to get a better look.

He headed straight toward my bedroom window. With every step he took, the closer he got, the more handsome he became.

He looked up, straight at me.

I panicked and ducked down, thinking, *Oh my God, he saw me staring at him.*

Then I thought, *Why am I hiding? What am I so scared of?*

My heart thumped in my chest.

Never felt that way before.

Getting the courage to peek over the window sill, the boy had turned his back to me as he marched toward Momma's rose garden.

Jumping off the window seat, I ran to my closet. Tried on three blouses before I found the red silk top that looked right.

Scurried into my bathroom to view myself in the mirror.

Happy with my blouse and jeans, I ran a brush through my straight black hair.

Momma discouraged lipstick and makeup, but I got lucky in life.

My lips looked good without adding color. My black eyelashes and hazel eyes did not need eye liner.

Smiling to make sure my teeth looked white and spotless, I pinched my cheeks to make them rosy and scurried out of my bedroom.

Stay calm, Julia, I thought. *Don't let Momma know you're excited. Act normal.*

As I ran down the stairs, I realized I behaved like I had never seen a boy before.

"Calm down," I whispered under my breath.

Spotted my mother in the family room pushing a vacuum with one hand. Holding a glass of white wine in the other.

Shuffled through the kitchen and grabbed Crystal's hand.

The vacuum stopped.

"Momma, I'm going to take Crystal outside to play."

"Okay, but don't be long," she yelled, "I need help with the baby."

Out of my mind with apprehension, I strolled into the sunny backyard.

There he stood.

Pruning my mother's roses.

He didn't notice me as I strolled around our swimming pool.

I pulled Crystal along the red brick path that led to the formal rose garden. The walkway meandered its way toward the ocean cliffs. Every step I took toward him, he looked more and more handsome.

What are you going to say, Julia? What if he doesn't want to talk? What if he doesn't like you? Maybe he has a girlfriend.

"Jeremy!" Mr. Estrada shouted from the front yard, "I need your help!"

"Okay, Dad," he yelled.

Jeremy.

What a perfect name. It starts with a J, just like mine.

He tossed the rose trimmings in a cart, turned, and marched up the brick path—straight toward me.

We both stopped in our tracks.

Our eyes locked in a mutual, gratifying gaze.

I'll never forget how his wavy black hair moved against his forehead in the gentle ocean breeze. Only a few feet away, his hazel-brown eyes looked right through me, into my soul.

Crystal, who'd normally pull on my hand or fidget, stood still, staring at the boy.

Pushing the garden cart with his muscular arms and chest, he strolled up to me and asked, "Hello. Are these *your* roses?"

My lips felt unmovable, like they had been sown shut.

So, I nodded, *yes.*

"Then, you must live here," he said, grinning.

Before I could respond, he reached into the pile of thorny green stems and handed me the loveliest red rose I had ever seen.

"Thanks," was the best response I could come up with.

I knew my flushed face looked as red as the rose petals.

He likes me, I thought. *He likes me and he's here, in my backyard. Momma can't tell me that no boys are allowed at our house. Jeremy's already here. He works here! He works for his father who is Daddy's friend. I hope that—*

He interrupted my thoughts by asking, "What is your name?"

"Julia," I said, trying not to make a foolish grin or look stupid.

By this time I'd unconsciously let go of Crystal's hand and she'd run back to the house.

"That's a great name," Jeremy said, smiling.

His delightful smile revealed straight white teeth and huge dimples.

"I guess so. I mean, thank you."

"I'm working for my dad this summer," he said. "He wants me to take over his business one day, but I have other plans."

"What school do you go to?" I asked.

"Pacific Grove. I'm a senior next year."

"I won't hold that against you. I'll be a senior at Carmel High."

He laughed, knowing that his high school was our cross-town rival.

Before he spoke, his father shouted, "Son, I need you out here, now!"

"I have to go," Jeremy said, grabbing the handles of the cart. "Maybe I'll see you next weekend."

"I'd like that." I grinned, trying to look coy as I moved off the brick path so he'd have enough room to walk past me.

He smiled from ear to ear.

Never, *never* had I seen such a beautiful person in my whole life. I admired his every step as he paraded around the pool, flexing his muscles.

Jeremy disappeared out the wrought-iron gate.

My thoughts ran wild: *He's absolutely gorgeous. He'll be back next weekend. That's only seven days away. What will I wear? What am I going to—*

Momma interrupted my thoughts, yelling from the back

door. "Julia, please come in the house. I need your help. Right now!"

"Don't worry, helpless mother of mine. I'm coming," I whispered to the ocean breeze.

That first week of summer I hardly slept.

Still sweet sixteen and a magical boy had entered my backyard from nowhere.

My father told me that Metamorphosis taught him, 'All things happen in perfect order'. The sage also said, "People come and go, in and out of our lives, at the right and perfect time."

The Sage of the Ages knew what he was talking about.

I felt a deep connection to Jeremy, yet I hardly knew him. But I had this good feeling about him. It wasn't just his comforting voice, it was the way he talked to me. It was the special way he looked at me with his dreamy eyes. I felt his positive energy.

The anticipation of seeing him again filled me with happiness.

I wrote page after page of joyous feelings in my journal.

Joy soon ended.

Like that saying, "Gone in a heartbeat!"

As it turned out, he did not return to see me the next weekend. His parents were divorced. His mother, who had become seriously ill, lived on Plum Island, Massachusetts, with her new husband.

Jeremy had to travel to the east coast to be with his mom at the hospital.

My life is cursed, I convinced myself. *When would I see Jeremy again? Would he stay in Massachusetts? What if he never came back?*

Momma asked me what's wrong, that I acted moody, that I

wasn't myself.

"Nothing's wrong," I replied. "I'm fine."

"Well, *act* like it then," she said.

There was no way I could tell her I was lovesick for a boy I had met one time.

One time, for ten minutes.

The night before my seventeenth birthday, Daddy brought me into his library and sat me at his desk in front of his computer.

Frowning, he asked me, "Who is Jeremy?"

In shock, I did not answer him, fearful he'd be mad at me.

Thoughts got lost in my head: *How did he find out about Jeremy? I've never said a word to anyone.*

Daddy hugged me and told me he wanted the truth.

Showed me an e-mail on his computer screen.

I stared at the message:

> Hello Julia,
> I hope you get this soon.
> Sorry I couldn't see you for the past two weekends.
> I had to travel to Massachusetts.
> My mom's been sick, but she's okay now.
> I'm flying home this week.
> I'll be working at your house the weekend of July 4th.
> Can we spend some time together?
> I can't stop thinking of your smile, it is beautiful.
> Your friend,
> Jeremy

I exploded with joy. Couldn't catch my breath.

Feeling exhilarated, high on happiness, I thought, *Jeremy somehow got Daddy's e-mail so he could contact me. That means he must love me! Of course he does, he can't stop thinking of my smile, it says so right here on the screen!*

My father stood there, waiting for an explanation. I gathered my composure. Instead of crying, I told him who Jeremy was and how we had met for a brief time in the backyard.

I told the truth.

When you tell the truth, you don't have to think up a bunch of stupid stories that you can't remember later.

Putting his hand on my shoulder, he said, "Well, I better have a talk with Mr. Estrada about his landscape crew."

"Please don't get Jeremy in trouble."

"What I mean is, we'll have to invite his son for lunch, get to know this boy."

My father smiled and chuckled. "I need to know if your new friend can prune your mother's roses properly."

"Oh, Daddy, you're such a kidder."

I grinned and blinked my big hazel eyes, trying to soften him up for a request that would require my mother's approval. "Jeremy's coming home tomorrow. Can he eat lunch with us? It's my birthday."

I held my breath, hoping my wish would come true.

Then it hit me.

"Wait," I said. "We're not going to be here tomorrow."

I remembered that our family planned to celebrate Hunter's and my birthday in Monterey.

He patted my shoulder. "You can wait until next weekend. Be patient, Julia. You have your whole life to see Jeremy."

My parents always told me I had this *huge* amount of time, my entire life ahead of me. But when you're in love, tomorrow seems like forever.

Hugging me, he said, "I'll tell your mother we're having a guest for lunch next weekend. I'll talk to Mr. Estrada about this, make sure it's okay for one of his workers to take a lunch break with one of his clients."

"Thanks, Daddy. Love you."

I hugged my father for being so understanding. He didn't get angry or upset that a boy had communicated with me.

That evening, I couldn't sleep.

At midnight, I jumped out of bed and pranced to my favorite spot at the bay window to gaze at the twinkling stars and the blue moon's reflection shimmering on the calm ocean.

Snuggling into the window seat pillows and turning my faithful book light on, I tried to read the first chapter of *Charlotte's Web*.

For the first time in my life, I found myself drifting away from the words on the page and into a magical self-fulfilling fantasy.

Into a boy's arms.

I stayed up that entire evening thinking of Jeremy.

And Millennium.

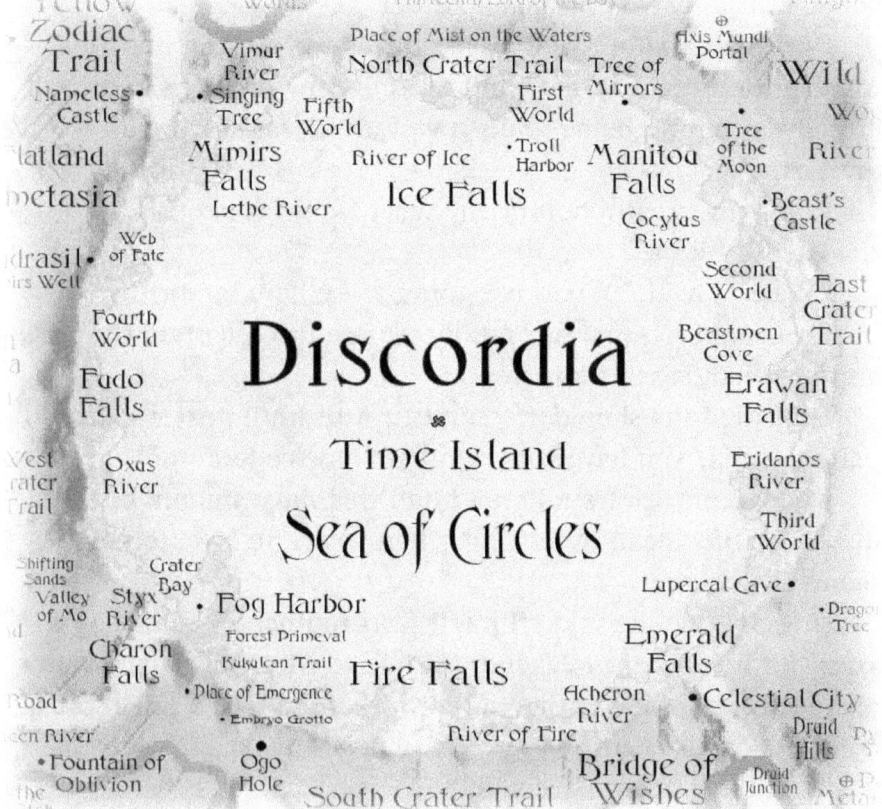

Chapter VI
Hunter

Waves crashed against the cliffs below our home. Sea gulls squawked and sea lions barked as the morning sunlight poured through my bay window. Sleepless, but feeling energized, I sat up in my canopied bed and gazed across the room at my full-length mirror. Smiling at my reflection, I felt so alive, so happy. Happier than I could ever remember.

My bedroom door creaked opened.

Momma peeked her head in, frowning.

Sighing, she said, "I know it's your birthday, but I need help with Sebastian. He wants you to feed him. He won't stop crying."

She closed the door.

Still smiling, I jumped out of bed.

"Be right there," I yelled, humming a happy tune while I opened the bay window and inhaled the cool morning air.

Like thousands of ivory swans swimming in formation, white caps rolled across the turquoise ocean in perfect symmetry. Gulls and terns dotted the pink and purple sky, diving and soaring to the rhythm of the pounding surf below. The ancient sea cliffs and grottoes behind our home eagerly embraced the endless waves that arrived, one by one, in a timeless sequence.

Tuesday morning, the 8th of July, 2014.

A great day.

My thoughts were not of birthdays, but of Jeremy.

In less than a week I'll see him again. It will be like a real date. We'll have lunch in our home together. I pray we can be alone. I hope Hunter doesn't embarrass me. Ruby will probably be in one of her cranky moods. I wonder if Daddy has talked to

Momma about the lunch next weekend? What if she freaks out that I have a boyfriend?

While I put on my jeans and a blue blouse, my brothers and sisters giggled and teased each other as they ran up and down the hallway. I had to hurry and help Momma get them ready for our trip to the Monterey Bay Aquarium.

Because of summer vacation, Daddy promised to stay home more, to spend quality time with the family. After the aquarium visit, Hunter's and my birthday dinner would be at a fancy restaurant in Monterey, on Cannery Row.

As for birthdays, when you're a twin, you never feel special. You never have a birthday alone—your very *own* party.

I thought about asking Daddy if Jeremy could talk to his father and take off work early and drive to Monterey with us.

Why should I have to wait an entire week to see him?

Thoughts of Jeremy were abruptly interrupted by a loud, distressed yell from the hallway.

"Ohmygod...aaaggghhh!"

The yells turned to screams.

"Hunter, wake up!" Momma shouted in desperation. "What's wrong, sweetheart? Please, talk to me!"

I ran down the hall and pushed through my brothers and sisters who blocked Hunter's doorway.

My mother shouted, "Call 911...he's dying! Get an ambulance!"

Before I reached Momma, my father pushed me aside and stood by the bed, shouting, "Gloria, stand back! Let go of Hunter! Let me see him!"

Daddy grabbed my hysterical mother and pulled her away. She wouldn't let go of Hunter's arm.

My father shook her by the shoulders and yelled, "Don't worry, he's unconscious; he's not dying. He might be in a coma."

Red-faced, Momma stared at my father like a wild tiger ready to attack its prey. She hit him with her fists on his chest and shoulders, slapping his face, hard.

"What do you mean a coma?" she screamed. "How could you let this happen? I told you to get rid of that medallion! You bastard!"

We seldom heard Momma curse.

While Daddy called for the paramedics, Ruby stood in the corner, emotionless.

Emily, Grace, and Astrid acted hysterically, crying and holding each other. Zachary and Alexander stood on the other side of the bed shaking Hunter and telling him to wake up.

Unable to cry, I knew that my mother was right about the gold medallion.

Hunter never told me, but I knew he had stolen my father's Triamulet. Knowing where the sacred medallion had been hidden, my brother often talked about how easy it would be to get into Daddy's desk and open the grey metal box.

Hunter really did it!

My rebellious twin brother had worn the Triamulet.

He had escaped, just like we always talked about. He planned to accomplish a quest that his father had failed to complete ten years earlier. I know this to be true because Hunter always tried to prove his manhood.

Daddy never accepted the reality that his oldest son wanted to be an artist. From the time he first held a pencil, Hunter loved to draw. He especially liked fantasy and science fiction artwork. His bedroom walls were covered with drawings and paintings of castles with knights fighting dragons, hideous trolls, vampires, and mythological beasts.

Hunter often stayed up all night creating video games and fantasy artwork on his computer.

He'd rather draw than do his homework. His rebellious behavior really upset my parents, especially my father.

The rumor among my gossiping relatives was, "Dr. Wainright demanded too much from his oldest son."

Hunter always got into trouble for failing to get good grades in school or for spending too much time, as Daddy said,

"Drawing those strange creatures," or "Going to those ridiculous renaissance faires," or "Wasting time on role-playing games."

My brother had to hear, "Why can't you get straight A's like your sister, Julia?"

He spent a lot of time on restriction. Daddy punished him by taking away his computer, or his surf board, or his guitar. Demanded that his oldest son go straight to college and get his Ph.D. to become a professor or a doctor.

Hunter was continually told to stop dreaming and to get his head out of the clouds by the father who claimed to have visited another planet!

Can you believe that?

No wonder my brother left home.

Hunter spent two weeks in the same hospital as Daddy.

My father managed to pull some strings, those were his words, and got an early release from the doctors to bring my twin brother home.

Without my mother's approval, Daddy had already prepared for other Coma-X patients to visit the Wainright home. He knew the exact medical equipment requirements for a comatose person to stay at our house.

Little did my father know that one day he'd need the research equipment to care for his *own* son.

The doctors gave Hunter the long-term status of PVS. My mother sobbed when she heard the doctor say, "Within four to six weeks, if Hunter does not wake up, he will enter a persistent vegetative state."

The medical diagnosis made Momma a nervous wreck. I'll never understand why doctors want to frighten people by announcing some worst-case scenario for the patient.

The ambulance brought Hunter home the end of July, 2014.

Daddy hired a contractor to install an elevator in our home.

By Labor Day, we were able to wheel my brother from his upstairs bedroom to the downstairs family room, where my mother had set up a nursing station.

Based on the doctors' diagnosis, she hired an R.N., a registered nurse, to train her in the complicated task of caring for a person with the worst, debilitating coma—PVS status.

Momma learned the names of the various medical equipment machines and the function of each apparatus.

She told Daddy that she didn't need nurses to visit our home, she would care for Hunter herself.

Can you guess why?

That's right, she had *me* to help her!

It didn't take long for her to fire the nurse and train me in the use of the intravenous tubing and the arterial line that had been attached to a monitor.

I hated the nasogastric tube. That horrible thing went down Hunter's nose and mouth. I was so happy when Hunter got a PEG tube inserted. It hooked directly through his stomach wall. So he'd receive proper nourishment.

Hunter never lost weight. He never required a respirator or ventilator. His breathing, slower than normal, remained an independent function. Looking perfectly healthy, it was like he was sleeping with his eyes open.

It's a lot of work caring for a comatose person.

I wanted to scream, "Mother, I plan to major in literature, not nursing!"

But I kept my mouth shut. "My lips buttoned", as Daddy would say.

Never let Momma down in her hour of need.

I learned to read the EKG—electrocardiogram information—on a second monitor. Hunter also had an ICP, an intracranial pressure monitor, attached to his head.

Tubes and pads and wires everywhere.

Our family room, with the nursing station, looked like the

emergency room at the hospital.

Hunter's bedroom had the same medical equipment.

He lay in a special hospital bed that housed all the monitors and machines built into the lower portion of his home on wheels.

Hunter's bed inspired many family nick names.

My twisted sister, Ruby, called the bed "Ectomobile". Weird Alexander called the bed "Batmobile". Emily, Grace, and Astrid called the bed "Herbie", after some movie.

Not amused by the bed names, my mother became obsessed with Hunter's care. My brothers and sisters complained, nagged, and constantly sought her attention.

They failed.

I tried to make up for my mother's lack of parenting skills. I did the best I could, but kids know who their real mother is.

Momma spent her waking moments at Hunter's bedside. If she wasn't attending to his medical needs, she clutched her rhinestone-beaded rosary and prayed for hours on end.

Raised Catholic, my mother made sure that all of us attended Mass every Sunday.

Except Daddy.

He never went to church with us. Claimed to be an agnostic; that is, *before* he lapsed into his coma.

When he awakened, he told us he had found God.

My parents argued about religion.

They also fought over politics.

No wonder. One was a Republican and the other was a Democrat.

They'd spend hours debating who was the greatest president of all time, or which political party had the best social programs. Stupid stuff like that.

Whomever the person was who came up with the motto, "Never discuss religion and politics," knew exactly what they were talking about.

More often than not, Momma would wear herself out

arguing and then dose off, excuse me, *pass out*, in her favorite rocking chair next to Hunter's bed.

Sometimes, she'd sleep all night in that chair.

Sometimes, Daddy carried her upstairs.

Then, I'd take over.

Come to my mother's rescue.

I'd sit in her chair, caring for Hunter, rocking back and forth.

Back and forth in the dark.

Dreaming of Jeremy.

After Hunter's coma, life in the Wainright home became even more chaotic.

Remember that lunch with Jeremy that my father promised me? It was supposed to have been the week after my birthday.

Nothing ever happened.

No lunch.

My selfish parents thought of one thing, and one thing only. Hunter!

My twin brother ruined my seventeenth summer on Earth with his selfish decision to leave us.

No, it was my mother's attitude.

Actually, *both* of them were responsible for interfering with my relationship with Jeremy.

Hunter did it unintentionally. He had no idea the boy of my dreams had come into my life.

Momma did it to hurt me.

I know this because, when she found out from Daddy that Mr. Estrada's son wanted to have lunch with Dr. Wainrights' oldest daughter, she fired the landscape company.

Fired them without a notice of any kind.

How cruel and thoughtless is that?

The nerve of her to do that without talking to me first.

Daddy acted really upset. He and Mr. Estrada had known each other for ten years. But my father didn't do anything about it. Said nothing.

Sometimes he acted like he was afraid of Momma.

No one admitted it, but we *all* walked on egg shells around her.

Feeling betrayed, I thought about running away from home, going to find Jeremy on Plum Island.

But I didn't have my own car. I was afraid to drive the family SUV across the country.

Afraid I'd get lost on some lonely road to nowhere.

The only time I drove was to take my mother to the store or the mall and back.

My father took me to my martial arts lessons in his favorite black sports car.

One school night, instead of doing my homework, I stayed up until three in the morning studying a map of the east coast, all the major highways.

Staring at the roads to Massachusetts.

Looking for Plum Island.

How was I going to leave home when Momma would surely fall apart, have a nervous breakdown, without me by her side?

Abandoned my crazy plot to run away. That would have been the dumbest thing I ever did.

If I didn't *physically* go see Jeremy, how was I going to get in touch with him?

No computer. No cell phone.

How was I to contact him?

I felt so helpless, so frustrated with my stupid, worthless life.

The summer of 2014 ended miserably.

No boyfriend and no life.

Loneliness overcame me.

Night after night, tossing and turning in my canopied feather bed, I prayed for relief. Prayed for Jeremy to return to Carmel.

"Please, dear God, let school begin."

Since grade school, the first day of class had always been special.

Like a rebirth.

My senior year in high school began with high anticipation.

The first day, I gave a note to a girl who's stepbrother went to Pacific Grove. He had been friends with Jeremy.

The next day, I received a message.

Not from Jeremy, but from his friend.

The note read:

Jeremy has gone to live with his mother in Massachusetts.

Stared at the note for an hour, two hours, three hours. I don't remember school that day.

Cried myself to sleep that evening, sobbing until my eyes hurt.

The next night, wrote in my journal for four hours.

Forty pages of pain.

My father told me a storm does not last forever.

He got *that* right.

Three months later, one week before Christmas, my love sickness ended.

Mr. Estrada told my father that Jeremy would attend Pacific Grove High in January, 2015, to live with his father again.

Hurray!

Jeremy was moving back to Carmel By-The-Sea.

I screamed for joy.

Finally, something to live for.

I'm sorry for sounding so down, but it broke my spirit to be away from him. It didn't matter if we had spent but a few minutes together, I had fallen in love with him. I knew by reading his *one* e-mail that he felt the same about me.

A girl has a sixth sense about these things.

Knowing that Jeremy would soon return, Daddy had a long talk with my mother.

Told her that I was a senior and should be able to date. She refused to answer him, saying she needed time to think it over.

I mean, what's wrong with a seventeen-year-old girl dating?

Having a boyfriend is not against the law.

How much time does it take to make such a simple decision?

At the Thanksgiving dinner table, my patience ran out. I openly begged my mother to consider allowing Jeremy and me to start seeing each other in January.

To date like normal teenagers.

The family sat in rare silence.

Momma answered, "I'll let you talk to him on the telephone."

Finished her glass of Merlot and looked at Daddy, who wore a frown.

"Okay," my mother said, "Julia can go to her senior prom with the gardener's boy."

The prom, I thought, *is five months away.*

She sighed and said, "I hope he's planning to go to college, make something of himself."

Daddy said, "Jeremy's father is a successful business man."

Gulping down more red wine, my mother said, "I don't want Julia spending too much time with a boy. I need her to help me with Hunter. I can't take care of him all by myself."

Momma pointed across the room at my twin brother, lying peacefully in his hospital bed, oblivious to the drama taking place in front of him.

Everyone ate in silence, knowing not to speak.

We didn't want my mother to become more upset than she already was.

My father poured more dark-red Merlot into my mother's crystal glass.

It didn't take long for the boys to tease and kick each other under the table. Within minutes, the dining room returned to its normal chaos—everyone talking at once.

Except for me.

Staring at Hunter, I wondered what he had been doing on Millennium.

How truly free he must have felt.

At least I had my prom to look forward to.

My first date.

The next day, my father apologized to Mr. Estrada and rehired his company to maintain our estate. Seeing the landscape trucks in the driveway reminded me of Jeremy.

I would spend the entire holiday season waiting impatiently for the first of the year, for Jeremy's return.

"Happy New Year" really meant something special for the first time in my life.

Found myself taking care of Hunter more often, especially when Momma needed rest.

Locked in her bedroom with the curtains drawn, she required more "down time". That's what Daddy called it. I think he meant, "Time to recover from her hangovers".

We couldn't help but notice she drank more.

A *lot* more.

Chapter VII
Wainright Foundation

Dressed warmly in my black workout clothes and breast-cancer-pink running shoes, I grabbed a bath towel and climbed out my bedroom window, down the trellis, through the pet door entry in the garage door, between the expensive cars in Daddy's auto court, and into the back side of the aquarium cabinet.

Earlier, we had eaten dinner with four of the Wainright Foundation doctors.

My mother acted irritated.

No, she acted mad as hell.

Daddy told her an emergency had occurred, that the doctors wouldn't stay long.

After dinner, I had finished washing the dishes when Momma came into the kitchen and yelled, "The nerve of them to show up on Christmas Eve."

She ordered me to go upstairs and put the kids to bed while she finished wrapping presents in the family room.

Told her I had a headache and asked if I may stay upstairs after I finished my chores.

Sighing in disappointment, or maybe disgust, she motioned, *go away.*

I tucked Crystal and Sebastian under their covers and waited for them to fall asleep before I snuck out my window onto the slippery tile roof and climbed down the trellis to the garage.

A series of nasty winter storms had brought us heavy rains for the holidays.

I settled into my secret hiding spot inside the cabinet. I had just finished drying my wet hair with my towel when my father escorted four of his top colleagues into the library.

In the corner of the room, twinkling white lights adorned a green Christmas tree. I loved the smell of a freshly-cut pine tree.

The black-shaded lamps cast an amber glow on the bookshelves of the library.

My father climbed up a wall ladder, holding the rail as he reached for a dictionary-sized book, *Mythology Compendium*. The single volume rested on the seventh shelf of his one-story-tall book collection featuring cyclopedias, rare mythology and fairy tale collectibles, literary classics, and medical publications.

"I'll need this when Van Campbell gets back in town," Daddy said, stepping down from the ladder.

Offering his guests cigars and wine, he strutted to his desk and opened the thick book.

"What if I can get Van Campbell to give us his Triamulet?" Daddy asked.

"Are you talking about the Millennium volunteer idea?" Dr. Dustin asked.

"Yes," my father replied. "All we need is one famous person to make the trip, stay a few months to gather information, and return."

He flipped through the pages of the mythology book while the four foundation doctors sat on the leather sofa and chairs. They glanced at one another apprehensively, sipping red Merlot from crystal wine glasses.

"Wayland, we've spent nine years, almost a decade, on the medical research," Dr. Herrick said, pointing his cigar at Daddy. The foundation's expert on teleportation frowned. "Can we please focus on *that* instead of mythology?"

"Okay, calm down," my father replied, returning the frown. "I'll talk to Johan about his Triamulet as soon as I see him. Let's get on with the report. We *do* need to talk about the media event so I can get you guys out of here and back to your families for the holidays. We'll talk about mythology later."

My father's announcement "to hurry" made me happy. I know how upset Momma acted at the dinner table, giving her four guests the evil eye.

If looks could kill, the doctors would have all dropped dead!

She yelled at Daddy, scolding him with, "Christmas Eve should be for family, not business associates."

Dr. Fletcher removed five manila folders from his briefcase and handed everyone a *Planet Millennium Report*. "I'll briefly mention the key points that Wayland will announce to the media."

"I'm still nervous about going public," Dr. Dustin said, "without first publishing our findings to the scientific community."

My father forced a grin. "Thank you, Paul, but we've already discussed that subject at length."

"I know we have, but—"

"Our fellow scientists will take *years* to test our evidence," Daddy said, interrupting. "In the meantime, they'll ridicule us and discredit our foundation. That's why I'm going to the media first. Let the public decide."

The doctors puffed nervously on their cigars.

If I didn't know better, I'd say they were all pouting.

Extending his hand in apology, my father said, "I'll tell you what we'll do. We'll publish the scientific report a few days prior to my media announcement. Does *that* satisfy everyone?"

The four doctors nodded in unison, *yes*.

I silently rolled onto my side, getting into a more comfortable position.

My father pointed at Dr. Fletcher, motioning, *you may begin*.

The foundation's parapsychologist nodded and said, "After Wayland describes his visit to Millennium, he'll present irrefutable scientific information of how our Coma-X study group lives in two bodies. He'll show photographic evidence of how our patient's muscles have not atrophied.

"He'll explain our hormone study, that we have charted

exactly when our patients eat, drink and sleep. The research proves they are alive and well on Millennium."

"That's good stuff," Dr. Dustin, the foundation's quantum physicist, said.

Dr. Herrick raised his hand. "One more thing. According to Hunter's daily activity analysis, we're correct about the time difference, the fifty to one ratio. Hunter averages forty days without sleep. He's awake more than one month at a time. His sleep periods last from 8 to 11 days."

My father pointed to Dr. Richardson. "Tom, give us the fMRI updates."

The foundation's neurosurgeon pointed to the twinkling tree and said, "The functional MRI scans of Hunter's brain indicate that he's consciously perceiving his environment on Millennium. When we show him photos of mountains, oceans, and nature scenes, his neuro-image reactions to visual stimuli are all positive. When we place his illustration of Metamorphosis in front of his eyes, his readings light up the monitor screen like a Christmas tree."

My father said, "As soon as we begin using the new brain computer interface equipment, we'll be able to communicate with Hunter in the next few weeks. If that's successful, we'll add *that* to the report."

Communicate? I wondered what Daddy meant by that. The thought of interacting with Hunter sounded intriguing.

"I know we're all excited about Dr. Shankar's BCI research, but I have something special to tell you," Dr. Richardson said, raising his almost-empty wine glass. He grinned and flicked the rim with his index finger, causing the crystal to ring—*ping*.

"It appears Hunter has fallen in love. The magnetic impulses of his *nucleus accumbens* has increased several times in the past five months. Really lit up the screen. The boy's fallen head over heels for someone."

The doctors smiled and raised their right thumbs. All except for my father.

"In love? I hope it's just infatuation and he doesn't get distracted," Daddy said. "He never seemed that interested in girls in high school. I wonder what kind of girl he's managed to find on Millennium. Hmmm?"

As surprised as my father, I held my hand over my mouth and giggled silently. Hunter never dated. Had a couple of girl friends that he and his surfer buddies hung around, but my brother never acted serious about any girl.

Fletcher smiled at the "Hunter's in love" announcement, closed his report booklet and said, "I believe this concludes the information that Wayland's going to present. Any questions?"

The other doctors shook their heads, *no.*

My father stood and slammed the *Mythology Compendium* shut. The loud bang scared me, causing me to accidentally bump the cabinet louvers with my hand.

Daddy turned his head and looked straight at the cabinet. I felt like he stared right into my eyes.

I froze, knowing that if I tried to sneak out the back doors, I'd make more noise. Closed my eyes and held my breath, thinking, *Please don't walk toward me. Don't open the cabinet.*

"What's the matter, Wayland?" Richardson asked.

"Nothing," Daddy replied.

I opened my eyes to see my father take a gulp of wine and say, "I've made my decision. I'm going to wait on the mythology report. Unless, of course, Van Campbell changes his mind."

The doctors shook their heads affirmatively.

"One last thing," my father said, holding up three documents. "I'm still considering having our three Coma~X survivors, the one's with *these* birth certificates, attend the television interview. I really like this Elizabeth Dow woman."

"That's not a bad idea," Richardson said.

Fletcher raised his hands in the air and said, "For God sakes, I thought we already agreed that the awakened survivors would be a total distraction."

"Dennis is right. The media will have a feeding frenzy,"

Dustin yelled, pointing his cigar at Richardson.

My father waved the three documents in the air. "We have their birth certificates. They don't look anywhere near their ages. They've never experienced muscle atrophy or coma health issues."

I liked the birth certificate idea. I wanted the doctors to stop arguing and let my father have his way. After all, it was *his* foundation, *his* money, not theirs.

"I think Paul might have a point." Herrick held up the report. "When our awakened guests tell the press they are all over one hundred years old and they look more like thirty, the whole focus will be on them, not our *Planet Millennium Report.*"

"I agree," Fletcher said. "The media will have their cameras focused on our three patients, not Wayland. The headlines will be, 'Fountain of Youth Discovered,' or some other Paparazzi sensationalism."

"There's bound to be a media frenzy," Daddy responded, "especially when I announce I've returned from another planet in another dimension, that my son, along with five other people, are now visiting the same planet in cloned bodies wearing Triamulets. Might as well bring the awakened Coma-X survivors to the—"

A loud knocking on the door interrupted my father.

Startled, we all turned our heads.

The library door swung open and slammed against the wall.

Momma stood there with her arms crossed.

Let's just say she was not smiling.

"Wayland, for heaven's sake!" she shouted. "Tonight is Christmas Eve! There are still presents to wrap and you've got to put Sebastian's tricycle together. The children are asking about you. They need their father!"

Daddy blushed. "Sorry, darling. We'll wrap this up so I can wrap presents."

My mother's face turned red. She stood in the doorway, glaring at my father while the foundation doctors put down their smoldering cigars and half-empty wine glasses.

"Wait, that sounded stupid," Daddy said, turning off his desk lamp. "I wasn't trying to be funny."

My aggressive mother pointed at the doctors and yelled, "Don't you men have homes?"

Daddy's colleagues looked at each other with bewildered expressions, refusing to make eye contact with Momma.

I felt sorry for my embarrassed father. He looked so weak in front of his friends.

Daddy hurried toward the door, knocking over his half-full glass of red wine onto his *Planet Millennium Report*.

He picked up the wet, dripping booklet and told her, "We're almost finished. The guys are leaving in a few minutes; they have planes to catch."

The four foundation doctors grinned nervously at my mother.

She rolled her hazel-brown eyes in disgust, turned, and slammed the door behind her.

My father held his hands out in apology. "Sorry, men. Things have been a little stressful around here."

"We understand." Richardson gestured toward the door. "We'll be on our way."

"No, don't get up," Daddy said. "Before you guys leave, do we all agree that the hormone study, the fMRI research, and the latest BCI studies will be released at my media event?"

The renowned scientists nodded *yes* in unison, tucking their report folders under their arms.

"I'll hold off on the mythology and fairy tale research. I'm still not sure about bringing the three awakened Coma-X survivors to the media event. I'll decide soon."

Richardson asked, "Shouldn't we wait until Hunter awakens before we announce our Millennium discovery to the world?"

Daddy sighed and ran his fingers through his black hair while the doctors fidgeted in their seats, chewing on their cigar stubs.

"I believe we have enough scientific evidence to go public," my father announced, gloating.

"Okay, Wayland. Our fate is in your hands," Richardson said, crushing out his cigar in an abalone shell ashtray.

"When will you make the announcement?" Dustin asked.

My father combed his fingers through his goatee, studying his colleagues while they stood and put on their raincoats.

"In the next ninety days, my friends. Sometime in March. Maybe early April. The date depends on Howard Blake."

Daddy turned off the library lights and shut the door after his staff shuffled out of the room. As the voices faded away down the hall, I scurried out the back of the cabinet, between the cars, out the garage pet door, up the trellis, onto the roof, and through my bedroom window. I undressed and climbed into my canopied feather bed. After hearing that Hunter had fallen in love, my curiosity for Millennium grew stronger.

Stayed up half the night, gazing at the Milky Way.

Mesmerized by each shooting star's fiery white tail blazing through the night sky, I wondered what it felt like to live on another planet, but still have a body back on Earth.

Two bodies, like my brother.

Maybe I'm more like Hunter than I realize.

After all, we *are* twins.

Overly curious, he always got into everything. My father told him that his curiosity would get the best of him.

Daddy had *that* right.

That's how Hunter ended up on Millennium.

By New Year's Day, 2015, my *own* curiosity had begun to get the best of me.

That Thursday afternoon, my mother told me that Daddy and Professor Van Campbell were on their way to our home from the Wainright Foundation's headquarters in San Francisco.

The day was easy to remember because Jeremy was scheduled to return on the following Saturday. Overwhelmed with joyous anxiety, I hadn't seen his gorgeous face since July, the week before my birthday.

Hung over from her New Year's Eve party that she celebrated all by herself in the family room, my cranky mother complained all day long about Daddy hiding in the library, about his "crazy foundation", about high government taxes, the outrageous price of gasoline, the lousy weather—anything she could think of.

Negative energy.

It was difficult to be around her that day.

Happy New Year, Momma.

After dinner, she demanded I clean the upstairs bedrooms while she attended to Hunter.

I never disobeyed her.

Standing in front of the bathroom mirror with a toilet brush in my hand, I waved the white handle back and forth like a magic wand, convincing myself it was time for some well-deserved mischief.

Full of rebellious energy, I decided to sneak downstairs to find the *Planet Millennium Report* that Daddy had shown to his colleagues. I *had* to read it.

Tiptoeing down the winding staircase, I scurried past my mother. She rocked back and forth in her favorite chair next to Hunter's hospital bed. I sprinted down the marble corridor and into the library.

After closing the doors, I sat at my father's cherrywood desk to catch my breath.

The report laid in the top drawer.

Holding a flashlight, I read the booklet.

The *Planet Millennium Report* revealed detailed information of what had happened to all the people after they wore the Triamulet and went to sleep. Into a coma.

Coma-X.

At that very moment, I knew Hunter's fate.

For some reason, *reading* the report made it factual.

Tears ran down my cheeks.

I know why I cried. It was the realization that Hunter lived so far away—that my brother might never come home.

Or, if he did come back, I'd be an elderly woman and he'd still be a teenager. Sobbing, I heard four footsteps and two voices approach from down the hallway.

Professor Johan and Daddy marched toward the library!

Fumbling with the flashlight switch, I ran across the dark room and hid behind the leather sofa. I held a handkerchief against my nose and mouth. Tears welled in my eyes.

The mahogany doors opened and the library lights came on.

While the latches clicked and the doors shut, I crawled to the end of the sofa and peeked through the legs of the end table.

"I wish I had stayed longer," Daddy said. "I might have seen some of the gods and goddesses, like you did."

"I saw one, just *one* god," Professor Johan replied.

"If there wasn't such a huge time difference, I'd have stayed longer. But, if I'd have stayed as long as I wanted, Gloria would have been an old woman by the time I returned. My kids would have grown up without me around."

"I hope Hunter remains on Millennium long enough to answer some of our questions."

"Don't let Gloria hear you say that. She'll get really angry."

"Sorry, Wayland. I didn't mean it that way."

Daddy patted Professor Johan on the back. The same back that had the most beautiful tattoo I had ever seen.

Held my breath while the professor, my father's best friend, sat on the sofa and continued the conversation.

"Wayland, I see you have all your mythology and fairy tale books out on the table."

"Hey! What's my *Millennium Report* doing out of the drawer?" Daddy shouted.

Julia, you idiot, I thought. *You left the report on the desk. How could you be so careless?*

"Excuse me?" Professor Johan asked, watching Daddy pick up the report.

"Nothing. I thought I had put this back in my desk drawer this morning," he said, holding up the booklet. "I need you to review this report in the next few days."

"Make me a copy and I'll read it."

"Johan, this *is* your copy," Daddy said, laying the *Planet Millennium Report* on his desk.

"I'll get it on the way out."

My father stepped to the wet bar and poured two scotch on the rocks. "I just wish the report could be completed properly," he said, handing a drink to his friend.

"Come on, Wayland, you're not going to start begging me again to get involved in this thing, are you?"

"Johan, you've been there. You're an awakened survivor. You're world famous. You are my only reliable mythology connection."

"I will not be interviewed," Professor Johan said, gritting his teeth. "Sorry. I don't want my years of respected work to be discredited."

"Don't worry, your work will always be revered."

"As I've promised, if you can convince the world that Millennium is real, I'll consider coming forward. Other than that, end of conversation."

Daddy threw his hands in the air. "I give up. You win. I respect your decision. I won't ask again."

"Much appreciated." Professor Johan held his drink in the air, toasting my father's surrender.

"Did you bring it?" Daddy asked.

The professor swallowed a gulp of scotch, patting his coat pocket. "Against my better judgment, yes."

My father grinned. "Since you refuse to get involved with my media event, I *do* need your expertise on mythology. I'm considering adding it to the report, even if I don't have you as a witness. I still have time before I go public. Don't worry, you won't have to write anything. I'll do the report myself."

"I thought your foundation staff doesn't believe the mythology evidence is solid enough for the report, especially the fairy tale study."

"Those guys are great scientists and medical doctors, but they've overreacted about my upcoming media event. They're paranoid that something's going to go wrong."

"Well, you have to admit, it will be the most amazing announcement of all time. There are going to be negative reactions. A lot of radical responses to your Planet Millennium declaration."

I wondered what the professor meant by *radical responses*. His comment bothered me. I had a feeling that something terribly bad was going to happen by the tone in his voice.

"I'll deal with all the negativity as it comes," Daddy said, confidently. "Now, let's get down to business. Tell me what myths and legends and fairy tales to put in this report and what to omit. I'm a bit overwhelmed."

"Keep it simple. First of all, focus on the fact that all the mythological information is accurate, that every myth described since the beginning of human history is real.

"Second, you must make people understand that all the gods and mythological creatures, that all the fairy tale characters and the fantasy lands really exist. On another planet.

"Third, you must explain that over the centuries, people returning to Earth from Millennium brought back factual information that became the myths, legends, and fairy tale stories that have become so ingrained in our culture. Myths are real."

Professor Johan took a sip of his drink and asked, "When are you going public with the report?"

"I have a major media event scheduled."

"After Hunter's awakening?"

Daddy walked to the conference table in the middle of the library.

Ran his hand over the stacks of mythology books and ancient maps covering the cherrywood table. He pointed to the color map on the wall. "Thank God you had your tattoo done so we have accurate geographical information."

"Let's not discuss my tattoo right now," Professor Johan said. He took a deep breath and asked, "Wayland, you're *not* considering an announcement before Hunter returns, are you?"

My father picked up a pen and yellow pad from the table. "We'll discuss that later. Please, help me decide what mythological names to put in my report."

The professor said, "During my brief visit with the great sage, Metamorphosis, I learned a lot about Millennium."

"Brief? You were in a coma for more than two months. You stayed a lot longer than I did. I only got to see Time Island and visit with Metamorphosis for a few hours. You sailed the Sea of Circles and saw Poseidon, a *real* god."

"I got lucky when the old sea god surfaced next to the *Skipbladnir.* Unfortunately, Poseidon taught me very little. Most of my mythology knowledge came from their sacred Book Of Wisdom, the *Magnum Opus.* I wish I had a copy of that fabulous text."

"If only I could have spent as much time with Metamorphosis as you did."

"I sense jealousy in your voice."

The professor was right.

Daddy *did* act jealous. He never got over his decision to leave Millennium.

Throughout my childhood, I heard him complain about, what he called, "his horrible choice to leave."

"Can you blame me?" My father asked, shrugging his shoulders. "Sorry, Johan. Go ahead. I'll stop whining."

The professor nodded and continued. "The wise sage allowed me as much time as I needed to study the *Magnum Opus.* As I turned the sacred book's parchment pages, it became clear that all the mythological history on Earth, all the gods and goddesses, all the legends and fairy tales, all of our grandest myths originated on Millennium.

"In fact, we need to thank Metamorphosis for our entire cultural heritage. Our language. Our customs. Our knowledge of the sciences. Our philosophical beliefs."

Daddy scribbled on his yellow pad while the professor talked.

"Wait until people realize that our roots, everything human, came from Millennium. The great sage, Metamorphosis, also taught our spiritual masters, the prophets.

"Before I went to sleep on Time Island to return home, I'm glad I had the foresight to study the names engraved on the rock platform's surface. I was blown away by all the great explorers and writers and poets and philosophers who had visited Millennium before me.

"People like Socrates, Lao Tzu, Homer, Galileo, Dante, Shakespeare, Grimm, Leonardo Da Vinci, Thoreau, Emily Dickinson, and so many more."

While my father lit a cigar, I tried to comprehend what I had just heard.

No wonder people were calling Dr. Wainright a lunatic.

Daddy blew three smoke rings into the library air and said, "The media is going to go crazy when I announce this stuff."

Professor Johan sipped from his glass of scotch. "As for the gods, they are alive and well on Millennium. In the Utopian's sacred Book Of Wisdom I saw descriptions and drawings of all the gods and goddesses.

"Zeus, Hades, Odin, Freya, Thor, Osiris, Isis, Brahma, and Manitou. Hundreds of them, all alive on Millennium.

"I was dumbfounded when I studied the Millennium maps and discovered the locations of Atlantis, Wonderland, Enchanted Forest, Sleeping Beauty's Castle, Camelot, and all the Arthurian legends and fairy tale lands and fantasy kingdoms."

My father opened a wooden humidor, offered his friend a cigar, and said, "I wish I had boarded the *Skipbladnir* so I could have seen the *Magnum Opus* and the maps of Millennium."

"I should have stayed long enough to see the First Great Treasure of Octilogy, the Eternal Rose," Professor Johan said, accepting the cigar from my father, who flicked open his chrome lighter and lit the havana.

The professor rolled the cigar between his lips and blew a puff of blue smoke into the library lights. "I loved the fabulous illustrations of the mythological beasts and creatures in the *Magnum Opus*. The gryphon, unicorn, pegasus, cyclops, centaur, faeries, dragons, and hundreds more described in perfect detail."

Daddy pointed to the map on the wall. "We need proof that all our myths originated from Millennium. We need a volunteer, an eye witness who everyone trusts."

"I'm not sure about your Millennium volunteer idea. If I were you, I'd be patient and wait until Hunter wakes up, or until one of your *other* Coma-X patients awaken."

"I'm not waiting any longer."

"All right, have it your way. I've spent my entire career proving that myths are important to our civilization. Not once have I confused the issue with my Millennium experience."

"Well, it's time to clarify the origins of myth. Clear the air. Let the world know the truth."

"I'm not sure the world *wants* to know the truth," Johan declared, frowning at my father.

I sensed the professor knew something that my father could not comprehend.

Daddy stared into the professor's eyes, turned, and walked back to his desk. He gulped down his drink and said, "You told me you brought it."

Professor Johan nodded, *yes*, and reached into his pocket. Laid his Triamulet attached to a gold necklace on Daddy's desk and said, "Please, for the love of God, don't lose *this* one."

My father grabbed the medallion by the gold chain and held it up to the light. From behind the sofa, I watched the shiny medallion gleam in the amber lights, swinging back and forth between my father's fingers.

I felt an attraction to the sacred Triamulet.

Like a moth to a flame, I was drawn to her golden glow.

"This is the undeniable evidence that will prove that Millennium exists. All I need is one volunteer, someone with a healthy ego who has not traveled there, and we can prove the Coma-X patients' whereabouts. The origin of myths, legends, and fairy tales."

"Be careful. You must select the right person for the journey or people will think it's a huge hoax."

"Don't worry, I know what I'm doing."

Daddy stepped to the library shelves, pulled out a weathered red book, and opened it.

"A book safe?" Professor Johan asked. "Why not a *real* safe?"

"I had my Triamulet locked and hidden in a safe deposit box and look what happened. No one will look here."

He placed the gold medallion and chain into the fake book and closed the lid. "I've hired some armed security guards for the television appearance, so that the Triamulet is protected."

"Guards?"

"Damn right," my father said, sliding the red book back into its original slot on the library shelf, directly behind his leather chair. "You can never be too cautious."

Without warning, the library doors opened.

Daddy turned and yelled, "Who is it? Who's there?"

"For God's sake!" my mother shouted. "It's your wife!"

"Oh. Sorry, darling."

"Dinner in ten minutes," she said. "Let me guess. The professor will be joining us?"

"If you don't mind," Daddy said, smiling at the professor, "Johan just loves your delicious home-made meat loaf."

Momma had already rolled her eyes and stormed away in the middle of my father's sentence.

His face flushed with embarrassment, he handed Professor Johan the *Planet Millennium Report*, turned off the lights, and shut the mahogany doors behind them.

The footsteps disappeared down the corridor.

Switching on the flashlight, I pointed the light at the bottom bookshelf behind my father's desk, steadying the white beam on the red book.

Afraid to look at, or touch, the sacred Triamulet, I stood there and trembled, unwilling to open the book safe that evening.

Backing away, I turned and crawled through the secret cabinet passageway to return to my bedroom before Momma discovered me missing.

Have you ever prayed for something?

I have.

My prayers were finally answered.

The third week of January, Daddy called me into his library.

Sat me down on the leather sofa and said, "Someone wants to talk to you."

He hugged me, handed me the cordless phone, and smiled as he hurried out of the room, closing the door behind him.

"Hello?" I mumbled.

"Hi, it's me. I'm home."

"Oh, Jeremy! I thought I'd never hear your voice again!"

I couldn't believe how needy I sounded. So desperate.

My voice quivered when I spoke.

"Yeah, I know what you mean. I wasn't sure if I'd ever get back to California."

We both laughed and he talked about his mother in Massachusetts and the stress of moving back and forth across the country. I calmed down as I listened to his charming low voice.

"Never mind me, what about *you*?" he asked. "What have you been up to?"

Didn't know what to say. I wanted to tell him I spent every moment dreaming about him, but instead, I told him about school and the books I had read and really silly stuff. I knew how boring I must have sounded.

"Now that I'm back in school, my dad won't let me work weekends," he said. "I think it has something to do with your mom not wanting me over there."

My heart sank.

He knew Momma had a problem.

Before I answered, he said, "It's okay. Your mom's probably worried I'll fall in love with you or something."

While he chuckled at his humor that I did not find funny, I tried to say something clever. I decided to tell the truth without revealing too much about my family.

"My mother is old fashioned. She worries about me a lot. I'm sure when she meets you, she'll like you."

"Okay, when will I meet her?"

Oh no! I had opened my big mouth. He wanted to meet Momma.

I blurted out, "Well, I'm not sure. If you call me back, I'll have an answer."

"Great. I can't wait to see you again."

My heart raced in my chest.

Did you hear that? I thought. *He can't wait to see me!*

I giggled nervously and we continued to talk about school.

It seemed like we had only talked for a couple of minutes when my father opened the door and said, "You've been on the phone half an hour, sweetheart. Time to say goodbye."

How could I have talked thirty minutes?

It felt like a brief moment in time.

"Goodbye," I said, dying to tell him I really liked him. But I never found the courage, afraid to hear his response. I think he felt the same, but he never said anything terribly romantic.

It didn't bother me, I felt reconnected to him.

Like a prince, he had come to rescue me.

So, we said goodbye and I hung up the phone.

I hugged Daddy as I pranced out of the library and floated up the stairs, oblivious to all family members.

Or the endless household chores.

Or problems of any kind.

When I got to my bedroom, I plopped on my feather bed. With a smile on my face, my head spun with thoughts of Jeremy. I felt so good about myself.

Finally, I had a boy calling me.

A boy friend.

Portal   • Haenthal
Celestial City   Balan   Acre of
Druid   Pyramid of   Bacham   the Undying
Hills   Yonaguni   Bridge   Dwarve   Zavendis
Druid   Micromona   River
Junction   ⊕ Portal of
          Metamorphosis   Glittering   Tom   • Milosis
Doubting   Palatine Hills   Plains   Sawyer's
Junction   Island
The • Doubting Castle
Point Stonehenge   Turnaround
                              World   Land of the   Oneida
Cardiff   McDougal's   Lesser Gods   Lyrcea
Hill   Caves
       Montesino's   Astral Plain
       Cave

Utopian   **Pellagus**
River
Gorge   Hemakuta   Conscia   Rharian
        Lake Hill   Field
        Makhalinda
                          Griddhraj Parvat Hills
        Phoenix • Midella   **Regnum**   Animal Repa
        Hill   Tree   Mediterra

        Gates of   Land of the
        Dawn   Greater Gods   • Telepylo

                          Phlegra
          Theleme   Hills of   White
        Place   Cleito   Zodia
        of   River of   Trail
        Generation   Pleasure

medaciuat • Lubee   Anostus
Junction
Open Road and   River of
South Caravan Trail   Grief   • Escalot
          Mt. Penglai   Mt. Horai   • Hygeia
Gaste
Forest   Melody   • Cavershall Castl

80

Chapter VIII
Millennium Report

Wagging his tail, faithful Pooh licked Hunter's hand. *The poor dog,* I thought, *he wants Hunter to play with him, take him for a run on the beach like they used to do.*

"Quiet Pooh! We're watching Daddy on television," I yelled, snapping my fingers at the submissive golden retriever.

The dog whined and lay next to Hunter's bed.

Momma sat next to us in her winged back chair, in front of the flat-screen television.

Hunter lay in his hospital bed by the fireplace while we listened to the live interview.

"Finally," I said, "After all these years, Daddy gets to tell the world about Millennium."

My mother looked at me with daggers in her eyes.

Have you ever had one of your parents look at you with *that* look? You know, when their eyes reach deep inside your mind and they extract all your deepest secrets?

"Momma, please," I said, "Let's watch the show."

Couldn't blame her for being upset.

She begged my father not to go public with, as she put it, his "crazy ideas".

All ten of us kids shared the sectional sofa. The girls giggled and teased each other while they waited for Daddy to appear on television.

Momma held a glass of her favorite night-time beverage—whiskey on the rocks. When the show began, she hushed my brothers and sisters with her *better-be-quiet* stare.

"Good evening, ladies and gentlemen. From our live studios

in New York, I'm Howard Blake, host of *Innovative Americans*.

"Although it's April Fools Day, our show promises to be an insightful one. Our special guest tonight is Dr. Wayland Melvin Wainright, founder of the Wainright Foundation. Welcome to the show, Doctor."

"Thank you, Howard. I'll ignore the 'April Fool's' reference."

Blake smirked. "As I read the information in front of me, I find it quite unbelievable. It says here that you have evidence of intelligent life forms on another planet."

The live audience responded with mixed emotions. People cackled, while others whistled and cheered.

Blake allowed the crowd to calm down. "It goes on to say that you have published a report, released last week to the scientific community."

"Yes. In fact, my staff has already received numerous calls and e-mails from all over the world."

"Do these other scientists believe your *Planet Millennium Report?*" Blake asked, holding up the document.

The cameras zoomed in for a close up shot.

The report cover filled the screen.

I was dying to yell out that I had read the report.

"So far, we have mixed reviews," Daddy said.

"Fair enough. You claim to have proof that a planet with intelligent life forms is out there somewhere?"

"Correct. I have documented evidence, as well as three witnesses, that will verify that Millennium truly exists."

"You say, Millennium. Who came up with *that* name?"

"It comes from the inhabitants. I learned the name from a great sage named Metamorphosis, who lives on the planet."

"This report states that you visited the planet yourself, that it's located in the Andromeda Galaxy, that it's 200 million light years from Earth."

"That's correct."

"Please, tell us. How does one get to this planet?" Blake asked, with a sarcastic tone in his voice.

Daddy explained how he wore the Triamulet and lapsed into a coma—how he traveled to Millennium via dimensional shifting on the Astral Highway—his experiences on Time Island—his meeting with Metamorphosis—his return to Earth—the formation of the Wainright Foundation for the purpose of Coma-X research to prove extraterrestrial life exists.

Allowing my father time to explain his visit to Millennium without an interruption, Blake then asked, "I understand you've brought more of your fellow intergalactic travelers with you."

The audience erupted into cheers and applause.

My father stood and introduced his three guests, the Coma-X survivors with verifiable birth certificates.

Momma said she liked the appearance and the confident attitude of the woman who spoke with an English accent—Elizabeth Dow.

During their interviews with Blake, the three guests told the same story: they had fallen into a coma wearing a Triamulet—were transported to Millennium—met a sage named Metamorphosis—learned about the Secrets of the Universe—returned to Earth.

They emphasized how their Earth body had not aged after spending decades in a coma—Coma-X.

Confirmed they had never suffered from muscle atrophy or other health-related coma symptoms.

The audience sat in silence, listening attentively.

At the end of the interviews, the Millennium returnees gave their age.

The Coma-X survivors all claimed to be over one hundred years old.

While Howard Blake raised his eyebrows in disbelief, the audience mumbled to each other with mixed emotions, believing that none of the travelers could possibly be as old as they claimed.

Elizabeth Dow really shocked the crowd when she announced she was 139 years old!

The camera zoomed in for a face shot and I noticed she wore a Triamulet with a shiny crystal mounted in the center of the medallion.

She's still got her Triamulet, I thought. *I like the stone set in the middle of the medallion. It's prettier than Daddy's.*

After the three guests had exited the stage, Blake asked my father, "Well, their stories are certainly fascinating. Out of this world, so to speak. Do you have more evidence, so our curious but skeptical audience can make an intelligent evaluation?"

"Hunter, my oldest son, wore my Triamulet and now lives on Millennium. His Earth body has been in a coma since July 8th of last year. We believe he'll wake up any day now."

"Okay. If that happens, we'll surely have *him* on the show. I understand you brought us a Triamulet."

My father raised his hand, motioning to his right.

Two armed guards carried a canvas security bag to the table, unlocked the bag, and handed it to Daddy. He reached inside the canvas sack and pulled out a golden necklace and medallion.

"This Triamulet is just like the one that I wore back in 2004."

He handed the necklace to Blake.

A hush fell over the audience as the host dangled the shiny medallion by the gold chain.

"So, if I wear this necklace to bed tonight, I'll wake up on Millennium?" Blake asked, examining the Triamulet.

"As long as you have a healthy ego and truly believe that Millennium exists; yes, you will."

Blake made a comical face, handing the gold medallion back to my father.

The audience laughed and cheered.

"This is the exact reaction that I expected," Daddy said, half smiling and half smirking at the host and the audience. "In fact, we're now in the process of interviewing several volunteers, one of whom will wear this Triamulet, travel to Millennium, and visit Metamorphosis. Then, return to Earth."

"May I throw my hat in the ring?" Blake asked, chuckling.

"I'm not sure your level of self-esteem meets the qualifications," Daddy replied. "Your enormous ego might prevent you from making the trip."

The audience roared with laughter.

Blake smirked and announced, "After a short commercial break, we will bring out our panel of experts in the field of molecular engineering, astrophysics, astronomy, quantum physics, mythology, parapsychology, theology, and philosophy."

Daddy nodded with a defiant, *bring-on-the-experts* look, while he dangled the Triamulet between his fingers.

He sat back confidently and crossed his leg, mentally preparing to answer the barrage of critical questions. When the camera zoomed in on his hand holding the Triamulet between his fingers, my mother recognized the necklace and medallion.

"There's the necklace your father wore when he woke up in the hospital," Momma said, putting her crystal glass on the end table. "I never found out who put that weird trinket around his neck."

Not thinking, I pointed at the television and said, "That's a different Triamulet than Daddy wore."

"You act like you've seen it before," my mother said, glaring at me like a detective about to solve a murder mystery.

"I heard Daddy talking about it."

"So, you've *never* seen it in person?"

I swallowed and looked straight ahead, refusing to answer.

"We need to talk, young lady."

"Momma, please. Let's watch the interview. I don't want to talk about the necklace."

"Sorry, I'm a little out of sorts watching your father be crucified by the media," she told me while the show paused for a commercial break.

She looked over at Hunter resting peacefully. Sipping from her glass of whiskey, she pushed the lemon twist deeper into the ice cubes.

"I think Daddy's doing really well," I said, "holding his own against all the negativity."

We dipped our fingers into a mixing bowl of buttered popcorn and turned our attention to Howard Blake, who introduced the eight distinguished panelists.

The guests bowed their heads and waved while the audience applauded.

"Due to time restrictions," Blake announced, "we're going to allow one question from each member of our panel. Ready?"

The panelists nodded.

My intuition told me they were eager to "interrogate Dr. Wainright". I used that phrase because the panelists looked determined to criticize my father.

Discredit him.

Momma sensed it too.

Both of us were right.

The heated interview proceeded with Daddy answering eight questions that centered around the *Planet Millennium Report*. They focused on:

• Coma-X data.

• Dimensional shifting.

• Time-space travel on the Astral Highway.

• The non-aging process and the 50:1 time ratio between Earth and Millennium.

• Myths, gods and goddesses alive on Millennium.

• Fairy tale characters living on Millennium.

• The bizarre physical appearance of the inhabitants of Millennium.

• The ramifications of a sage, a philosopher king living on another planet who offered a peaceful message of non-violence and unconditional love; an ancient sage who influenced the great prophets and philosophers and writers and poets; a wise being who was responsible for our culture and heritage—everything human. The interview did not go well for Daddy and his Wainright Foundation.

My father, who wore his pride like a suit of armor, had to tolerate accusations of:

• Fabricating the three birth certificates.

• Bribing the Coma-X patients.

• Manufacturing the Triamulet himself.

• Hiring nutty professors at his Wainright Foundation.

• Falsifying medical records of the Coma-X patients.

• Inventing a planet with a cast of characters that would result in his financial gain.

Only Meta Viola, the renowned psychic, supported my father's theories and reported stories. The clairvoyant claimed, according to her telepathic powers, that everything Daddy said had been the truth.

"Thank you, Dr. Wainright," Blake said, "for one of the most exciting hours of *Innovative Americans* we've ever had."

The audience, mumbling and restless, responded with mixed emotions. Many people cheered. Many people booed my father.

"From our New York studios, good night."

Howard Blake stood and shook the hands of the panelists while the cameras faded to a commercial.

"My God, that was horrible," Momma said. "I feel so sorry for your father. He didn't deserve all that criticism. Whether I believe him or not, he's worked so hard, spent so much money to prove Millennium exists."

She raised her hands to cover her face.

Cried her eyes out.

I jumped to my feet.

"Okay, kids. It's bedtime," I announced, turning the television off with the remote control. "Ruby, please help Emily and Grace with the babies while I talk to Momma."

With tears in their eyes, the older girls picked up Sebastian and Crystal, who had fallen asleep. Zachary and Alexander punched each other in the arms while they chased Astrid and Pearl up the staircase.

I held my mother's hand and comforted her while she

sobbed. Gently stroking her black hair, I swore to myself I'd do something to help my mother feel better—something that would stop her depression.

Hunter, lying peacefully in his bed, could not respond to his mother's anguish.

Momma grasped my hand, tightly.

We sat silently, listening to the steady *beep—beep—beep* of my twin brother's monitoring equipment.

If I told you that Jeremy and I never got to physically see each other—be together—would you think I lived in the dark ages?

Only phone calls. I was only allowed to talk on the phone.

Jeremy asked me to e-mail him, text him, or tweet him.

Embarrassed, I had to tell him I didn't have a computer.

Or a smart phone.

Only an old-fashioned land line telephone with a big, clunky hand set.

Daddy and Mr. Estrada worked out a schedule where Jeremy called me two nights a week.

Because we went to different high schools, we had to tolerate our exile from each other.

The phone calls were all we had.

Then, in April, after Daddy's television appearance, my mother started drinking more and Jeremy was allowed to call me three nights a week.

More drinking. More phone calls.

At night, Momma didn't seem to care anymore. In the evenings, while Daddy hid in the library, she hid in her bottle.

Every morning, her hung-over personality, what Daddy called her "dark side", would dominate her unpredictable behavior.

Finally found the courage to ask my mother if I may go on an official date with Jeremy. I had already asked Daddy, and he said, "It's okay with me, but you better talk to your mother."

On a school night, I asked her.

Momma sat in her rocking chair next to Hunter's bed. She had just finished saying her rosary and she seemed to be in a good mood.

Told her the senior prom had been scheduled for the third week of May.

Stared at me for a long time before she spoke.

"I imagine you want that boy you've been talking with since January to take you on a date."

"Yes, Momma. To the prom on May 15th, on a Friday night. His name is Jeremy."

"Your father seems to approve of this boy."

I nodded, *yes*.

"Well, I guess it's time to meet the gardener's son."

His name is Jeremy, I wanted to scream, *not the gardener's son!*

Gathering my composure, I asked, "You mean I can go?"

"I guess so. But the young man has to come *here* for dinner. Your father and I need to meet him, see what he's like."

My thoughts swirled in confusion. I didn't want Jeremy to see my mother drinking, or see comatose Hunter lying in a hospital bed, but I had no choice.

All I cared about is that I'd finally get to go on my first date.

"When?" I asked. "What should I tell Jeremy?"

"The night of the prom, of course. Tell him he won't have to spend his money on some fancy dinner at an expensive restaurant. He's going to eat *here*, with the Wainright family."

I pictured Jeremy sitting at our dinner table with all my brothers and sisters screaming and acting like complete idiots. But I didn't complain. The last thing I wanted to do was upset my mother. After all, she had given me her blessing. Wait until you hear Momma's follow-up statement to her prom promise.

She announced, "I'll talk to your father about you dating next year when you attend Stanford."

Oh my God! She was going to let me date when I got to college!

Can you believe that? I was too embarrassed to tell Jeremy, tell him that we had to go all summer without dating.

Hiding my smirk, I thanked my mother.

She hugged me.

"I trust that you'll be a good girl on your prom night."

"I've always been good, Momma."

It seemed like I had to constantly justify my behavior. My inherent goodness. My unblemished purity.

She took a gulp of her wine.

"Yes, dear, of course you have."

That evening, when Jeremy called, I told him the good news.

"My parents want us to eat dinner over here."

"That sounds okay," he said. "I was going to take you to a nice restaurant, but I can do that this summer."

Scared to tell him I was forbidden to date until I attended college, I said, "Thank you for understanding. My parents just need to meet you. Once they see how wonderful you are, they'll let us be together more."

Before Jeremy could respond, my mother yelled, "Julia, please get off the phone. I need you to help me with Hunter. Now."

"I have to go," I said. "I'm excited to see you on prom night. Thank you, Jeremy."

"Good night, Julia. I love you."

Speechless, I sat there, stunned.

Holding the phone, the dial tone hummed before his words really hit me.

Unable to move, I allowed his declaration of affection to ring in my ears. He loves me!

Tears of joy filled my eyes. Jeremy loved me from the moment we met. I saw his passion for me in his expressions. Heard it in his voice.

Someone loves me, I thought. *Jeremy and I are going to start dating and—*

"Julia, where are you?" Momma shouted, interrupting my loving thoughts.

My joy soon dissolved as I hurried to the family room and found my mother in one of her drunken moods. She had finished an entire bottle of vodka. Sat in her rocking chair, next to Hunter's bed, arguing with my father.

"You need to go to bed before you fall asleep in your chair," Daddy told her.

He did not mean to say, "fall asleep", he meant, "pass out".

Daddy lifted my fatigued mother to her feet. Slung her arm over his shoulder as he helped her climb the winding staircase.

"Take ga~good ca~care of yer brother," she said to me, slurring her words.

When Momma passed out from exhaustion, my father carried her to bed. Late at night, I often found myself alone, caring for my comatose twin brother.

Since I had no one else to talk to, Hunter got an earful.

Telling him how angry I felt that he had done this terrible thing to his family. Scolding him for being so self-centered. Cursing him for keeping me away from Jeremy, my true love.

"Shame on you for leaving Momma the way you have," I mumbled. "You know how she totally freaked out when Daddy had *his* coma."

I tapped Hunter's forehead, hard.

Then, I thumped him with my index finger on his cheek.

When he didn't move or blink, I thumped him again, harder.

"You are so selfish, Hunter Wainright. You've been gone for almost a year. I hope you're having fun on your stupid trip to Millennium."

The week before my senior prom, a military officer came banging on our front door. You could sense something was wrong by the way my parents nervously escorted the intelligence officer into the living room.

What was he doing at our house this time at night? I thought, standing at the top of the stairs, listening to my parents talk to Lieutenant Colonel Blatt of the Homeland Security Division.

The colorful ribbons and medals pinned to his military jacket gleamed in the lamp light. The officer's uniform reminded me of formal clothing.

Getting dressed up.

Reminded me of my upcoming prom night.

The day before, I managed to get my mother out of the house so I could drive her to downtown Carmel By-The-Sea to pick out my prom dress.

Jeremy had already selected a white tuxedo with tails and a black bow tie.

The dress I liked, the powder-blue formal gown, fit perfectly.

Surprisingly, Momma allowed me to buy a low-cut top.

She told me that I filled out the dress nicely. I had matured physically during my senior year of high school.

Before we tried on the gown, the saleswoman measured me.

Five foot ten inches tall.

I can't grow any taller, I told myself.

Ruby is over six feet tall.

She's always been self-conscious, referring to herself as an "Amazon freak of nature".

Daddy told me to be proud of my height, but I think anything over six feet puts you in the *hard-to-get-a-date* category.

Luckily, Jeremy stands six foot two.

So, I don't feel like an Amazon.

On the way out of the dress shop, Momma suggested I become a model because of my height and my slender figure and my high cheek bones and my thin, turned-up nose.

I wished she'd make up her mind.

One day it's a teacher, the next day it's a nurse, and the next day it's a model.

Do professional models wait until their senior prom of high school to go on their first official date?

My father frowned at the military officer. "What is so important that you had to come out here at 8:30 in the evening?"

The Lieutenant Colonel cleared his throat. "As you're aware, all your Wainright Foundation offices located overseas have received bomb threats from various radical organizations. We believe we have that situation under control, internationally. Unfortunately, our intelligence sources have informed us that the threat is now here, in the United States."

"What kind of threat?" Daddy asked, motioning for my mother not to speak.

"Our sources tell us that an assassination plot, or possibly a kidnapping, has been planned."

Momma held her hand to her mouth while Daddy threw his arms in the air and yelled, "Assassinate who?"

The officer stared at my father with a *don't act so stupid, you know who* look.

"Okay, I understand. What about the kidnapping?" Daddy asked while my mother pulled a handkerchief from the pocket of her white capris.

"According to our surveillances, one or more of your family members are being targeted."

"What does that mean, for the children and me?" my mother asked, drying the tears in her eyes.

"For your protection and safety, we have contacted the FBI and CIA, as well as local law enforcement. Their representatives will be here in the morning. Our department requests that you keep the children home from school tomorrow. It is just a precautionary measure until we establish security and surveillance around your property. We also request that you and your husband remain here, at your home, until someone contacts you. We have officers patrolling the area this evening."

My mom burst into tears.

She looked at Daddy and shouted, "This is insane! Now the children can't go to school, can't go outside! Your oldest son is lying upstairs paralyzed! Tell the world you made this whole thing up. Tell them Millennium is not real. Tell them it's all a joke! We've been through enough hell! For God's sake, Wayland, make this all go away!"

Before my father responded, Momma jumped up and ran through the foyer.

She sobbed, crying hysterically.

I hid in the hallway closet with the door cracked open so I could see downstairs.

Just as I found a flashlight hanging on a door hook, Momma raced up the stairs with a handkerchief held to her face.

As she ran past me, Daddy ask the officer, "Is that all?"

"That covers the main issues," Lt. Col. Blatt said, standing. "Someone else will fill in the details tomorrow. I am sorry I had to be the one to bring you the bad news. I will leave now so you can be with your family."

"I need to be with my wife," Daddy said.

My father escorted the officer to the door, slammed it shut, turned the deadbolt lock, and hurried up the staircase.

I remained motionless in the closet while my father ran up the stairs toward the master bedroom. Before the door slammed shut, my mother screamed at Daddy, calling him names I'd rather not repeat.

During the chaos, I tiptoed down the stairs wearing my silk pajamas.

Ran down the glass corridor. Opened the library doors.

Breathing heavily, I turned the flashlight on and pointed the white beam at the books behind my father's desk.

For several weeks in a row, I'd become a late-night visitor to the library, obsessed with seeing the gold Triamulet, holding it in my hands.

I always returned the sacred medallion to the red book safe.

Holding my breath, I stepped behind Daddy's desk chair, removed the red book from the shelf, and placed the safe quietly on his desk.

Opening the lid, I shined my flashlight on the gold necklace and medallion.

Then and there, I realized how much I loved the darkness, the suspense, the thrill of doing something I knew would change my life.

Setting the flashlight down, I picked up the gleaming gold Triamulet between my trembling fingers.

Grinning, I put the necklace over my head.

Knowing the talisman's hidden promise of unimaginable adventure, the Triamulet gave me a sense of power I had never experienced.

Something changed inside me, a feeling of freedom.

The amulet felt magical around my neck.

Returning the book safe to the shelf, I switched off the flashlight and shut the library doors behind me.

This time I acted differently.

This time I took the Triamulet with me, out of Daddy's library.

A strange premonition drove me to take it. A exhilarating feeling I had never experienced before.

I was afraid to leave Momma. I was in love with Jeremy and dreamed of being with him.

So why in world would did I take that Triamulet?

There was no way I could leave my family.

A yellow, waxing moon rose steadily above the black ocean as I snuck down the glass-walled west corridor.

The gold Triamulet looked mystical under the starlight.

I kept thinking, *Take the medallion back, Julia. Take it back to the library.*

But instead, I lifted the gold chain and dropped the medallion inside my purple pajama top.

High on adrenaline, I ran past the kitchen and tiptoed up the winding staircase.

Familiar *beep—beep—beep* sounds came from Hunter's monitor.

Trembling, I stopped and listened for my mother and father.

Their argument had escalated into a shouting match.

Sneaking past my parent's bedroom and down the hallway, I silently closed my bedroom door.

With each beat of my pounding heart, I felt the warm Triamulet pulsate up and down, up and down, up and down against my sweating chest.

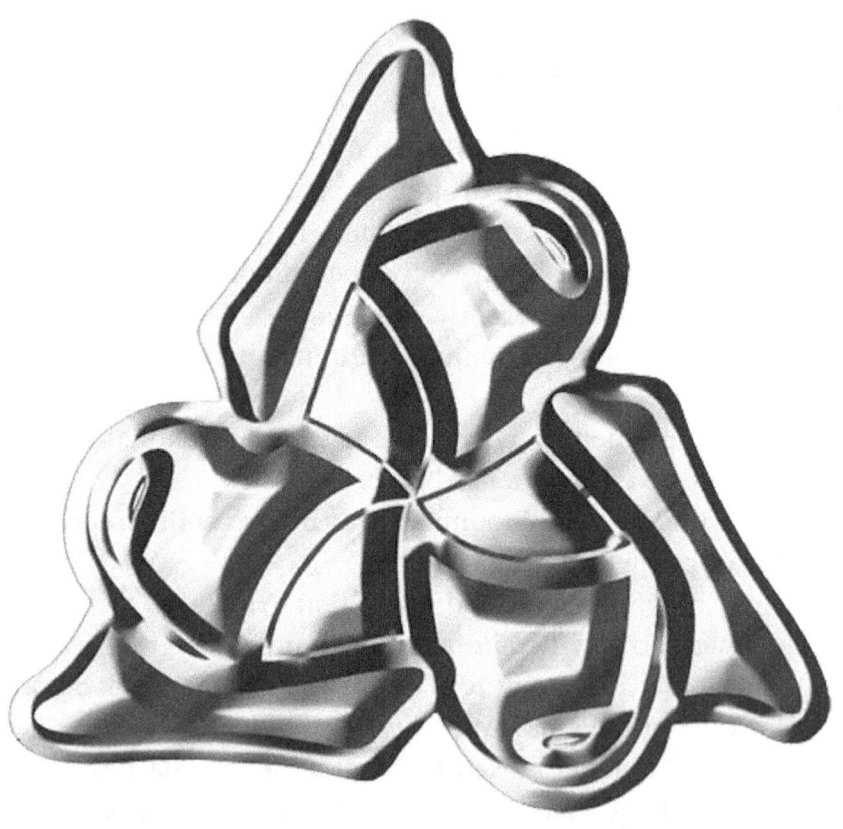

Julia

DAYNIGHT OF THE SPIDER

Chapter IX
The Triamulet

During that second week of May, my emotions were torn between Jeremy and the Triamulet. Between love and the unknown. Between my first kiss and seeing far-away lands. Instead of doing my homework that week, I'd leave my unfinished assignments in my school backpack and call Jeremy.

I didn't have to sneak downstairs to make a call.

Guess why. Finally got my *own* telephone!

My father talked my mother into buying me a cordless phone for my bedroom. So what if it wasn't a cell phone. Didn't care, as long as I could call Jeremy. Having our prom night to look forward to, each phone call got better and better, more intimate. The anticipation of going on a date and kissing a boy gave me goose bumps.

One night, I found the courage to tell Jeremy I loved him. Saying the words was not as difficult as I thought it would be. I said them without thinking. It felt so natural to say, "I love you."

Although completely lovesick—consumed with visions of Jeremy—something more powerful had overwhelmed me.

The Triamulet. The irresistible gold necklace had cast its spell on me. My mind never stopped thinking of the sacred medallion that held such mystery, that promised such high adventure.

Each night after I talked to Jeremy, I turned off my night-stand lamp. Lying in the dark, I listened to make sure the family was asleep. I had hidden a key under my mattress. The key opened my jewelry box. Daddy gave me the gift on my fifteenth birthday. The hand-crafted miniature chest also played music.

Maybe I should call it a music box. The fairy-tale song that came with it, *When You Wish Upon A Star,* happened to be old fashioned, but I learned to love the melody while the movement turned and the enchanted music danced around my bedroom.

What's that movie where the cute little cricket sang that song?

My hands trembled as I turned the key in the lock and lifted the lid of the chest. The Triamulet laid hidden under the purple velvet tray that covered the gold musical movement.

Carefully lifting the shiny Triamulet from the velvet lining, I tiptoed to my bay window and studied the sacred necklace under the starlight. Never, never had I seen anything so captivating.

I crawled back into bed with one of my favorite novels. Not to read, but to use the battery-powered book light. Laying the necklace across the open pages, I admired the Triamulet's radiance as the tiny light shined on the magic medallion.

The divine beauty of the gold talisman wasn't the only thing that intrigued me. I'd been captivated by the awesome power the sacred amulet possessed.

Distracted, I tried to read *The Golden Compass,* but how could I finish the book when my mind was overwhelmed with thoughts of Millennium?

I stared at the divine Triamulet, sensing my destiny.

Across the room, my powder-blue prom dress hung proudly on the closet door hook, beckoning me to try it on.

Dear God, I thought, *I'm going to miss the dance on Friday night. That's only three days away. What will Jeremy think? Maybe I should have told him about my plans so he doesn't worry. I haven't been honest with him.*

My heart pounded in my chest. Have you ever felt light-headed when your mind becomes filled with too many ideas?

My head spun with a barrage of thoughts: *How is Momma going to care for Hunter if I leave? Who's going to watch the babies when I'm gone? What will Jeremy think of my decision? Maybe I can return home soon enough for my prom. With the time difference, I'm not sure if that's possible. I hope Daddy doesn't discover the Triamulet missing. What will I say if he asks me about it?*

Breathing deeply, I gazed out the bay window at the river of stars drifting across the night sky.

What if I go to Millennium and I can't get back? I wonder what it feels like to be in two different bodies? Will I feel my Earth body when I'm on Millennium? I wonder if Hunter's comatose body can see me? What if I can't find my brother if I travel to Millennium? Momma is going to freak out when she sees me in a coma.

With my mind spinning with thoughts of the unknown, I stared at the Triamulet. While I held the triangular-shaped medallion and felt its incredible power, I agonized over making the right decision. The choice of a lifetime.

Tuesday.

I decided to leave home on a Tuesday. At 3:33 a.m., on the 12th day of May, 2015, I placed the Triamulet over my head, around my neck. I made the decision to go find my brother and bring him home.

Lying in bed, clutching the medallion, one of Daddy's favorite poems came to mind. He told me it had been written by one of the Millennium visitors.

The verse went like this:

"Thus grew the tale of Wonderland,

Thus slowly, one by one,

Its quaint events were hammered out,

And now the tale is done,

And home we steer, a merry crew,

Beneath the setting sun."

Am I really going to Wonderland, I thought. *Somewhere magical, like Daddy dreamed about?*

Closing my eyes, I murmured, "Go to sleep, Julia. Go find Hunter and bring him home. You'll be Momma's hero."

Pretending I breathed air into my lungs from the other side of the universe, I stopped worrying and slowed my mind down, imagining myself floating above my bed, looking down at my body.

Floating. Detached. Free.

"Relax, Julia. Let go."

The exact moment I fell into a dream state I felt warm all over. Completely weightless. A fantastic white light flashed and then pulsated within my mind. Not in my eyes. Within every cell of my body.

The light never blinded me, it had *become* me. The warm illumination overtook my body, radiating and absorbing itself within my spirit, my soul. The glowing light lifted my spirit up and pulled me toward somewhere mysterious.

Upward. I sensed the light carried my body to another dimension, to somewhere else. To a place far, far away. Like I had been lifted up and shot out of a cannon—from slow motion to an incredibly-fast warp speed.

What a wild, exhilarating feeling I had. A true, out-of-body experience. Everything seemed to be happening at once; yet, all things remained static—the same.

Time stood still while I sped through endless space.

A timeless void overwhelmed me. A magical place with no sky and no physical boundaries. The experience felt real, nothing like a dream.

Chapter X
Astral Journey

Without warning, the uplifting, inner white light within me dimmed. The warm illumination disappeared and my body became heavy again. My astral journey, dimensional shifting as Professor Johan called it, lasted but a moment in time, but to me, it lasted an entire lifetime.

My bright world had gone dark.

Immediately, I knew what had happened. I had awakened. Or, at least I thought I had.

Remember those times when you woke up out of a dead sleep and you couldn't tell if you were still dreaming?

When I opened my eyes, everything looked blurry. Blinded, I held my hand in front of my face to shield my eyes from the glare of a red sky. The atmosphere looked on fire.

Sitting up to gain my bearings, I looked down to see a glowing blue circle with an illuminated Triangulum symbol beneath me. The opaque surface felt warm to the touch. Streaks of white and blue light emerged from the glowing circle. The radiant beams shot straight up into the atmosphere.

I knew I had arrived on Millennium, having traveled across several dimensions to awaken on Time Island, atop the platform that my father and Professor Johan had described so many times.

The air felt cool and damp as I gazed at a layer of crimson-grey fog that encircled the stone platform. In the far distance, above the eerie mist, a 360° circle of towering vertical cliffs surrounded me, what Daddy described as the rim of Discordia. The only sounds were the crashing of waves below and the occasional squawking of white sea birds overhead.

Directly above me, ghostly stars hid behind the scarlet haze while a trio of moons crawled across the heavens. On the horizon, the red sky melted into a blue sky. On the opposite horizon, a black sky hugged the crater's rim.

Looking down at myself, I couldn't tell if the goose bumps covering my body came from the cool air or my adrenaline rush.

I grabbed the gold Triamulet hanging from the gold chain around my neck. The medallion glowed against my purple pajama top. As promised in the *Planet Millennium Report*, the medallion had materialized with me during my cloning while I traveled through the traversable wormhole.

Climbing to my feet, I immediately noticed eight white stone paths radiating from the center circle and connecting to each of the eight stone pedestals. These were the eight Time Oracles.

Suddenly, one stone path began to glow and pulsate, like a heartbeat. The three-foot-wide illuminated path led straight to a stone pedestal marked EARTH.

To the side of the path sat a stone bench and a weathered leather trunk, just like the one Daddy described during his meetings with Professor Johan. The trunk, twelve feet away, had EARTH engraved on the side.

Knowing exactly what to do, I ran to the trunk and opened the lid. The ornate hinges creaked and popped. The escaping odor of musty air reminded me of my home attic—old creaky chests stuffed with moth-eaten clothes and moldy books.

A reddish-brown fur laid folded inside the chest. After rubbing my hand over the soft pelt, I picked it up and put on the bizarre coat with four arm holes, two on each side. Lined with satin, the fur smelled musty. I didn't care; the full-length coat made me feel secure—warm and cozy.

The trunk also contained clothing, swords, knives, a rope, two unmarked bottles filled with liquid, and a bag of gold coins.

Not sure what to do with any of the weapons or coins, I closed the lid and turned my attention to the end of the illuminated path, to the Time Oracle with the perfect replica of planet Earth spinning slowly while it floated magically above the rock pedestal. I walked to the pedestal, then moved my hand back and forth under the globe, feeling a strong magnetic force.

A twelve-inch-long parchment scroll laid on the pedestal's rock ledge. I unrolled it and read the message inscribed on the yellow papyrus:

Welcome to Millennium,

As our esteemed visitor from Planet Earth, please be aware that I, or one of my eight fellow Utopians, are racing to greet you and inform you of your circumstances, which, as you shall soon discover, has happened at the right and perfect time in your life. Grow from your journey, wherever it may lead you; however it may unfold, for all things happen in perfect order. Please place your hand on the Earth globe to discover your Time Dilation.

Be strong and survive your trials,

Metamorphosis, Master Utopian

Putting the scroll back down on the ledge, I placed my hand on the globe. The Earth stopped spinning and a deep voice from within the globe announced:

"Greetings. You have arrived on the Daynight of the Spider, the 14th of Aires, Year of the Dragon, 9001 A.E.. Therefore, your Time Dilation from the 3rd dimension to the 11th dimension has been calculated at fifty to one, 50:1 E/M, Earth time to Millennium time."

I couldn't recall exactly what the Time Dilation meant, but I knew time, as I knew it, was no longer the same.

Staring at the pedestal, I noticed engravings had been chiseled into the sides of the pedestal's stone surface.

"The names," I mumbled, "those must be the famous people."

Daddy and Professor Johan described the engravings on the

Time Island pedestals and how they wished they'd written down all the Earth visitors, the people that had visited Millennium and returned to Earth to share the wisdom of Metamorphosis, Sage of the Ages.

I knelt down to get a closer look at the names that had been chiseled in the Time Oracle's surface.

It was true. Many famous people had visited Millennium before me:

· LAO TZE · SOCRATES · PLATO · PYTHAGORUS · ARISTOTLE · GAUTAMA BUDDHA · ZOROASTER · COPERNICUS · HOMER · AESOP · NOSTRADAMUS · PLINY THE ELDER · CLEOPATRA · HYPATHIA OF ALEXANDRIA · RUMI · JOHN MILTON · GALILEO · DANTE · MICHELANGELO · NICCOLO MACHIAVELLI · SIR WALTER RALEIGH · LEONARDO DA VINCI · HAFIZ · JONATHAN SWIFT · CHARLES DARWIN · CERTEUX · RENE DESCARTES · EDGAR ALLAN POE · VOLTAIRE · HANS C. ANDERSON · PERCY BYSSHE SHELLEYS · ELIZABETH BARRET BROWNING · CERVANTES · LEWIS CARROLL · WILLIAM SHAKESPEARE · FRANCIS BACON · NIETZSCHE · WILLIAM WORDSWORTH · SIR ISSAC NEWTON · JACOB GRIMM · WILHELM GRIMM · DANIEL DEFOE · EMMANUEL KANT · RALPH WALDO EMERSON · ROBERT L. STEVENSON · DISRAELI · SIR THOMAS MORE · WALT WHITMAN · NATHANIEL HAWTHORNE · AMADEUS MOZART · JOHN LOCKE · OSCAR WILDE · SAMUEL CLEMENS · TATANKA YOTANKA · VICTOR HUGO · BENJAMIN FRANKLIN · KENNETH GRAHAME · HERMAN MELVILLE · CHIEF SEATTLE · HENRY DAVID THOREAU · CHARLES DICKENS · SIR JAMES BARRIE · HENRY W. LONGFELLOW · HARRIET BEECHER STOWE · H.G. WELLS · JOEL C. HARRIS · JULES VERNE · KAHLIL GIBRAN · LOUISA MAY ALCOTT · WASHINGTON IRVING · L. FRANK BAUM · EMILY DICKINSON · JOHAN VAN CAMPBELL · WAYLAND M. WAINRIGHT

At the bottom of the carvings, two names stuck out like they had been written in neon lights.

JOHAN VAN CAMPBELL
WAYLAND M. WAINRIGHT

I knew for certain that the stories my father told about his brief visit to Millennium were true. His belief that famous people had visited Millennium and returned to Earth with untold wisdom had also been correct. As he told everyone, "These people changed the course of human history!"

Wary of any movement, I turned in a 360° circle, studying the platform.

Eight trunks sat behind eight stone benches, all arranged around the center circle emitting the beams of light, the galactic entry portal of Time Island. Four raised platforms at each corner displayed giant fire pits with flames leaping and dancing into the air. Between the corner platforms, I could see four openings, the top of four stairways leading downward.

I walked several paces to my left and stopped at the top of a stone stairway. Standing there, I couldn't believe how steep the steps were. They reminded me of a Mayan or Aztec temple. I peered down through the gray mist at the foamy-white waves breaking on the jagged rocks below.

Intuition told me not to go down the steps, so I decided to walk around the entire circle of Time Oracles, reading the names on each pedestal. The seven other planets were named Leda, Triton, Metis, Phobos, Phaethon, Deimos, and Epiphany.

The spinning globes suspended above each pedestal looked fantastic. Some of the bizarre planets looked Earth-like, especially the one named Epiphany.

Having seen all eight planets, I walked back to the stone bench in front of the EARTH trunk and sat down.

From my galactic seat, I gawked at the fiery-red sky and the towering granite cliffs in the distant horizon.

The feeling of freedom overcame me. Independence.

I no longer felt afraid of anything. At that moment, a peaceful calmness overcame me, an inner feeling I had never experienced before.

Surrounded by the surreal landscape, I waited for the unknown.

The Skipbladnir

DAYNIGHT
OF THE
WOLF

Chapter XI
The Skipbladnir

rom my stone bench, 200 million light years from Earth, I stared in amazement at the surreal, tri-colored sky. The blue, red, and black atmosphere became a constant reminder of my unworldly location.

Two shadows!

Staring at my double shadow, I remembered that the bizarre heavens held a pair of shining daystars—two suns. Having read the *Planet Millennium Report*, I recalled how Helios shone at one end of the binary solar system, and its twin star, Sol, burned brightly at the opposite end.

Relentless waves broke on the granite rock that surrounded Time Island.

I questioned my fate.

Have I made a mistake coming here? What if no one shows up? I have no food or water. What am I going to do when it gets dark?

Interrupting my chaotic thoughts, the faint sound of voices broke the silence.

"Someone's coming," I mumbled, jumping on the bench and holding my breath.

The steady splashing of oars and the cadence call of a ship's crew cut through the pinkish-grey blanket of fog.

"Rrrooooooooow!"

"Rrrooooooooow!"

"Rrrooooooooow!"

Three masts emerged from the gloomy mist, cutting the primordial fog like a giant knife. The carved figurehead of a dragon adorned the front of the mystery ship.

The cadence call stopped. The splash of an anchor and clacking chain broke the silence.

I prayed the vessel was the *Skipbladnir*, the ship that Daddy always talked about sailing on.

My heart pounded in my chest as I jumped down from the bench, ran across the platform, and kneeled down at the top of the stone stairway.

Who is on that ship? I asked myself.

One wooden boat emerged from the swirling patches of fog. A gigantic man with red beard rowed the skiff. Curved horns protruded from each side of his metal helmet. He looked like a Viking.

I rubbed my eyes in disbelief.

In front of the huge man, a white rabbit stood upright, on two legs. A blue dorsal fin ran from her forehead, over her head and down her back. Her torso and tail were covered with scales, like a fish, or a mermaid.

Professor Johan had described the captain of the *Skipbladnir* as a Vanir giant, but the professor and Daddy never talked about any creature half rabbit and half fish. A rabbitfish!

The two strangers swayed up and down on the waves, smiling and waving.

Three hundred feet below me, the giant yelled, "I be Captain Gog, und dis be Nyx der Utopian. Ya, she needs ta tell ya somethin' now."

The rabbitfish spoke, yelling between the crashing of waves. "Hello, young lady. I must talk to you and explain your fate. May I come up?"

I waved, motioning with my hand, come up.

Still in awe, I did not know what to expect. If it hadn't been for Professor Johan's descriptions of all the bizarre creatures on Millennium, and my father's stories about Metamorphosis, I'd have totally freaked out when I first saw Nyx.

While Captain Gog tied the skiff to a metal pole mooring

with a yellow rope, she dove into the swirling water, head first, with her ears pinned back.

Within seconds, Nyx shot up and out of the waves, landing on the rocks below. She shook the water off her white head and body, then she climbed up the rocks, leaping from ledge to ledge with ease.

Within minutes, she was climbing up the pyramid's stone steps. As I backed up a few steps, she entered the top platform, right in front of me.

She smiled and walked toward me with her right paw extended.

"Greetings, I am Nyx, your humble friend and escort," she said. "On behalf of my fellow Utopians, I welcome you to our planet, Millennium."

Nyx looked like a character from one of my wildest fantasy books. Other than her human, furry-white face, hands and legs, her body was covered with silver-blue and green fish scales—the translucent color of abalone shell. Her blue dorsal fin rose from the bridge of her nose and ran over her head, between her upright bunny ears and down her back. Her mermaid-like tail fin almost touched the ground. Six red gills, three on each side, protruded from under her jaw line.

I can't believe I'm standing here with a human rabbitfish, I thought. *Welcome to Millennium, Julia.*

Stepping forward, I shook her paw. I mean, her hand that had five, human-like fingers.

My hand, then arm, then body, tingled with energy, like a mild electric current. White spots appeared before my eyes. I could not comprehend what had happened, but I felt exhilarated.

She smiled and let go of my trembling hand.

The Utopian stood my height, including her upright ears pierced with ten gold earrings, five in each flesh-colored ear. She had a human-like face with a snout adorned by long whiskers. Her two front teeth reminded me of the Easter Bunny. So did her long rabbit feet. Don't get me wrong; Nyx was quite beautiful, in her own unique way. She wore a coral-pink chemise. A shiny, triangular gold buckle adorned her braided rope belt.

Her facial expression had a calming effect on me. Nyx's blue-green eyes looked hypnotically tranquil. Her pink nose twitched, making her translucent whiskers move up and down.

"I am Julia," I said with a quiver in my voice. "Julia Wainright."

Nyx raised her black eyebrows and asked, "Wainright? Did you say Wainright?"

I nodded, *yes.*

Before I responded, she asked, "Do you have a brother named Hunter?"

"Do you know where he is? I need to find him and take him back home to my family. My mother is worried sick and Daddy is in trouble and—"

"Slow down, young lady," Nyx said, interrupting. She pointed to the bench with her furry index finger. "Please, have a seat so we may talk."

"I'm too excited to sit down. Just tell me where he is. I won't cause any problems. Hunter will listen to me. We are really close."

"I'm sure you are, my dear." Nyx removed a leather water bag from her braided belt. "You must be thirsty after such a long galactic journey. Here, have a drink of amrita."

Telling her I had heard of Millennium well water from my father, I drank from the leather bag.

The cool amrita tasted delicious.

After I swallowed, I felt a rush of euphoria from the mystical mineral water, the feeling of being light headed, but clear thinking.

Nyx grinned. "Because you are a Wainright, I assume you are familiar with our planet, as well as astral body travel."

I nodded, yes.

"How about dimensional shifting, or the power of the Triamulet?"

"I've heard about them," I answered. "I'd like to learn more, if I'm here long enough."

"I sense you are in a hurry. Is that because of our time difference?"

"According to my father's *Planet Millennium Report*, human travelers to Millennium cross the dimensional plane and experience Time Dilation. I heard him say that for every day that Hunter's here, fifty days pass on Earth."

"I am not familiar with such a report, but you are correct."

Pointing to the Time Oracle marked EARTH, I said, "When I touched the globe over there, it told me my ratio was 50:1, Earth to Millennium. I knew right away that was the same as Hunter."

"Does the time ratio concern you?"

"Well, yes. I need to get back home. I don't want too much time to go by. My mother is getting worse; I mean, she is stressed out. Depressed. I need to get home as soon as possible."

"I am sorry to hear your mother has inflicted herself with severe anxiety. Perhaps I can recommend a cure for her ailment."

"All she needs is Hunter to come home and she'll be fine. Please, help me find him so I can take him back to Momma."

"Your brother is traveling with Metamorphosis. I shall send a messenger to locate them."

"How long will it take to find Metamorphosis?"

"My, you can pronounce his name," Nyx said, smiling.

"Yes. My father also called him the Sage of the Ages."

Nyx wiggled her rabbit nose and whiskers. "I shall know the great sage's whereabouts by tomorrow. That is the Daynight of the Scorpion. Does that meet your time schedule?"

"It will have to do."

She nodded to affirm my response and pointed toward the ship. "The *Skipbladnir* awaits us. We have appropriate clothes for you to wear. I am sure you shall enjoy them."

Thank God. I thought. *This fur smells like Pooh after a bath.*

Above us, the cosmic ring that formed the black sky crept closer as I followed Nyx down the steep stone steps to a ledge at the bottom of the stairway. As we descended the steps, I looked to my left and right, amazed at all the hieroglyphic symbols carved into the sides of the pyramidal walls.

We reached the bottom step and stood on the stone ledge that stopped at some natural rocks.

Nyx reminded me to be careful, that the gravity on Millennium was three-quarters that of Earth—that I'd be much lighter and I'd be able to jump farther.

Within minutes, she led me down to the bottom rocks. As I leaped between the jagged rocks toward the skiff, crashing waves splashed warm, foamy water in my face. I loved the powerful feeling of being able to jump twice as far as normal.

When we reached the rocks next to the skiff, Captain Gog reached out and lifted me into the boat. For a giant, he had a gentle touch.

Nyx jumped into the skiff as it swayed up and down on the waves.

The captain grabbed the two oars and rowed rapidly toward the ship. His powerful arms lifted the front of the boat out of the water with every stroke. The waves had grown larger by the time we pulled along the port side of the mighty *Skipbladnir*. Twenty-four wooden oars jutted from the hull. That meant the vessel had forty-eight oars.

I followed Captain Gog and Nyx up a rope ladder and over the brass railing. The wooden planks felt warm when my bare feet touched down on the main deck.

Just as I had imagined from Professor Johan's descriptions, the three-sailed ship looked magnificent. Although the hull of the *Skipbladnir* had the appearance of an ancient Viking galley, the upper deck looked like a Spanish galleon. The stern's aftercastle rose three levels up and around a deckhouse.

Captain Gog rang the ship's brass bell and the *Skipbladnir* surged forward. Forty-eight wooden oars moved in unison to the rhythmic cadence.

"Rrrooowww! Rrrooowww! Rrrooowww!" bellowed from

the bowels of the ancient ship.

Gog rang the bell two more times.

"Vee best be gettin' der first mate on das yonder ship's vheel und bringin' ze crew up on der deck."

"Of course, Captain," Nyx said. "Secure the vessel; I shall take our guest below."

Gog strutted across the deck. The eight-foot-tall giant wore a leather vest, brown breeches, and black boots.

The captain shouted an order, "All hands on der deck, now!"

One by one, a crew of green-skinned creatures emerged from below deck. The tallest one ran to the ship's wheel, shouting orders.

Although smiling, they looked scary. Nyx explained that they were half-orc sailors, the finest sailors on the Sea of Circles.

"Sailors?" I asked, unable to take my eyes off the huge beasts.

Every bit as tall as Captain Gog, the half-orcs' faces revealed large teeth and fangs protruding from their lower jaws. Their pointed ears and long black hair gave them a primitive, wild appearance.

The wooden deck bustled with the green-skinned sailors, each performing a task while Captain Gog barked orders.

Nyx placed her hand on my shoulder and said, "Your cabin awaits. Please, follow me."

Still amazed by the scene of bizarre sailors on deck, I followed the Utopian toward the prow of the ship.

By this time, the black sky belt—cosmic ring—had moved over Discordia. Twilight had arrived. The sky had lost her two-sun daylight.

As I gazed up into the river of sparkling stars, a frightening creature flew over the *Skipbladnir*.

The half-orcs pointed upward while Captain Gog shouted, "Dat der Kraken has spotted der girl!"

Nyx grabbed my arm. Hurrying me along, she said, "An Extractor, Captain Kraken, has flown over the *Skipbladnir*."

Under the light of three Millennium moons, the hideous

Kraken, a humanoid, lizard-like creature, rode atop the winged sea monster, Tyrannus.

The Extractor waved a gleaming saber above his head as he disappeared into the darkness. They flew so fast over the ship that I only got a glimpse of the two bizarre creatures.

Before I could ask, Nyx said, "Pay no attention to Kraken the Intimidator. He is nothing but a bully. I shall explain the evil Extractors another time. Right now, we must get you below deck."

Although Nyx showed no fear and made Kraken sound like a minor issue, I sensed the grotesque captain could be extremely dangerous.

Following Nyx, I kept a watchful eye on the black sky.

The cadence call quickened, reverberating from the deep, unified voices of forty-eight bellowing half-orcs rowing below deck.

"Rrrooowww! Rrrooowww! Rrrooowww!"

Nyx stopped at the entrance beneath the forecastle deck's staircase, swung the door open, and shouted, "Princess Julia aboard!"

I grinned and thought, No one has ever called me a princess before. I like that royal title.

I would later learn that all female visitors from other planets were call Princess. Boys were addressed as Master.

Nyx stepped three paces forward and descended a narrow stairwell lined with oil lanterns.

"Please watch your step," she said.

Shutting the door, my eyes adjusted to the flame-lit stairway. I held the brass railing at the top of the stairs.

Nyx walked to the bottom of the steps, signaling, *come down.*

Descending the stairwell, I followed Nyx to my cabin—a room fit for a queen. Excuse me. A princess.

The oil lamps mounted on the walls made the cabin glow with a warm, yellowish hue. My reflection shined in the reddish teak walls and the oak-beamed ceiling. A purple silk spread covered the canopied bed and a parchment map of Millennium hung on the cabin wall next to a full-length mirror.

A leather-bound book sat on a marble podium. The embossed, gold-leafed letters read:

MAGNUM OPUS

Nyx gestured with her arm. "Go ahead, get comfortable. Alfrigga shall bring your clothes. She is a Dockalfar, a dark gnome from the northern highlands. You shall enjoy her company."

I had so many questions but I just nodded, unable to speak.

Before she shut the cabin door, Nyx said, "Dinner shall be served in one hour. Everyone is looking forward to meeting you."

"Who is everyone?" I mumbled, as Nyx closed the door.

Alone in my cabin, I walked to an open porthole, gazing out at the Sea of Esteem.

A cool breeze brushed my face. Through the patches of swirling fog, a curtain of shooting stars lit up the black sky.

The *Skipbladnir* surged forward to the rhythm of the forty-eight oars simultaneously slapping the water.

Breathing the pure Millennium air, I believed, deep in my heart, I had made the right decision. Soon to be reunited with Hunter, I knew I would bring him home to Momma.

Turning in circles, I stood in front of the cabin's full-length mirror admiring my new outfit. Just as Nyx had promised, Alfrigga had laid the clothes on my bed.

That's when I met the gnome.

When she entered the room, her plump body and jolly face made me smile. Alrigga's black hair, styled in a medieval beehive with a blue bow pinned to the front, accentuated her round face and rosy cheeks.

"Aye, Princess Julia, me brought ya some fine clothes ta wear," she said.

She grabbed the sides of her dark-blue surcoat and curtsied.

Her wooden clogs clacked on the cabin floor as she waddled out the door. Told me she had to set the dinner table.

I expected her to bring me a cumbersome, frilly, Victorian-style dress. Instead, I wore brown breeches, a long-sleeved white chemise, and a black waist-length bodice with crossed-laced leather ties. My Triamulet laid just above the top lace. I loved the puffy shoulders. My knee-high snakeskin boots were topped with brown fur.

The medieval outfit looked great on me.

If you've ever worn a fantasy costume on Halloween or dressed up for a masquerade party, you know what I mean. You feel totally different.

Sashaying back and forth in front of the mirror, I admired my unique look.

The new me.

I had just returned to my cabin from a festive dinner with Nyx, Captain Gog, Alfrigga, Fundin, Balder and Lycus.

Let me tell you about our earlier meal together.

The ship's dining room looked magnificent. The teak-wood wall displayed an oil painting of Millennium. The artwork depicted red skies, blue skies, and black skies radiating from the planet's circumference.

A crystal chandelier with hundreds of burning blue candles hung from the copper tile ceiling. Ornate crystal bowls, overflowing with fruits and vegetables, adorned the oak banquet table. Baskets of ambrosia laid at both ends of the purple and gold table cloth. The bread of life, as described by Nyx, smelled like corn bread and honey. Between two crystal candelabras, a silver platter held a humongous smoked fish.

My mouth watered from the aroma of the delicious food.

Famished from my galactic journey, I silently ate the entire plate of smoked fish and ambrosia before I found the courage to ask questions about Hunter.

Nyx, happy to satisfy my curiosity, told me she had not met my brother. I became frustrated when I learned that no one at the table knew of Hunter's whereabouts.

The two half-orcs, Balder and Lycus, had escorted Hunter as far as Ogo Hole—cave entrance to the Underworld. They told me that during their trek through the Forest Primeval, their party had been attacked by Extractors.

They told me not to worry, that Hunter had survived.

Relieved to hear my brother was okay, I looked at Balder and asked, "You said Hunter was attacked by Extractors but was not hurt?"

Balder nodded, describing how Metamorphosis and his small group had defeated Hocus, the Extractor captain and his crew of pirates.

The half-orc told me how Hunter had been attacked by a charging sea goblin and, the *Earthling*, as Balder called him, defeated the nasty Extractor by using his martial arts skills.

"Thank God, Hunter is all right," I said.

"Beggin' yer pardon, Princess Julia," Alfrigga said. "Marster Hoonter be fine, but me lost me mate, Andvari."

Lycus told me how Andvari, a Dockalfar gnome, had been killed. Stabbed with a dagger during the fight.

Alfrigga's brown eyes filled with tears. "Aye, 'twas a blooody mistyke for Andvari ta goo on sooch a dangerous trip."

Balder told me that Hunter became extremely upset over Andvari's death and considered returning home, back to Earth. The half-orc did not know who or what had changed Hunter's mind, but my brother, along with Metamorphosis and Eve, continued on their journey to the Upperworld.

"Eve?" I asked. "Who is she?"

Captain Gog told me about Eve, a teenage girl visiting from another world—Planet Epiphany. Eve had gone with

Metamorphosis and Hunter on their journey to the Upperworld to see the Eternal Rose, one of the Eight Great Treasures, what they called Octilogy.

I recalled one of the Wainright Foundation doctors had announced that Hunter had fallen in love. So, I asked Captain Gog and the half-orcs if my brother liked Eve.

The captain announced, "Ya, dat der boy ist sure liken' dat der girl."

I asked the captain how he knew of Hunter's feelings.

He replied, "Dat boy's eyeballs pop outta' his head every time he sees dat girl."

Alfrigga, Balder, and Lycus smiled and nodded, confirming Gog's observation.

"Aye, that lassie be a beauty. Eve's eyes be as green as emeralds," Alfrigga said in a high-pitched voice.

No wonder Hunter didn't want to return to Earth.

Thinking of home, I closed my eyes and visualized images of Jeremy and the prom I never went to and the kiss I had yet to experience. Loneliness overcame me, knowing that true love awaited me on the other side of the universe. The group remained quiet, finishing their meals, sensing I had drifted into deep thought.

Fundin, the ship's game master, broke the silence by asking, "Do ya play table games, Princess Julia?"

The elve wore an orange and green checkerboard shirt with black, white, red, and blue chess pieces dotting the silk fabric. Three bells dangled from his jester's hat.

I nodded. "My father taught me chess when I was a little girl."

"Pardon me," Nyx said, motioning to Fundin. "You may show our guest how to play *Gametasia Chess* on her return voyage. She shan't have time this evening."

The game master smiled, tipped his jester's cap, and excused himself from the table.

While Alfrigga cleared the plates and silverware, I asked Nyx to explain how I got to Millennium, what she called, astral body travel. Before the Utopian responded, Captain Gog and the two half-orcs stood and excused themselves from the room. Alfrigga followed them, waddling out the door.

With the room quiet, the Utopian replied, "Astral body travel is quite simple. Between Earth and Millennium, the Astral Highway allows dimensional shifting to occur. The shift between dimensions results in astral body transportation, all within the 11th dimension at the speed of thought."

Scratching my right temple, I mumbled, "I think I read about that in Daddy's report."

Nyx grinned. "It is time to expand your mind. I ask you to imagine you are in two different places at this moment. After visualizing it, believe it, because it is reality. After all, believing is Seeing. At this very moment in time you sleep on Earth, a deep sleep. And, you, the *other* you, sits here with me.

"Your astral journey from Earth to Millennium involved actual travel of your Id. Also, your body's atoms and DNA, every cell in you, experienced cloning as it traveled the Astral Highway's traversable wormhole from Earth to Millennium. The teleported journey included your gold Triamulet. The transfer of your Id and your physical cellular structure created the exact you. Not a replica, but you. There now exists two of you."

Understanding the concept of having two cloned, identical bodies, two bodies in two worlds, I nodded and remained silent.

"But there is something more important than your physical self that traveled the Astral Highway."

Nyx paused. "Can you guess what that might be?"

Thinking for a moment, I shook my head, *no.*

"Your thoughts. Your spirit. Your soul. The divine spark that makes you who you are. Although your body on Earth is alive and breathing, it no longer houses the personal energy of your thoughts. Your dormant body no longer contains your soul, that which sits in the center and knows."

She raised her furry eyebrows. "Am I making sense?"

"I think so."

"Allow me to clarify. We are what we think. When we talk to ourselves, the voice inside our head determines exactly who we are and how we behave. Thoughts are the most powerful force in the universe. As pure energy, they are more powerful than electricity. They last forever. Think of your thought waves as a radio transmitter that sends out a signal, your personal energy. Each of us, every creature in the universe, possess signals or wave patterns that radiate in all directions from the center of our being. Our personal energy transmits signals, energy waves that transmit out and into the vast cosmos. We call this energy the music of the universe. We all hear it, if we listen."

She paused and asked me, "Do you hear your own thoughts? Your self-talk? That voice in your head?"

Nodding, *yes*, I listened to myself think—the voice within me. I never realized my thoughts could be so incredibly powerful.

"Think of this energy as the invisible intelligence flowing through everything and between every creature. For instance, right now, your thought waves and mine meet exactly midway between us. Do you feel the energy filling the air between us?"

I closed my eyes. "Now that you describe it that way, yes, I do feel it."

Nyx nodded her head in approval.

"Think of all the air, the space in the universe, as a matrix, a vibrating grid filled with this personal energy. It affects everything. The energy field of the universal grid constantly shifts and changes, just as your own personal thoughts, feelings, moods, and behavior continually change.

"I believe you humans refer to this phenomenon of the thought matrix as collective consciousness. It affects every event on your planet.

"Everyone, every thing in the universe, emits energy in every direction."

She smiled and held up one index finger. "The first Secret

of the Universe, the first Universal Truth is, 'Like attracts like.' This means, like thoughts attract like thoughts throughout the universe. Good attracts good, bad attracts bad. This is the universal Law of Attraction."

I nodded, thinking of how Jeremy and I were alike.

"Your sleeping body on Earth is perfectly healthy, physically, but has no spirit. No soul. Your two bodies are chemically connected through space and time, but not spiritually."

"I'm trying to understand. All I know is, I feel exactly the same, like I just woke up."

Nyx raised her hand to prevent me from interrupting.

"I have good news as it relates to dimensional shifting. You are a girl. You have female energy. This feminine power allows your spirit to return back to your Earth body during Dreamtime.

"This evening when you sleep, your soul shall travel the Astral Highway, across the universe, to awaken in your Earth body. You shall see, hear, smell, taste, and feel everything as you remain motionless in your magical coma. When your dream ends—"

"What about Hunter?" I interrupted. "Can he visit Earth in his dreams? Does he see us when he lays there in his coma?"

"Please, relax and listen. There is wisdom in silence."

Nodding, I knew I had to learn to bite my tongue. Her smooth white fur glowed under the chandelier's candlelight.

"As I was saying, when your dream on Earth ends, when you awaken, your spirit and soul shall have returned back here, to your Millennium body."

She smiled. "Only women have this power. Dreamtime, as it is called, is a result of the female mystique, the immaculate purity given to us by the Great Mother. The gateway to the mysterious female is the root of creation, always birthing, never dying. Your mysterious female energy, your womanhood, is your greatest gift."

I stared at the Utopian, inspired by her words of empowerment.

"You asked about your brother. Hunter is a male, therefore, he does not possess the invisible female energy. This means he cannot enter Dreamtime to return to his Earth body. Hunter is a boy. Males do not possess the energy."

As I listened to her explanation, I liked to hear how powerful I was as a female, that I had the feminine mystique.

What I disliked was the uncomfortable thought of awakening in my comatose body and not being able to move or speak. Nyx made it sound like a sensational experience, but to me it sounded like a horror movie.

Can you imagine being trapped in a lifeless body and not being able to talk or move?

"What if I don't want to enter Dreamtime?" I asked. "Can I just sleep without returning to Earth?"

"My dear, do not fear what you have yet to experience. Dreamtime is a blessing, not a curse."

Before I responded, she said, "We have covered enough information this evening. We shall talk again, so I may explain the Astral Highway's origin, the Extractor Asteroid, and the Star of Evil. I shall also enlighten you on Ex and the Extractors.

"Now, at this moment, it is time to retire to our cabins. Our crew is going to row nonstop so we can arrive at Fog Harbor by morning. Whatever questions you may have shall be answered by Metamorphosis, our esteemed leader."

"When am I going to see Hunter?"

"If all goes as planned, sometime tomorrow evening, Daynight of the Scorpion."

Closing my eyes, I pictured the joyful reunion with my twin brother in my mind.

Nyx escorted me back to my cabin. Under the ghostly glow of three Millennium moons, we crossed the deck of the *Skipbladnir*. I looked up into a river of shooting stars and asked Nyx to point out the Sun.

She told me that the Earth's daystar was too far away to see with the naked eye. Her words stunned me with the realization that I now stood on the other side of the universe—200 million light years from home.

When we reached my cabin door, she reminded me that I was but a thought away from Earth as it pertained to time travel. I tried to comprehend the speed of thought, that everything happens at once, in an instant. Now.

The sage bid me, "Good daynight," and closed my door.

I paraded past the full-length mirror to take one last look at my medieval outfit. It again reminded me of the costumes that Hunter and I wore to the renaissance faires.

Full of restless energy, I sashayed back and forth in front of the mirror, admiring the new me.

Happy with my decision to visit Millennium, I smiled at my reflection, convincing myself that Momma would see me in a few short days.

Okay, maybe weeks.

Maybe months.

She'd understand why I left her, especially when she sees Hunter awaken. I knew, deep inside, that Jeremy would patiently wait for my return. I hoped he didn't freak out when he saw me lying in a coma.

Stopped worrying about home and family and everyone else and thought of myself.

I felt empowered. Ever since I was a young girl, I dreamed of exploring far-away lands. Now, as fate would have it, I lived on a far-away planet.

A leather-bound book sat on a marble podium.

The *Magnum Opus* had caught my eye.

I knew how pleased Daddy would be with me if I looked at the Millennium Book of Wisdom before I left the *Skipbladnir*.

Thicker than any of the dictionaries in my father's library, cloth ribbons of various colors divided the worn parchment pages of the magnificent *Magnum Opus*.

Opening the gold-leafed leather cover, I read the table of contents:

Curious, I turned to the section marked: *Extractors*

"Here they are," I said. "The dysfunctional creatures that Professor Johan talked about."

Turning the parchment pages, I stared at the illustrations of the strange creatures.

The Extractors looked really bizarre and had weird names: Captain Kraken, Vulcan, Hocus, Jinx, Lizardo, Rodanna, and Tarantulana.

When I got to the last page of the Extractor section, the description of Ex, the Master Extractor, depicted a hideous creature that looked like a devil.

The caption read, "Invisible Villain".

I looked around the room, thinking how creepy it would be if an invisible creature hid under the bed.

Wait. He doesn't have to hide, he's invisible, I thought. *I'll ask Nyx about the Extractors later.*

Closing the book, I turned off the oil lamps mounted on the teak-wood walls and latched the two porthole windows.

Light from the three Millennium moons poured into the cabin, giving the room a bluish glow.

Returning to my canopied bed, I undressed and slipped into a black silk night gown that Alfrigga had laid on the bedspread.

On the night stand table, a plum-colored candle provided a warm light. I sat on the edge of the feather bed and picked up a pearl-handled brush and a looking glass that laid on the tabletop. Gazing into the mirror, I ran the brush through my black hair as it fell onto my shoulders. My hazel eyes sparkled against my smooth porcelain skin.

Pleased with the way I looked, I couldn't help but smile in the looking glass.

I opened the top drawer to the night stand and picked up a parchment page that displayed an illustration of a man's face. My eyes were drawn to a signature that read:

HW

"It's Hunter's initials," I mumbled, grinning from ear to ear.

Studying the drawing of the man with a long beard, I knew it had to be Metamorphosis's portrait.

My brother can't stop drawing, even when he's on another planet, I thought.

Feeling closer to my brother than I had in a long time, I placed the parchment page on the night stand.

Blew out the candle and crawled under the purple satin sheets. With my head nestled into the fluffy feather pillow, I stared out the porthole above my bed. A blue Millennium moon, surrounded by a sea of Andromeda stars, seemed to stare back at me. Feeling alive, empowered; a barrage of thoughts entered my mind: *Even if the sky is weird, I like Millennium. Where will my quest take me? What bizarre characters will I meet along the way? Where do the Extractors live? I know they are dangerous.*

I'm sure Momma is crying her eyes out right now. I hope my brothers and sisters behave while I'm gone. Who am I kidding? They'll be holy terrors without me there.

I love that girls have special powers and boys don't.

I think I understand dimensional shifting and astral body travel, but I'm confused about Dreamtime. I can't imagine being trapped in a comatose body.

The mighty *Skipbladnir* surged forward. The muffled sound of the rowing cadence became hypnotic. The portholes above my bed displayed billions of twinkling stars.

Like a trance or magic spell, I turned my head and fixated on the Millennium map illuminated in the moonlight.

The mysterious map, with its eight kingdoms and eight treasures, beckoned to me. I stared at the ancient parchment, thinking about my journey to find Hunter. I studied the names of the Eight Great Kingdoms: Pellagus, Eremus, Harundia, Sallum, Saburra, Gellum, Nemoria, and Palludis.

Kept staring at the middle of continent at the colossal crater named Discordia. Time Island was located in the center of the crater, surrounded by the Sea of Circles.

Thoughts spun in my head while I stared at the map.

Will I really see Hunter tomorrow? I wonder what Metamorphosis is like? Daddy really liked the sage. Hope to see some of the fairy tale places like Wonderland. I pray my Triamulet will get me back home. What if Hunter doesn't have his Triamulet?

Finally, after hours of thinking, my eyes gently closed.

The distinct shapes of the map's Eight Great Kingdoms had been burned into the back of my eyelids.

I don't remember falling asleep.

Chapter XII
Julia's First Dreamtime

My mother's lovely face, her hazel-brown eyes and high cheek bones, came into focus. My mind cried out, *Momma, I'm awake!* But my lips remained motionless. My voice lay silent. It took me a moment to realize my vision *had* to be real. Dreamtime was indeed, a reality. I had returned home to my family.

My comatose body lay before me in an enamel-pink hospital bed with a purple headboard. It looked like someone else's body. That's because, no matter how hard I tried, I couldn't move.

I knew what it felt like to be paralyzed.

When I attempted to raise my arms, or turn my head, I found it impossible to use my muscles. Kind of like when your arm or leg falls asleep and you can't move it until the blood returns and you feel that tingling sensation. Well, imagine no tingling. Your limb is lifeless, like it's not part of you. But you can feel.

I couldn't speak or move. Not a peep. Not even a blink.

Although paralyzed, my senses felt keener and more powerful than they ever had.

Dreamtime vision allowed me to see like an eagle. What I mean is, my view looked panoramic. Everything in front and to the sides of me looked like a wide screen at the movies. What normally appeared unfocused on both sides of my line of sight looked clear.

Didn't have to focus on anything in my field of vision. Everything had become crystal clear—perfect eyesight.

Perfect hearing.

Every sound seemed to be magnified.

The familiar fragrance of home sweet home filled my nostrils. I could taste the saliva in my throat.

Feeling the air rush into my lungs, I breathed in and out. In and out. In and out.

My mother touched my forehead with her warm hand, kissed my cheek, and arranged my peach-colored bedspread to her liking. She sat at the side of my bed in her favorite rocking chair.

Trapped in a helpless body during my Dreamtime, I knew I'd be forced to observe my family through comatose eyes.

Julia, stop complaining, I thought, *at least you have returned home. You can visit your family even if they don't know you're here with them. See how they are doing. Be happy.*

The journey from Millennium to Earth took place instantaneously; that is, the experience happened at the speed of thought, as fast as you can say the word.

Don't remember falling asleep on the *Skipbladnir.* I only recall a dreamy vision of my home on Earth. The vision turned out to be the real thing. My spirit, along with my awareness, my senses, had returned home with me.

My hospital bed with the purple headboard faced the Pacific Ocean. The radiant sunrise poured through the floor-to-ceiling bay window as the Earth's daystar—the Sun—began its journey over the east side of our house.

Our backyard was visible through the picture window.

Three men dressed in dark suits stood on the swimming pool deck. They spoke briefly and then walked away in opposite directions, disappearing out of view.

Who were those strange men? I thought.

The clouds changed color, from purple to pink to yellow to white, while my mother sat next to my bed and prayed. She held her rhinestone rosary tightly, moving her fingers from bead to bead. With her eyes closed, she mumbled one "Hail Mary" after another.

Momma looked terrible. Her appearance shocked me.

Her tangled blonde hair hadn't been combed in days. She had slept with her makeup on.

Food and alcohol stains covered her wrinkled white pants and pink blouse.

A half-empty bottle of red wine and a plastic container of blue pills sat on the end table next to the sofa, waiting for Momma's embrace.

My mother needed her alcohol and prescription medication to keep the wolves of reality from her door.

Across the room, Hunter lay in his hospital bed. Propped up with pillows, he faced the picture bay window with a view of the ocean. He wore special headgear—BCI control cap—that Daddy and Dr. Shankar had talked about using on the Coma-X patients.

The special headset looked like a hair net with dozens of electrodes covering the surface. Wires extended from the cap to a computer under Hunter's bed.

As I watched him breathe, I knew he did not possess the female power of Dreamtime. Unaware of his surroundings, the morning sunshine accentuated the blank stare on my brother's face.

Pooh lay at the foot of Hunter's bed. The golden retriever looked at me with his head cocked. I could tell that the dog knew my spirit had entered my comatose body.

He pranced toward my bed; his toenails tapped on the oak floor. Pooh stared into my eyes and licked my left hand. His moist, warm tongue tickled my fingers.

"Pooh," Momma yelled. "Stop that. Go lay down, now."

The submissive dog whined, lowered his head, and slinked back to the foot of Hunter's bed.

Except for the beeping of the monitors and medical equipment, the house sounded quiet—empty.

The grandfather clock across the room chimed at 6:30 a.m.. Ever since I can remember, I've loved the sound of those gongs.

At 7:00 a.m., the Westminster chimes caused my mother to jump up and hurry out of the room.

Within minutes, the house came alive with people.

The sound of screaming children and the aroma of bacon and eggs cooking caused mixed emotions deep within me.

On one hand, I missed my home and my family.

On the other hand, it felt good to not have to jump up and feed the kids and do the dishes and make the beds and take care of Hunter.

I never thought I'd say it, but there can be advantages to lying in a coma. If you're Julia Wainright, that is.

Footsteps echoed down the corridor from the library.

"Daddy!" my mind silently shouted.

Walking straight at me, my handsome father carried the morning newspaper under his arm.

"For God sakes, Gloria, you haven't slept all night," my father yelled as he entered the family room. "Get some rest."

He checked on a video camera mounted on a tripod that stood next to the grandfather clock. The red light indicated that I was being filmed. Hunter also had a camera pointed at his bed.

Daddy glanced at me, then he came over and kissed my cheek.

Holding my hand, he whispered, "Good morning, Julia. I hope you come home today. Your mother needs you."

"Wayland, please come in here and help me with these kids," my mother yelled. "They need their father."

I felt his sweet breath on my face. His aftershave lotion had the aroma of cinnamon. Daddy's scent made me feel secure. His hand felt warm and strong.

He yelled to Momma, "Have Ruby help you, I need to watch the news. Johan just called and our Foundation is still being slandered...torn to pieces by the major news outlets."

Patting my hand, he trudged past Hunter to turn on the television, failing to acknowledge his oldest son.

My mother shuffled into the family room holding a brown

coffee mug in her hand. She yelled at Ruby to watch the children. My younger sister took care of her siblings in her usual way—yelling at them and calling them spoiled brats.

"Darling, here's your cappuccino, just the way you like it," Momma said. "I'm sorry I yelled at you. I'm really tired, that's all."

My father did not respond, holding up his hand for her to be quiet while he pointed the remote control at the flat-screen television. He increased the volume until the speakers got so loud that the children's screaming voices had been drowned out.

"Look at this propaganda!" he shouted. "No wonder we can't leave our house! The world's gone mad! They're all insane!"

Momma stormed out of the room with a scowl on her face.

My first surprise came when the news reporter announced, "Today, Tuesday, July 7th, our top news story features the controversial Wainright Foundation."

It was the day before my birthday. I had been gone for more than a month.

I wish the day of the month was my only surprise. Unfortunately, the news headline focused on *one* story—my father's research foundation.

Daddy kept changing the channels.

No matter where he switched to, the subject centered around the controversy of Millennium.

The news stations kept replaying my father's April Fool's television show interview. Because of the Internet and social media, his story had gone viral.

According to one news correspondent, the *Planet Millennium Report* was the most popular, the most widely read document on Earth, having the most hits on the World Wide Web.

The television screen showed a news reporter standing in front of our house.

They kept showing the same scene over and over again—our estate surrounded by military guards patrolling the property. I knew then who the strangers in the dark suits were.

News media trucks and reporters and Paparazzi waited across the street for any movement, any sign of Dr. Wainright leaving the house.

No wonder the children couldn't go out and play.

No wonder my brothers and sisters were not allowed to attend school.

No wonder Momma was so upset.

Ruby screamed at the kids to get dressed because the tutor was on her way.

We never had a tutor before. Especially on a Saturday.

According to the media reports, the military officer who visited our home the week I fell into a coma had been correct about the assassination attempts reported by several government agencies.

The headlines read:

Radical Terrorist Groups Threaten To Kill Dr. Wainright And His Foundation Staff

The crazy terrorists claimed the *Planet Millennium Report* insulted their ancient ritual beliefs. They were upset that Daddy's report stated:

Metamorphosis, Sage of the Ages, enlightened the great prophets and the most influential people in human history.

Life on a planet in the Andromeda Galaxy had been rejected by the majority of the scientific community. Millennium had made my father the laughing stock of the world media.

As the news of the gyro planet spread, more and more people got caught up in the controversy.

People loved to debate, I thought. *No, people loved to argue who's right and who's wrong.*

The barrage of negative news reports made me realize I needed to find Hunter and get home as soon as possible. When both of us awakened wearing our Triamulets, my father would have proof that Millennium existed. He'd have us on film waking up as the gold medallions magically materialized around our necks.

I lay there thinking, *I must find Hunter and get home.*

At 9:00 a.m., the tutor arrived.

All the children, except Crystal and Sebastian, shuffled past me to the den that had been converted to a makeshift classroom.

The instructor, who the children called, "Ms. Keller", had trouble controlling my brothers and sisters. The more they misbehaved, especially Ruby, the less the children learned. School on a Saturday didn't sit well with the Wainright kids.

Can you blame them?

The tutor served as nothing more than a baby sitter for my mother and father.

That upset me.

I wanted to scream, but I was unable to utter a single sound.

Every hour Momma hurried into the family room to attend to Hunter and me, to all our medical needs. She'd go through the coma care routine that I knew so well.

Why couldn't she have a nurse assist her?

Momma had always been so strong willed, refusing to accept outside help.

Her excuse?

Didn't want strangers in her house.

She looked so tired and frustrated caring for us. I wasn't surprised that she drank white wine before lunchtime. I wanted to scold her, or hold her, but I lay helplessly in my hospital bed on wheels.

Daddy paced the floor, watching the sensational news reports. Visibly upset, he scribbled notes on a yellow pad while he sighed and groaned and yelled statements like, "That's a lie!" and "Why don't they read the report?" and "Who'd want to hurt us?"

Momma reminded my father to keep his voice and the TV

volume down and, "Stop upsetting the children, they are trying to study."

I spent the entire day watching and listening to my family fight and argue.

Daddy acted impatient with my mother.

About the time she finished her third afternoon cocktail, she became verbally abusive to him *and* the children.

Momma carried her anger around with her like a favorite purse.

Gone forty days and my family had changed for the worst.

One thing for sure, my father had gotten himself in serious trouble.

Have you ever had someone threaten to assassinate one of your parents? It is the most horrible experience imaginable. It became clear to me that I would save my father's life if I could find Hunter and bring him home.

On my first evening back on Earth, Hunter and I were wheeled, one at a time, into the elevator and upstairs to our bedrooms. My room looked completely different. To make space for the medical equipment and nursing station, my dresser had been moved to the opposite wall next to my desk.

My music box laid on the desk chair.

Someone had been playing with it, the lid had been left open. It looked damaged.

How silly of me that I worried my little sisters had broken it. That was a selfish thought, worrying about my stupid jewelry box when the family was under siege by terrorists and the news media harassment and agents and guards patrolling our yard and my poor mother was falling apart in front of my eyes.

At midnight, Momma kissed my cheek and said, "Good night, sweetheart. Tomorrow's your birthday."

She checked all the monitors and wrote the data on a clipboard that hung on the rail at the foot of my bed.

Turning off the light, she closed the bedroom door.

I knew the time because a digital clock with red numbers set on top of the monitoring equipment.

At half past midnight, a cat meowed.

Maddie!

I wondered where she had been, I hadn't seen her all day. Ruby brought the crying kitten home from the animal shelter and, to my surprise, Momma let her keep it.

My sister could never care for anything.

The cat was supposedly Ruby's, but Maddie always slept with me. Animals know where to find the most love.

I heard a commotion in Ruby's bedroom. Her door creaked opened, and the next thing I knew, Maddie came running into my room and jumped on my bed.

She immediately sniffed my face, tickling my cheeks with her whiskers.

Then, she licked my chin and nose with her rough tongue.

Not a pleasant experience. You can't move. Itch your nose.

Maddie, I thought, *love you, but please stop licking my face.*

Just like the dog, the kitty knew my spirit had come home.

Finally, my faithful cat yawned, curled up on my stomach, and purred herself to sleep.

My bed faced the bay window I loved so much.

The weather looked nice enough for Momma to leave the panes open, so I could smell the Monterey pines and the salty sea air. The ocean waves crashed against the rocks below our sea-cliff home.

Wanting to sit in my bay window and read a book, I had no choice but to lay there, motionless, all night long.

Most of that evening I thought of Jeremy.

Where was he? Did he know what had happened to me?

Did he freak out when he found out I was lying in a coma? Would he still want to see me?

Regretting not going to the prom with him, I wondered if I'd ever get kissed by a boy, let alone go out on a real date. I pictured just the two of us alone.

Crying inside, I did not feel tears run down my cheeks.

But I cried.

Can you imagine going days without sleep, yet experiencing no fatigue? It's an odd sensation to lie in bed and never get tired.

As I listened to the beeping of my monitors and the sound of waves below our home, I knew my Millennium body slept soundly on the *Skipbladnir*.

My other body heard waves, but from the Sea of Circles, not the Pacific Ocean.

Or at least, I assumed I must be sleeping in my cabin; otherwise, I wouldn't have been on Earth. I mean, if I woke up on Millennium, my Dreamtime on Earth would stop.

Right?

Am I making any sense?

That first night alone in my bedroom, time really dragged on and on. Try to imagine being wide awake and just lying there. You can't get up.

I did the time conversion calculations in my head and realized if I slept four hours on Millennium, my Dreamtime would last eight days on Earth.

Happy to see the first light of dawn, I wished I could have smiled. Outwardly. Instead, I smiled inside and felt the positive, happy brain chemicals being released by every cell in my body. What a wonderful feeling.

Maddie stretched and jumped off the bed. She ran to the bay window and sat on the cushioned seat to stare at the sea gulls flying over the cliffs.

Momma, wearing her pink robe and red slippers, came in and kissed my cheek.

I had never seen her look so weary and unkempt.

Her breath smelled like alcohol as she wheeled my bed downstairs to the family room.

Hunter, already there, faced the ocean, propped up in his usual spot across from the picture window.

Daddy meandered through the door and managed to tell me, "Good morning, Julia."

"For heaven's sake, Wayland, can't you wish the twins happy birthday?"

My father came over and kissed me on the forehead, then whispered, "Happy Birthday, Sweetheart," in my ear.

"I've got two cakes in the oven," Momma said. 'We'll celebrate when I return from church. I'm going to confession."

"I'll try to make the birthday party. I've got an important meeting with my top doctors."

"Today?" she yelled. "Can't you take off one lousy day and be with the children?"

"Sorry, the guys are on their way."

After Daddy watched the world news on television, after he complained about the negative Wainright Foundation coverage, he disappeared into his library with three of his colleagues. They had arrived at ten o'clock.

Lying there listening to the negative news reports about Millennium, I daydreamed about Jeremy. About how we would be together one day soon.

Ten minutes later, Momma arrived home from church. She always looked calm and at peace after she confessed her sins.

The smell of cake mix baking made me smile inside. I mean, who doesn't like to eat their own birthday cake? Then it dawned on me. I couldn't eat anything!

At noon, Momma and Ruby paraded into the family room carrying two birthday cakes—one with white coconut frosting and one with chocolate.

Each cake displayed eighteen burning candles.

Zachary, Alexander, Emily, Grace, Astrid, Pearl, Crystal, and baby Sebastian wore pointed party hats and carried pink and blue balloons. Moody Ruby wore black.

My mother counted to three.

Ten voices sang:

> "Happy Birthday to *both* of you,
>
> Happy Birthday to *both* of you,
>
> Happy Birthday, Dear Hunter and Julia,
>
> Happy Birthday to *both* of you."

Sung off key, it still sounded wonderful.

Momma cried while the children blew out the candles and opened the birthday presents wrapped for their comatose brother and sister. My mother always went overboard with presents. I couldn't believe all the stuff Hunter and I got.

Clothes and watches and jewelry and smart phones and new cars. That's right! We each got a brand new vehicle.

Mine was a red Corvette. Hunter got a yellow Hummer.

What's up with that?

Unbelievable, I thought. *I have the red convertible sports car that I always dreamed about sitting in my driveway and I can't even move.*

"Julia can't drive," Ruby announced, smirking. "Can my boyfriend and I borrow her car? Dylan is eighteen."

Momma gave my sister that sinister stare that only a parent is capable of making.

Ruby knew what that meant: *No. Never ask again!*

I couldn't believe my ears. Dylan? Since when does my little sister have a boyfriend? Ruby's only sixteen and she's dating?

The next thing you know, Emily and Grace will have boyfriends.

My brothers and sisters ate their cake like wild animals and ran out of the room, leaving my mother with a pile of wrappings and ribbons and paper plates to clean up.

She chose to leave the mess and sit in her rocking chair, crying and drinking wine.

The doorbell rang.

Momma scowled as the children ran to open the door.

Another Wainright Foundation doctor had arrived to meet with my father.

Within minutes, someone else knocked on the door.

It was those men and women in dark suits and sun glasses, the security personnel who came into our home three times a day to report to Daddy.

My mother treated them disrespectfully. She didn't like the parade of strangers in her domain. They always wore dark glasses and barely spoke.

That upset Momma.

She told the kids, "They look like morticians and act like zombies."

For being so consumed with her own misery, at least my mother dressed me in acceptable clothing.

Instead of drab, boring hospital gowns, I wore a powder blue satin robe with a white, lacy nightie.

She also brushed my long hair and kept my face washed, applying all sorts of beauty creams and skin conditioners.

For a coma patient, I looked really good. At least, that what I heard Momma say to my father.

And so it went. The same routine every day for my first five days home. I became depressed lying there in a coma, day in and day out. Although surrounded by people, I felt lonely.

No, I felt like I had wasted precious time.

Where was Jeremy?

Although I wanted to be home to see what was happening, all I thought about was waking up on Millennium so I could go find my brother.

Find Hunter. Resume the journey that beckoned to me from across the universe.

On Sunday, July 12th, things got better.

A *lot* better.

A spectacular sunset had illuminated the clouds with streaks of deep purple and gold.

Momma sat in her rocking chair next to my bed with a glass of white wine in her hand.

The doorbell rang.

Daddy entered the room with a smile on his face and announced to Momma, "Darling, someone is here to see Julia."

My spirit soared when I saw Jeremy!

He looked so incredibly handsome as he followed my father toward my bed. I couldn't believe my eyes. It was really him! His name hadn't been mentioned since my Dreamtime began.

He must really love me to come see me like this, I thought. *I'm glad Momma brushed my hair this morning. I know I look really creepy with all these tubes and wires attached to me. I wish Momma would have put my makeup on, at least my lipstick and my blush.*

"She looks really peaceful, Mrs. Wainright," Jeremy said, walking toward my bed as he stared at me with a look of concern.

Refusing to smile or acknowledge my boyfriend's presence, Momma did not stand up to greet her only guest.

My mother took a sip of white wine. "Still waiting for that date, are we?"

"Come on, honey," Daddy said, clenching his jaw. "He just wants to see how Julia's doing."

"She's doing the same as she was last week, and the week before that." Momma frowned as she talked, looking Jeremy up and down.

His bewildered face turned red.

He looked handsome even when embarrassed.

"Have you met her twin brother, Hunter?" she asked. "He's over there. Go on, introduce yourself."

Momma pointed across the room at motionless Hunter, propped up, facing the floor-to-ceiling picture window.

"I look forward to meeting him someday," Jeremy said, grinning in a gesture of friendship.

My mother chuckled and said, "Sure, as soon as he wakes up. I'll probably be an old woman by then. Or dead."

Daddy grabbed my mother's arm to quiet her.

Jeremy stood at the end of my hospital bed and gazed into my open eyes.

He didn't seem upset that I lay in a coma. His arched eyebrows looked compassionate.

His eyes told me, *I'm here for you, no matter what.*

"Why don't you let Jeremy spend some time alone with Julia," Daddy said. "His voice might stimulate her."

"I'm all the stimulation she needs. There can be nothing more soothing than a mother's voice."

Jeremy raised his eyebrows and looked at my father like, *Help me, Dr. Wainright.*

"Darling, let's go in the kitchen," Daddy said. "I'll open a bottle of our finest Pinot Noir. It's 2001. I just brought it up from the wine cellar."

"I've got to get dinner started," she said. "I'll be back in ten minutes, young man. Go ahead and visit, but don't touch anything!"

"Yes, Mrs. Wainright," Jeremy said. "I understand."

My father helped Momma out of her rocking chair and out of the room.

Jeremy's face radiated in the light of the setting sun as the glowing orange ball disappeared beyond the dark-blue ocean.

He walked to the side of my bed and held my hand.

Oh my God! It felt so fabulous to have him touch me.

Squeezing my fingers, he said, "Hi, Julia. If you can hear me,

I want you to know that I'll take a rain check on the prom date. I looked kind of stupid in the tux anyway."

His voice quivered as he spoke to me.

He looked at me like he expected me to respond.

His hand trembled. His deep dimples appeared as he nervously grinned.

If I could have just made a sound.

Nodded my head. Or blinked.

Anything to let him know I could hear his soothing low voice. Feel his touch. Smell his pheromones.

"I'd have been here sooner but I had to get security clearance. Your father is on the news a lot. He seems like a nice person. He just told me I can come by once a week to visit you. I hope your mom is okay with that."

Jeremy looked over his shoulder at Hunter.

"My dad says your mom is really nice, but all the media stuff and you being in a coma and all the threats and the security are too much for her to deal with."

Jeremy's cologne carried the fragrance of sweet vanilla.

He wore a sky-blue sports shirt with beige khaki shorts and leather sandals. His muscular biceps filled the sleeves. His hands felt strong but soft.

"I just read your father's *Planet Millennium Report* on the Internet. I'm not sure what to believe. If you are really in a Coma-X condition, it means you are on another planet right now. If you are, I hope you're okay. I don't want you to be hurt. I never expected our relationship to start this way. I'm a bit confused, but I promise I will always be here for you."

"Young man!" Momma shouted from across the room.

Jeremy dropped my hand and stepped away from the bed.

"Honey, let the boy talk to her," my father yelled. "It can't hurt."

"I have to attend to my daughter's medical needs."

Her black eyebrows lowered, my mother stared at Daddy and said, "He'll have to leave, now."

Oh no, not yet, I thought. *He's just begun to talk to me. Please, Momma, let him stay. Just for a while longer.*

"I have homework to do," Jeremy replied, bowing his head in submissive reverence to my domineering mother.

As my boyfriend followed my father out the family room's arched doors, my heart sank.

Thanks a lot, mother, I thought. *You always want me all to yourself.*

The Wainright Foundation doctors visited our home three times a week to meet with Daddy. Because of the terrorist threats, they traveled with armed federal agents.

"He has way too many meetings with his buddies," Momma mumbled.

I'd often catch her talking to herself. Especially at night.

She acted so lonely and withdrawn after dark.

On Monday, July 13th, she wheeled Hunter and me into the conservatory. What a great open space. It looked like a sun room, only with a towering domed roof. The view of the ocean, the curve of the Earth, looked spectacular through the glass walls and ceiling.

My mother raised my upper bed, so I rested in a sitting position. Thank God she kept me in an upright position most of the time.

Grey clouds drifted across the sky, hiding the Earth's daystar, the Sun. White caps dotted the dark-blue ocean as the sea gulls and pelicans rode the swirling winds.

Momma cracked open a window, allowing me to smell the ocean air and listen to the sea lions bark while the waves crashed onto the majestic cliffs behind our home.

Daddy entered the conservatory and announced that four research doctors were on their way to the house.

After arguing about the reason for the doctor's visit, my mother finally gave in and yelled, "Okay, Wayland. Just for a few minutes. I'm tired of your staff showing up without *my* approval."

"It's time you hear what's going on with the twins," Daddy said, staring at me from across the room. "You cannot ignore the truth anymore."

While Momma sulked and drank wine from her crystal glass, Daddy got on his smart phone to check his e-mails and text messages.

Within twenty minutes, his top staff members stood in the conservatory looking over Hunter's charts and medical print outs. I recognized all four of them, having observed them many times from my secret hiding place in the library.

My mother gazed at the ocean through the conservatory windows while the doctors huddled around Hunter's bed.

Holding metal clipboards, they compared chart data.

Daddy turned to my mother and whispered, "The doctors are going to give you a presentation, I mean an *explanation*, of Hunter's condition. In the next couple of weeks, we'll also have an update on Julia."

Momma frowned. "I don't know if anything's going to help me right now."

"You really need to hear what my colleagues have to say," Daddy said, gritting his teeth. "Please, sit down over here."

I liked when my father took charge. He had allowed Momma to get away with her rude behavior for way too long.

He led her to her rocking chair next to Hunter's bed. She forced a smile and sat on the cushioned seat.

"When are you going to take that damn cap off his head," she asked. "I need to wash his hair."

My father kept his composure and did not raise his voice in front of his colleagues.

"Gloria, we've already talked about the importance of the control cap."

"Do any of you brilliant scientists know when my son's going to wake up?" she asked, smirking. "That's all I care about."

My stubborn mother had refused to listen to what Daddy or the Wainright Foundation doctors had to say about my brother's coma condition.

Momma trusted the doctors at the hospital in Monterey more than my father's renowned staff of medical experts.

Daddy said, "Go ahead, Tom. We're ready."

Dr. Richardson placed his clipboard at the foot of Hunter's bed saying, "Thanks, Mrs. Wainright, for your hospitality these past few months, especially under these unusual circumstances.

"Before I can explain Hunter's unique condition, Wayland's asked me to take a moment to explain EEG and neuroimaging, how they relate to your son's condition. Then I'll explain the brain computer interface information."

She tried to smile but gave him a forced grin. "I'm listening."

"First of all, it is important to understand that your son has never entered into PVS, a permanent vegetative state. He continues to defy medical experts by remaining in the first stage of a coma. As you are aware, he breathes on his own and does not experience muscle atrophy or—"

"Yes, I know all that," Momma said, interrupting the doctor.

"Of course," Richardson replied. "We've recorded Hunter's brain activity for the past ten months, specifically, his EEG and neuroimaging data. EEG is an acronym for electroencephalograms.

"We record the electrical impulses in his cerebral cortex, the nerve center of his brain. The functional MRI imaging, called fMRI, gives us reports, colored scans on the metabolism of Hunter's brain. The colors allow us to read your son's mind, so to speak."

After no response from my mother, he continued. "Without getting too technical, we'll first explain the brain waves that relate to his condition. Then, you'll understand why we move Hunter to the mobile fMRI vehicle for brain scanning."

The doctor opened a graph chart for Momma to read.

She remained emotionless, refusing to look at the chart.

My father gestured with a nod, *continue.*

"See these Beta waves?" Richardson asked, pointing at the chart's graph lines. "They indicate that a person is awake. They also indicate mental activity and sensory input typically found in waking consciousness, not in people asleep or in a coma. We've discovered that our Coma-X study group, including Hunter, has recorded EEG readings that showed active Beta brain waves, indicating that all our patients experience bodily activity somewhere else, shall we say, in another state of mind."

Dr. Dustin smiled at my mother, but she remained stoic. The corner of her mouth raised slightly. The doctor showed her the data on the chart, pointed to a graph and said, "See, right here. This green line is the active Beta waves."

She pointed at the graph paper's printing and asked, "Can you tell by those charts if my son is in pain?"

The doctors glanced at one another. Then, they looked at my father. He answered, "That's an excellent question. According to our research, all the Coma-X patients, including Hunter, are resting peacefully. To put it another way, all their physiological indicators appear normal, no pain that we know of."

Momma held back her tears.

My father's explanation comforted her.

Dr. Herrick added, "His Beta wave data also indicates he is experiencing emotional stress, another awake activity."

"Emotional stress?" She grimaced and looked at Daddy with anger in her eyes.

He glanced at Herrick, who extended his right hand to apologize to her.

"Please, don't be upset Mrs. Wainright. I've used misleading terminology. By emotional stress, I mean the daily activities that we *all* experience. Prehistoric man had to hunt for food. For modern man, grocery shopping has its own stress level; specifically, we have too many choices on each grocery isle, causing brain overload. There's also job stress, parenting stress, operating-a-smart-phone stress. Technology overload. What we Americans call the 'stress express'."

I loved the doctor's explanation.

Wish he would have added my favorite: *being-the-oldest-daughter-and-having-to-do-all-the-housework* stress!

My mother never realized how she had turned me into a servant.

Herrick drew a breath and sighed.

Momma frowned.

"Many of our daily decisions are stressful. Our brains have not evolved properly to handle the Information Age, the stress of multi-tasking. Does that make sense?"

My mother glared at Herrick. "I suppose so, but what does that mean for my son?"

Dustin interrupted. "It means he is registering brain waves that indicate he is awake, not asleep. That is why we know Hunter is somewhere else conducting daily activities, making decisions. Doing normal, you know, stressful things."

She shook her head in disgust and took another gulp of wine.

Daddy patted her shoulder and said, "Dennis, tell Gloria about his Gama waves. Make it quick."

Dr. Fletcher said, "The most interesting find is Hunter's Gama waves. These record the fastest frequencies, over 40 cycles per second, and they are associated with bursts of insight and the high-level information processing of the brain. Your son's Gama readings have been off the chart several times. This means Hunter's mind is in a superior high state of consciousness."

Momma nodded. She wanted to hear anything positive, especially that Hunter was in a high state of intelligence. I would find out later that my brother's higher state of mind came from being around Metamorphosis, Sage of the Ages.

My father smiled. "Okay, let's finish with Hunter's neuroimaging study, then, the BCI control cap."

Herrick pulled fMRI charts from an envelope and said, "The

most compelling data that Hunter is awake and active comes from his weekly fMRI readings. These axial and sagittal fMRI scans show bold red signal overlays."

"You've lost me!" my mother shouted, throwing her arms up in the air.

Richardson replied, "Sorry. The fMRI images indicate changes in his blood flow to his brain associated with neural activity. The scans indicate perception, thought, and action. According to these scans, he is awake and extremely active."

My mother interrupted by saying, "If he's awake, can any of this equipment allow me to communicate with Hunter?"

"We were counting on the BCI equipment," Daddy replied. "We're still trying to connect with Hunter."

Dustin nodded and said, "Based on his fMRI scans, we expected Hunter to be 'locked-in'. This is a medical term that means the coma patient is paralyzed but fully conscious, aware of his surroundings.

"Unfortunately, we were wrong. Your son is not 'locked-in'. His mind is active, but not as active as we had hoped. We are unable to communicate with him."

"Is he awake, or not?" Momma asked, firing eye daggers at Daddy.

My father extended his hand in an apology. "Yes, but not as it relates to the term 'locked-in'. Hunter fails to respond to our Brain Computer Interface because he's not fully conscious *here*, on Earth. He is chemically connected to his Millennium body, but his brain is unaware. Non-functioning as it pertains to perceiving his outside environment from his hospital bed."

Daddy pointed at me. "However, we believe we *can* communicate with Julia."

"What makes *her* different than Hunter?" my mother asked. "They *are* twins."

"We have new information," my father said. "It's a female thing."

Momma wrinkled her nose.

That *what-are-you-talking-about* squint she was known for.

"At this time, all our Coma-X patients are males," Daddy said. "Based on Elizabeth Dow's account of her coma, she claims that she returned and re-entered her Earth body during her Millennium dreams. She claims that only females are locked-in and conscious during Coma-X."

"You mean that English woman on television?" my mother asked.

"Yes," Daddy replied. "Elizabeth will visit us soon and explain her Dreamtime, as she called it."

Oh my God! I thought. *They have figured out Dreamtime!*
Put the cap on me!
I can communicate right now!
Bring the cap over here!

"Next week," Dr. Fletcher said, "we begin our fMRI scans and BCI studies with Julia. We will fit your daughter with a special cap that will allow us to study her brain, so you can communicate with her via the computer."

Momma stood with her glass in her hand, spilling wine on the hardwood floor, pointing at my father and shouting, "I don't want you or your quack doctors attaching any more gear or contraptions to my children! They are not guinea pigs!"

Her response made me sick inside.
Please, Mother, don't be so ignorant!
Stop throwing a hissing fit!
Listen to your brilliant husband and the doctors!
They've got it right!
Put the cap on me and I'll show you they're all correct!

Daddy rushed to her and held her while she cried uncontrollably.

"Thank you, men," he said. "That's enough information for today. I'll take it from here."

The four Wainright Foundation doctors eased out the conservatory doors while my father calmed her down.

Sat her in her rocking chair next to Hunter's bed and poured her another glass of wine.

After he got Momma to stop crying, he explained dimensional shifting and teleportation.

He must have said, "Hunter's two bodies" a dozen times.

Knowing that she overreacted to the simplest concept, I don't know why he told her so much information all at once.

She couldn't handle it emotionally.

My father should have known better.

Couldn't help himself. He just kept talking, blurting out stuff like, "What this all means is that Hunter and Julia are resting unconsciously here on Earth while their newly cloned bodies live and breathe on another planet."

"Other bodies?" she asked, trying to comprehend that her son possessed a second body.

Squeezing Hunter's hand and crying, she listened to Daddy's incredible explanation of how her son and daughter possessed two bodies—one asleep, one on another planet.

One active body with a soul. One dormant, comatose body *without* a soul. I was dying to scream out, but all I had were my silent thoughts.

Put the cap on me. I have returned to my dormant Earth body because I am a girl—a female. I have traveled across the universe because I possess magical female energy. Let me wear the cap and I'll prove it.

While Daddy knelt down and held Momma in his arms, I watched him stare at Hunter.

My father lifted her chin with his hand, kissed her cheek, and said, "Hunter has decided to stay on Millennium for a bit longer. He and Julia will return soon. Wake up."

My mother stood and leaned over to lay her head on Hunter's chest.

Daddy stood beside her, silent, knowing he had told her too much information.

While she held my brother, the smell of ocean spray mixed with Monterey pines and cypress reminded me of my childhood.

The sun had been blotted out by a fast-moving marine layer. A fog bank drifted in from the ocean, covering the glass room like a solemn grey veil.

I always loved to walk on the cliffs in the thick fog.

Hidden from view, no one could see me.

Sobbing, my mother leaned over and kissed Hunter's forehead.

Tears dripped down my brother's face.

Not *his* tears.

Momma's.

I admit, I felt jealous that Hunter got all her attention. He had always been her favorite child.

Oblivious to the world outside the conservatory, she obsessed over having her oldest son back, now.

On Wednesday, July 15th, my eighth day back on Earth, I found myself crawling out of my skin. The night before, Daddy locked himself in the library. As a payback, Momma drank two bottles of red wine.

At midnight, she passed out in her rocking chair next to Hunter's bed. That meant the three of us stayed in the downstairs family room overnight.

Alone with only my thoughts, I gazed out the bay window at the fading lights of a distant ship on the horizon.

I wasn't alone for long.

It turned out there was a lot of activity in our home in the late evenings. Actually, early mornings.

As the grandfather clock struck one in the morning, Emily snuck down the stairs and headed for the kitchen. After a few minutes she came out with a bag of potato chips and a candy bar and a soda in her arms. No wonder she was overweight.

At 2:12 a.m., Ruby tiptoed across the family room and

opened the patio door to let her boyfriend in. She whispered his name. Dylan was in our home!

Wearing a black hoodie with torn blue jeans, he looked really creepy. At first, I thought Ruby had let a prowler in. From what I saw of his face—his beard and nose ring and pierced lip, I don't know why Ruby was so attracted to him. One thing he had going for him, he was taller than her. My drunken mother snored while the two teenagers walked by her. Holding hands, they played kissy face as they ran up the staircase.

It wasn't just the issue of Ruby taking advantage of her alcoholic mother and absentee father, it was the fact that Dylan somehow managed to sneak onto our estate and into our home without the government surveillance team spotting him. If he could outsmart the security guards, couldn't the terrorists?

At 3:18 a.m., Daddy finally came out of his "library hideaway", as Momma called it, to check on Hunter and me.

After reading our monitors, he covered my mother with a blue checkered blanket. He got an energy drink from the kitchen and returned to the library.

As the grandfather clock gonged four times, I lay in the darkness thinking.

Thinking about how my sisters and brothers misbehaved and took advantage of my depressed mother and workaholic father. Especially Ruby.

Thinking about how Jeremy had failed to visit me the day before. Where was he?

Thinking about how my family had grown apart since I lapsed into Coma-X.

Thinking about Millennium and how I had to find Hunter and bring him home as soon as possible.

From my calculations, I had slept four hours on Millennium.

As I lay there, I knew my Dreamtime might end at any second.

What I didn't know is how my Earth dream would end—on the spur of the moment or by slowly fading away.

Dreamtime ended at five o'clock on that Sunday morning.

Dylan snuck past my mother and slipped out the patio doors into the darkness.

Moments later, Momma awakened from her stupor, threw off the blue blanket, and stumbled into the kitchen.

Ruby came downstairs holding baby Sebastian in her arms.

Pink and purple clouds drifted above the Pacific Ocean as the smell of cinnamon-flavored coffee awakened the family.

Momma's irritated voice echoed from the kitchen, "Feed the baby now!"

Ruby attempted to take care of baby Sebastian, who fussed and cried. Pouting, he wanted *me* to feed him.

Sorry everyone, I thought, *I'm no longer available to do all your work for you. No more servant at your beckon call.*

Thinking about my Dreamtime, about being awake for 192 hours in a row, I began to feel dizzy.

Without warning, my view of the blue-green ocean became blurry.

Within seconds, my eyesight grew darker.

Darker.

Then, a void.

The pitch blackness transformed into a white glow.

Just like my earlier experience of traveling through time and space, a feeling of nothingness overwhelmed me, the sensation of weightlessness, moving from slow motion to an incredibly fast warp speed—the speed of thought.

As fast as you can say the word, my soul reentered my Millennium body.

Like the great philosophers and prophets have told us, "From the invisible, to the visible. From non-being, to being."

DAYNIGHT OF THE SCORPION

Chapter XIII
Fog Harbor

The radiant white light within me dissolved to blackness. My weightlessness disappeared as my journey across time and space ended. The instant my spirit entered my body on Planet Millennium, I came alive.

Awakened.

Opened my eyes.

The morning light poured into my cabin from the two portholes above my bed. From the bowels of the *Skipbladnir*, the muffled cadence call of the crew continued while the ship swayed back and forth to the rhythm of the splashing oars.

My Dreamtime experience on Earth, every moment of every day I spent with my family, swirled round and round in my head while I stared at the Millennium map on the wall.

Last night's dream, just a few hours, lasted eight days on Earth. But I wasn't dreaming at home, I was awake. So, that means I slept on the Skipbladnir, in my cabin.

My conclusion was: Because I lived in two bodies, my Millennium body *did* actually sleep during the night. I had been connected to my Earth body through the Astral Highway.

Nyx's explanation of dimensional shifting made sense. I had experienced the reality of being alive in two bodies, in two worlds, at the same time.

Have you ever had a dream where part of you is observing yourself? You know, the *other* you stands in a corner of your dream, hidden. Out of sight, but present. Like a silent watcher has entered your private world. And when you ask the observer, "Who are you?" they reply, "Who wants to know?"

Well, that's what my dream felt like on Millennium.

Satisfied with my self-revelation, my explanation of Dreamtime, I jumped out of bed and grabbed my clothes.

Negative thoughts of home flashed inside my head. In my mind's eye, I saw my mother agonizing over her two oldest children lying in hospital beds.

Don't worry about Momma so much, I told myself. *All you have to do is find Hunter and bring him home. That will solve everything.*

I had to go find my twin brother. It was as simple as that!

My energy level had risen to new heights.

Never felt so alive in my life. I was about to begin an adventure on a mysterious planet in the Andromeda galaxy to meet my brother in the Upperworld.

How great is that?

Images of landscapes never before seen by humans swirled in my head.

While I listened to the rowing cadence below deck, I dressed in my brown breeches with the puffy-sleeved white chemise and black, leather-laced bodice.

Stood in front of the full-length mirror brushing my hair when the blast of a medieval horn startled me. I ran across the cabin to open the porthole window.

"Fog Harbor ahead, mates!" Balder shouted from the crow's nest.

By the time I slipped on my wool socks and pulled up my knee-high boots, Alfrigga knocked on the cabin door.

The Dockalfar gnome, wearing a black hoop skirt with a white bodice, escorted me up the stairwell and onto the top deck of the mighty *Skipbladnir.*

Awestruck, I stopped and stared at the colossal cliffs in front of me. Through the patches of gloomy fog, the towering granite walls of Discordia's great crater disappeared straight up into the blue sky. The top of the crater's rim perched somewhere above the clouds.

In the distance, Fire Falls poured a river of red, molten lava down the face of the slate-grey cliffs.

Through the mist, Charon Falls, fed by the River Styx, fell from the heavens to the crater floor.

If you're wondering how I knew all these landmarks, Daddy and Professor Johan talked about them numerous times as they reviewed their hand-drawn maps of Millennium.

Plus, I had the real map on my cabin wall.

If I didn't recognize something, Nyx would identify the geographical landmark.

As we strolled past the aftercastle deckhouse, the ship entered Crater Bay and approached a lighthouse constructed of grey stone. A radiant white light from the glass tower cut through the fog.

"Aye, lassie, Alfrigga said, "yonder be Namo's Lighthouse."

The landmark stood stark against the blue-grey haze, rising majestically above the jagged line of evergreen cypress, pines, and monkey puzzle trees.

Alfrigga told me that Namo's Lighthouse beckoned ships to the safety of Crater Bay. A family of Selkies, seal-like sea fairies known for their hospitable nature, operated the stone structure.

A gentle breeze brushed my face as I inhaled the clean air.

The fragrance of pines and sea air reminded me of home.

Alfrigga waved to Captain Gog, who waved back at us while he barked orders to his bustling crew.

"Fog Harbor pier be one hundred yards ahead!" Balder shouted.

Nyx greeted me as I stepped onto the forecastle deck.

"Good morning, Princess Julia," she said. "How did you sleep last night?"

"I'm not sure," I replied. "All I remember is my Dreamtime, and it lasted a lot longer than last night."

"Did you enjoy that experience?"

"I liked being home and knowing what's going on, but I hated being trapped in my comatose body."

"I see. Are things peaceful at home?"

"Not really. That's why I need to find Hunter and get back to Momma."

"If all goes well, you shall see your brother by this evening, after the coming of the black sky."

I hope so, I thought. *I need to get Hunter home soon.*

Pointing at the wood and brass harpoon in her hand, I asked, "What is *that* for?"

"This is *Gungnir,* my royal spear," Nyx replied. "I carry her for self-defense. Speaking of protection, I have a gift for you."

Nyx motioned to Captain Gog, *come here.*

The Vanir giant lumbered across the deck and handed the Utopian a sheath attached to a leather belt.

"Ya, 'ere be der weapon," Gog said.

"We bestow this gift upon you, Princess Julia," the Utopian said. "This is *Galatine,* the sacred sword."

A sword, I thought. *Why would I need a sword?*

"No thank you", I said. "Momma does not allow me to accept gifts without her permission."

"If your mother knew that you needed the sword for your safety and protection, would she change her mind?"

"Maybe."

Looking up at the towering granite cliffs and the colossal waterfall, I immediately realized that it might be a good idea for me to carry the sword, just in case a wild animal threatened me.

Momma's not here, so I will make my own decisions, I convinced myself.

Accepting the sword from the Utopian, I buckled the belt around my waist, grabbed the jewel-studded handle, and pulled the sword from the leather sheath.

The single-edged blade glistened in the morning light.

Recalling the times Hunter had taken me to the renaissance faires, it dawned on me that I wore similar clothing with a sword strapped to my side at the Northern California Festival.

So, why not here, on Millennium? I thought.

"Use the weapon for self-defense only," Nyx said.

"Whatever you say," I mumbled, sliding *Galatine* into her leather sheath.

The Utopian smiled and pointed her spear toward the colossal cliffs. "Prepare to go ashore."

We stood at the ship's rail and watched Fog Harbor appear through the swirling fog.

The seaport fortress displayed a two-story stone wall with guard towers. Outside the main gate, beige buildings with walls of plaster over twigs and brown thatched roofs lined the street. Two revolving water wheels stood on the bank of a stream that emptied into the harbor. Stone chimneys belched sooty black smoke into the blue sky. A tall building with a glass atrium stood at the rear of the fortress.

The *Skipbladnir* navigated around the Namo's Lighthouse and docked at the end of the pier.

Balder and Lycus hoisted a gangplank from the ship's starboard side to the dock. In single file, Captain Gog led me, Nyx, Balder and Lycus down the plank toward the entrance to the cobblestone pier. Our boots and toenails clicked on the weathered wood. The sound of *tip—tap—clickity—clack* against the planks reminded me I was no longer on Earth.

I spotted figures moving about the decks of three fishing boats in Crater Bay.

"Who are they?" I asked Nyx.

"Those are the villagers, the Selkies and Roanes. They are quite harmless. Unless, of course, you upset them."

The creatures looked humanoid, but with flipper-like hands and elongated noses—seal snouts with fibrous whiskers.

Nyx passed the entrance to the main roadway, avoiding the main gateway to the fortress. Instead, she turned east and led our group around the outskirts of Fog Harbor walls, avoiding contact with the villagers.

Nyx reminded me that, since I was in a hurry to see my brother, we would not stop at the harbor town.

As human-looking tower guards waved at Nyx, the winding trail led us past the fortress and through a soggy marsh shaped by thickets of waist-high deer grass and tangled willows.

As the fog lifted, we hiked until we arrived at a fork in the trail. A wooden sign, nailed to a rotted cedar stump read:

That's the trail I saw on the cabin map, I thought. *It leads to the Forest Primeval, where Hunter fought the Extractors.*

We crossed the trail and entered an open meadow with ankle-deep grass swaying back and forth in the gentle breeze.

Gog held up his hairy arm, causing the half-orcs to stop.

"Is something wrong?" I asked Nyx.

"Our transportation to the Upperworld has arrived," she replied.

Nyx asked Gog, "Is that Ava?"

Looking up, the giant said, "Ya, dat be der gryphon."

As a child, I loved reading Daddy's mythology books. Hunter and I spent hours looking at all the amazing creatures. The illustrations of the gryphon—a winged beast, half eagle and half-lion—became one of my favorites. And the pegasus looked so magnificent. Hunter liked drawing giant birds of prey, rocs. He also became obsessed with winged dragons.

To us, any creature with wings that could fly was awesome.

Nyx pointed up at the slate-grey cliffs that towered into the swirling white clouds.

A four-legged creature soared downward, directly at us.

A gryphon!

Silhouetted against Charon Falls, the magical animal turned its black-feathered wings upward, slowing down for a landing.

"We're going to fly on the gryphon?" I asked Nyx.

"What did you expect?"

"A hot-air balloon," I replied, raising my eyebrows.

Logical answer. The first thing that came to mind was Dorothy, who traveled from Oz in a hot-air balloon.

Nyx grinned and said, "I thought you were in a big hurry to find your brother."

"You're right. I am."

Within moments, the gryphon touched down with its four bizarre legs. The two front legs had golden-brown feathers with orange eagle's legs and black, curved talons. The golden, short-haired torso, the back legs and long tail, looked exactly like those of a lion.

"Her name is Ava," Nyx said.

"She's gorgeous," I murmured, awestruck by the eagle's head, feathered chest and wings that adorned the lion's muscular body.

The gryphon stood twelve feet tall at the shoulder and thirty feet in length. To my surprise, a little person rode on the gryphon's upper neck.

"Who's riding on Ava?" I asked.

"Erda, the gryphon master," Nyx replied. "The Dockalfar gnome is the finest trainer of the flying beasts in all of Millennium. She will take us to our destination in no time."

The gnome, seated on a miniature saddle strapped on the gryphon's upper neck, just behind the white-feathered head, dropped the reins and pulled her goggles over her leather cap. Her braided red pigtails fell to her shoulders.

The freckled-faced gnome wore a green tunic, leather vest, and black breeches with grey snake-skin boots. Her smile revealed a missing front tooth.

She pulled a gold pocket watch from her brown vest, looked at the time and yelled, "Aye, we best put spurs ta the nags, the black sky's a comin', she is."

Erda grabbed a leather water bag strapped to her saddle and poured amrita down the gryphon's orange beak.

"Be right with you, Erda," Nyx yelled. She instructed Captain Gog to board the *Skipbladnir* and return to Time Island, telling him we would catch up with them in two daynights.

"Come, Princess Julia," the Utopian said. "Our ride awaits."

Don't ask me why, but I wasn't afraid to mount the huge gryphon, twice as tall as me.

Ava moved her front eagle's leg out and lifted me up, so I could climb onto the top of her shoulders, in front of the wings. I nestled down into white neck feathers.

"Aye, welcume aboard, lassie," Erda said, shaking my hand. "Jus' grab them saddle straps an' hang on tight."

I felt surprisingly comfortable and secure, like I wouldn't fall off if I held the leather handles tightly.

Nyx climbed behind me and signaled to Erda, *go*.

The gnome yanked on leather reins, causing the gryphon to flap her wings and race across the meadow at a rapid speed.

I'd ridden horses at full gallop. Ava ran much faster than any horse.

Erda waved to Captain Gog and the half-orcs as we lifted off the grassy meadow.

Too nervous to wave, I clutched the leather saddle straps for dear life as we soared into the blue crater sky.

Swooooosh!

So fast it took my breath away.

"Awesome!" I shouted.

It felt like a thrill ride at the county fair I attended every year with my family. I was never scared of all those crazy-fast roller coasters. That's why riding the soaring gryphon exhilarated me.

Once we became airborne, Ava rode the crater's warm air currents, climbing steadily.

You could feel the powerful rhythm of her jet-black wings.

Nyx sat behind me.

We were able to talk over the sound of the whistling wind in our ears.

She pointed to the fog forest below. "There is the Kukulcan Trail that winds through the Forest Primeval."

Awestruck by the Millennium scenery, I watched the winding trail snake its way into the dark woods.

Nyx explained that the Discordia Crater was the most dramatic geographical feature on Millennium—visible from space. The crater's vertical cliffs spouted great rivers of water, fire and ice, forming waterfalls and lavafalls like no others in the universe.

Pointing her spear at the river of red molten rock erupting from the crater's south face, she said, "That is Fire Falls. The lava plunges eighty-eight miles to the crater floor."

"How tall are the crater walls?" I asked, looking up into the heavens.

"The cliffs rise 150 miles above the Sea of Circles."

"No way," I mumbled, staring at the fissured granite walls honeycombed with hundreds of caves, grottoes, and tunnels.

Geography had always been one of my favorite subjects in school. I tried to imagine a landform six times taller than Mt. Everest, taller than anything on Earth.

Ava rode the warm crater thermals upward. Higher and higher. Soon, Namo's Lighthouse, Fog Harbor, and the mighty *Skipbladnir* became tiny specks far below us.

Watching the crater's primordial fog drift steadily over the Sea of Circles like a gigantic grey blanket, I suddenly realized I could no longer see Fog Harbor, or Time Island.

That's when it hit me.

You've done it, Julia Wainright. You must live with your decision. There is no turning back.

Chapter XIV
Doubting Castle

Ava spread her massive black wings, allowing the rising thermals to lift us higher and higher, toward the top rim of Discordia. Taller than any mountains you could possibly imagine, the towering granite walls of the crater disappeared into the white clouds drifting through the blue sky above us.

While Erda guided the gryphon in a southeasterly direction, Nyx pointed at a switch-back trail carved into the side of the vertical rock cliffs.

Pointing with *Gungnir,* her royal spear, the Utopian said, "That is the South Crater Trail, leading to the Upperworld. Balder told me it is the path that Hunter took up the face of the crater with Metamorphosis and Eve."

Hunter hiked that narrow trail? I thought. *Since we were young, he had always been deathly afraid of heights. He must be showing off for Eve. No way would he walk on anything that high back home.*

Ava screeched and banked to the right.

Amazed by the crater's incredible size, I asked Nyx how the cauldron had been created. She explained that an asteroid from the Dark Star—the Star of Evil—had collided with Millennium, forming the vast Discordia Crater, and with it, the Sea of Circles and Time Island.

As we flew along the southwest cliffs, Erda pointed at a triangular-shaped cave entrance bordered by a cascading waterfall that spilled into a rock pool.

"Yonder be Ogo Hole," the gnome yelled in her high-pitched, squeaky voice.

Nyx said, "That cave is where Hunter entered the Underworld with Eve, Metamorphosis, and a subterranean guide named Grimnir. That is the last time Balder saw your brother. It was the Daynight of the Bear."

Ogo Hole, an ominous cave in the side of the crater, looked really scary. Imagining my brother traveling through the dark underground world reminded me of that Jules Verne novel I had read, *Journey to the Center of the Earth*."

I remembered that Verne, like so many other great explorers, had visited Millennium and then returned to Earth to write down his adventures.

We climbed steadily as we approached Fire Falls, the great southern landmark. Her glowing, red-orange lava flowed down the face of the southern crater cliffs.

Nyx told me, "The lava falls is like no other in the universe."

Erda pulled hard on the reins and shouted, "These 'ere crater trade winds be weak as a bloody breeze!"

Ava screeched and flapped her wings faster to gain altitude.

Nyx yelled at Erda, "Dive!"

Sensing danger, I looked behind us.

Captain Kraken, riding the flying beast, Tyrannus, swooped down on us with his saber drawn. The infamous Extractor swung his gleaming blade at Nyx. The Utopian extended her spear and deflected Kraken's saber. Sparks exploded off the weapons as I closed my eyes and ducked down into Ava's neck feathers. Nyx saved my life.

Aggressive Kraken swooped under us, screaming, "Yer essence is mine, Earthlin', surrender!"

I felt that I'd be plucked from the air like an innocent dove grabbed by the sharp talons of a hungry hawk.

Tyrannus flew too fast for Ava to avoid his aerial attacks.

The sea monster with transparent wings hissed as he circled and soared over us.

Erda had her cutlass drawn, raising the blade above her head while she pulled on the gryphon's reins.

Kraken continued to dive at us, coming close enough for me to get a good look at the hideous creature. The white-fanged Extractor looked like a crazy man covered in lizard skin. His reptile scales shone metallic green under the Millennium skies. A row of blue tentacles ran from the top of his head, down his spine, and ended at the base of his serpentine tail that resembled an octopus arm. His wild eyes reminded me of the monsters in the movies my brother and I watched every chance we got.

Diving and flicking his dark-blue tongue at me, the drooling iguana man enjoyed seeing the fear in my eyes. I couldn't help but act scared. He looked like something out of your worst nightmare. He tried to hurt me. Kill me.

"Be gone, you big bully!" Nyx screamed.

Kraken made a final dive. Avoiding Nyx's spear, he swung his saber, cutting the feathers off the tip of Ava's right wing.

The gryphon screeched, watching her black feathers float in the crater sky as she banked hard to the left.

Cackling in a high-pitched voice, the captain flew upward, high into the crater sky. Within a few moments, the Extractor looked like a tiny bird above us.

"Aye, that Kraken be a sly devil. A sneaky one, he be," Erda said, sliding her cutlass into her leather scabbard. "Me gryphon ain't bleedin'. Ava lost a coople 'o feathers, that's all."

"Are you all right?" Nyx asked me.

"I think so," I replied.

My emotions turned from frightened to angry. The reality that a creature had followed me and had tried to capture me made me mad.

Who does he think he is? I thought. *I'm not looking for trouble. I have a right to find my brother. Just leave me alone.*

"The next time we face danger, Nyx said, "I highly recommend you draw your sword."

I grabbed the handle of *Galatine* and thought, *Why didn't I remember I had the weapon strapped to my side?*

Nyx was right. I needed to start looking out for myself.

Pay attention. Watch for danger.

As Ava climbed higher toward the top of the crater, my heartbeat returned to normal. I relaxed and felt safer. Well, as relaxed and safe as one could expect while flying a hundred miles above the crater floor on a gryphon navigated by a gnome on the lookout for hideous creatures attacking from nowhere.

Enjoying the warm wind in my face, I gazed at the surreal scenery—the towering granite cliffs and colossal waterfalls of fire and ice that fell from the heavens. Like a vision, it came to me. I realized I had become the girl protagonist in my own adventure novel. You know, the young girl who magically flies over the world and explores far-away lands.

Nyx announced, "Welcome to the Upperworld," as we soared over the top of the great crater at the southeastern rim. No longer inside the crater, I could see from horizon to horizon. The heavens opened up into an unworldly atmosphere, split into red, blue, and black skies.

Ava descended and glided a hundred yards off the ground.

To our right, the reddish-brown walls of an eroded river gorge came into view. No matter how beautiful the scenery, I became anxious to find my brother.

"Are we getting close to Hunter?" I asked.

"Not quite," Nyx replied. "We'll have another daynight's journey ahead of us."

"But, I thought we'd see my brother *tonight*."

"Patience, Princess Julia. All things happen in perfect order."

She explained that the crater thermals had not been as strong as normal, causing a delay. Kraken's attack slowed us down. Also, Erda avoided night flights whenever possible.

We had to spend the evening at Doubting Castle.

Wanting to complain, I realized it would do me no good.

I learned to never whine or nag around Momma. It always made things worse.

Relax, Julia, I thought, *enjoy the scenery. People would die to see such fabulous landscapes. As Daddy would say, "Live in the moment. Now is all you have."*

"That is our Utopian River Gorge," Nyx said, "one of our eight great river systems. The roaring river has carved out a magnificent canyon measuring 90 miles wide, 800 feet deep, and 3000 miles long.

The previous summer, I had visited the Grand Canyon with my family. The Earthly landmark looked like a narrow creek compared to the gorge we flew over.

Beyond the Utopian River, the Melody Mountains rose above the clouds, stretching beyond the horizons of Eremus.

Erda yelled, "Hang on," and yanked on the reins.

The gryphon dove straight down, leaving my stomach in my throat. She leveled off fifty feet above a yellow cobblestone road that hugged the east side of the gorge.

"Below us is the Open Road," Nyx said. "Hunter traveled that road, also called The Great Way, with Metamorphosis and Eve."

So, that's the famous road of life that Professor Johan wanted to see, I thought.

My father claimed that the "highway of life", those were his words, would take you to magical places and untold treasures. Wait until Daddy finds out that Hunter traveled the Open Road with Metamorphosis. Pine trees and noble firs and hemlocks grew from the edge of the cobblestone road to the top of the Druid Hills, creating the primordial Palatine Forest. The smell of fragrant pines reminded me of home sweet home as we followed the ancient roadway several miles.

Nyx announced we had arrived at Doubting Junction.

Ava turned inland over the crossroads and over a massive boulder formation—monolith.

When Nyx announced, "Stonehenge", I knew I had discovered the prototype for the upright stone formations on

Earth. Below us, a dozen blazing fires belched black smoke into the blue sky.

Erda looked back at Nyx and pointed down.

Knights on horseback wore armor and carried lances and broadswords, riding about the campsites tending to the flames.

"Those are funeral pyres," Nyx said. "A battle has taken place. We shall find out what happened when we arrive at the castle."

The smoky air smelled horrible, like when strands of tangled hair burn in your hair dryer.

You know that sickening odor, don't you?

We flew through the white smoke and followed a winding road up and over the Palatine Hills. Soon, Doubting Castle came into view, rising above the virgin forest. I marveled at the magnificent six-story-tall stone castle. Eight main towers with conical spires jutted into the Millennium sky. Four domes surrounded her central spire with red, white, and blue flags waving from the tops of the pinnacles.

By the time we arrived at the castle, the black sky had crawled over the landscape, crowding out the blue sky, creating a twilight atmosphere. I expected Ava to land at the draw bridge, the entrance to the castle. Instead, the gryphon flew up and over the towering fortress walls. Along the castle perimeter, a dozen armed ballistas and catapults had been positioned behind the balustrades, ready to hurl lethal javelins, rocks, and flaming balls of pine-sap pitch to any intruders who dared attack the castle. Bizarre characters dressed in medieval clothing—tunics, doublets, capes, cloaks, and surcoats—waved to us while we circled the main tower.

Too high in the sky to get a good look at their faces, I knew one thing—none of them were human.

Knights on horseback trotted down the main street of the courtyard. The armored soldiers carried lances, broadswords, crossbows, and scutum shields. Their horses wore champfreins over their heads and mail coif on their necks, shoulders and flanks. In the twilight, the stallions' pointed head ornaments gave them the appearance of silver-headed unicorns.

Erda landed the gryphon on an arched bridge that connected a single stone tower to the central spire.

We dismounted the gryphon and I followed Nyx across the bridge, through an iron-gated archway.

Two knights—boarman soldiers—stood guard at the gate.

Half my height, the hairy beasts had yellow tusks protruding from their lower jaws. Their shiny suits of armor rattled as they saluted Nyx. The husky boars wore pig-face basinet helmets and carried lances with royal shields. Snorting as they saluted us, the pair of knights made me feel safe.

The inside of the circular tower, illuminated by oil lamps mounted all the way up three flights of spiral stone steps, reminded me of all those fairy tale stories Daddy read us where the princess stayed in a lonely tower. I couldn't remember if the girl was Sleeping Beauty or Rapunzel or Cinderella or Snow White or Maid Marion. One of them, for sure.

Nyx led me up the winding staircase to the top of the tower, to a bedchamber. She pushed open an iron door that revealed a simple room with a bed, table, and two chairs. A wood-framed mirror hung on the wall. In the corner, orange and yellow flames danced in the stone fireplace.

"We shall spend the evening here," Nyx said. "Please, make yourself comfortable. I request that you remain in this room."

The Utopian grinned and closed the door. The blazing fire cast my shadow on the grey stone wall. It followed me as I walked across the chamber to an arched window, the only one in the room.

Opening the wooden shutters, I took a deep breath.

The twilight had turned to darkness. Torch lights burned in the courtyard far below. Unrecognizable figures moved about in the shadowed darkness.

Three Millennium moons glowed in the black sky filled with sparkling stars, some so bright they made me squint.

My mind played the tune, *When You Wish Upon A Star*, as my thoughts turned homeward.

I wonder if Jeremy is still visiting me. Please God, don't let him get discouraged because I'm in a coma. Keep his love for me alive while I'm gone. I hope Momma isn't drinking too much. The terrorist threats can't be real. No one wants to hurt Daddy. Do they? If they met him, they would know how loving and kind and gentle he truly is. Once I get Hunter home, Momma will be happy again.

My thoughts were interrupted by the creaking of rusted hinges as the door swung open.

Nyx carried a silver tray with food—bowls of porridge, ambrosia, and mugs filled with amrita.

We sat at the oak table by the crackling fire.

While we ate our dinner, Nyx explained that the bloody battle at Doubting Junction had been fought on the Daynight of the Wolf.

That was just yesterday, I thought.

The boarman soldiers, commanded by Malagig the Paladin, were defeated by Chax and his army of monstrous Grizzsects, led by Bodvar the Bearman. The battle, waged over Hunter and Eve, left many brave soldiers dead and wounded.

"My brother fought in a battle?" I asked. "Is he okay?"

"Calm down, Princess Julia. Hunter defended himself honorably, and he was not seriously injured."

"Thank God. Where is my brother now?"

"Hunter travels with Metamorphosis to the castle of Escalot."

"Why is he going there?"

"Unfortunately, Eve was captured by Ex and taken prisoner on the *Walrus*. The Extractor ship was last seen sailing south down the Utopian River toward Pellagus."

"You mean, Hunter's going after Eve?"

Nyx nodded, *yes.* "Metamorphosis ordered the great ship *Argo* to set sail from the port city of Hermopolis, to rendezvous with him and your brother at Kallipolis, farther up the coast."

"Hunter's going to get himself killed over a girl he just met?"

"Most likely, your brother has made the highest choice."

Not sure what she meant by the *highest choice*, I said, "He needs to come home with me, immediately."

"We shall see him tomorrow." She leaned over the table and patted my hand. "You may ask him yourself."

Pondering her words, I finished my elixir porridge and grabbed a slice of ambrosia. I asked Nyx to explain the Extractors, the ones I saw in the *Magnum Opus*.

"Allow me to expand your knowledge of the dark forces, the Extractors," Nyx said, taking a deep breath.

"Ex, the Master Extractor, also known as the Dark Master, the Invisible Villain, is the one creature who strikes the most fear in the hearts and minds of Millennians. Before his arrival, the most negative of emotions, fear, did not exist on this planet. Ex and his Extractors suffer from an *Emotional Virus*. Infected and highly contagious, they continue to spread the *Dark Essence*—Curse of the Universe, throughout the eight kingdoms and the Underworld."

"Is that the virus that Daddy described in his *Planet Millennium Report*?"

"Patience, young lady," Nyx said. "Allow me to focus on Ex. Then we shall discuss the *Dark Essence*."

I nodded, swallowing my last piece of ambrosia while Nyx continued her explanation.

"Unfortunately, Ex and his whereabouts remain a mystery. Defeating the *one who moves as a shadow* is a challenge that has alluded us all. A millennia has passed since the Dark Master's appearance and no one, not even we Utopians, have been able to stop his reign of terror, fear, and chaos. His underground fortress lies in Trikinus, Realm of Utmost Darkness, where he rules over his legions of Extractors."

I raised my hand. "Why is Ex so difficult to defeat?"

Nyx sipped amrita from her mug, then said, "Try to imagine dealing with an evil creature no one can see. Ex exhibits two devastating powers, invisibility and flight. To remain invisible, Ex wears the *Helmet of Darkness*. Also known as the winged *Cap of Invisibility*, someone stole the dog-skin helmet from the god Hades, ruler of Avernus. Soon after that, the fabled *Feathered Cloak* was pillaged from Asgard. Guarded by Fenris the Wolf, no one knows how the cloak turned up missing."

The Utopian wrinkled her nose. "The creature wearing the falcon-feathered cloak, a magical garment, can fly. Ex has both the cap and the cloak, making him seem invincible."

"Invincible?"

"We know he is mortal. We have discovered that he avoids Metamorphosis. The pulsating rays, the astral glow from the crystal ball on Metamorphosis's scepter, *Joyease*, has a negative effect on the Invisible Villain."

"So, can he be defeated?"

"Yes. But until we stop him, Ex and his Extractors continue to reek havoc and destruction throughout the Eight Great Kingdoms. Their sole purpose is to destroy the Eight Great Treasures—Octilogy—so that the Great Way, the Source, is lost forever. In the meantime, the diseased creatures continue to infect others with the *Dark Essence*."

Raising my hand in the air, I asked, "Where does the *Dark Essence* come from?"

"I shall quote our chief historian, Enoch, and his historical reference to, what we call, the Extractor Invasion. According to Enoch, *Eons ago, a race of malevolent beings, known as the Extractors, rose to prominence by feeding upon the life essence of sentient beings. These evil creatures realized that the darker the essence of the life form they consumed, the more power they accumulated. The Extractors quickly spread across their own dimension, the Tenebris Dimension, spreading suffering and pain to all sentient begins they came into contact with. Over time, they drained their own dimension of life. Soon, their race began to face starvation and extinction. A dominant one rose among them and devised a diabolical plan.*

177

"Ex, the Master Extractor, plotted to use the last of the life force energy they could gather to collapse the Tenebris Dimension down into a single, dense sphere known as the Dark Star. Shedding their corporeal existence, they forced the Dark Star to explode, sending gigantic shards of the star, Extractoroids, across nine dimensional barriers to other worlds. Ex and his Extractors, carriers of the deadly Virus, the Dark Essence, rode the shards of the Dark Star through the nine dimensional barriers so their evil race would be born again.

"The central worlds of the Amalgamation's nine dimensions invaded by the Extractors were the planets Millennium, Triton, Metis, Phobos, Phaethon, Deimos, Leda, Epiphany, and Earth. As the colossal shards collided with each of the nine planets, the Extractors unleashed their diabolical quest to feed upon the life essence of every sentient being, to control all the souls in all dimensions. All ways and for all time."

"There you have it," Nyx said. "A fragment from the Dark Star collided with Millennium and spread the viral plague, the *Dark Essence,* across the land. Prior to that cataclysmic event, our planet enjoyed an enlightened society, abiding by the Universal Truths. After the catastrophic collision formed the Discordia Crater, primitive tribes of dysfunctional Extractors emerged from the crater. Wars broke out. Disease and famine crept across the kingdoms of Millennium.

"Soon, our disease-free planet experienced major outbreaks of the *Extractor Virus,* infecting the thoughts of healthy creatures, inflating their egos, causing them to think selfishly, of only themselves and no one else. These powerful, egocentric thoughts turned them into greedy, self-centered beings, Extractors. Primitive civilizations with dysfunctional, ego-crazed creatures spread throughout our eight kingdoms, and much faster than we anticipated. Many Millennians, peaceful and non-violent, had their essence drained by the greedy and power-hungry Extractors, carriers of the *Virus.* The epidemic spread. Even the gods and goddesses became infected."

Wiping my mouth with a white napkin, I asked, "Is this *Extractor Virus*, this *Dark Essence*, on Earth?"

Nyx nodded her head*, yes.*

My mind searched for an explanation. I had to admit, many of the Extractor descriptions I read about in the *Magnum Opus* reminded me of family, friends and relatives I knew back home.

Some very close to me. It made me uncomfortable knowing that humans on Earth suffered from an *Extractor Virus*, a contagious disease. The Utopian told me the *Dark Essence* had been an epidemic on Earth since the beginning of civilization.

Pandemic was the word she used.

Nyx stood and said, "We have talked enough for this evening. You must get a good night's rest for tomorrow's journey."

"But I have more questions," I said, standing with the Utopian.

"I shall enlighten you tomorrow, Daynight of the Boar," she said, stepping to the chamber door. "The gryphon leaves for Escalot at daybreak. Please, get some sleep."

Frustrated with her response, I half-grinned and bid her, "Good daynight," as they say on Millennium.

Nyx closed the iron door.

Lying on the mustard-yellow bed that reminded me of that Van Gogh painting, I rubbed my Triamulet between my fingers, staring out the lone window. The sky reminded me of the painting, *Starry Night,* with the swirling rivers of sparkling stars.

As you can imagine, all I could think about was seeing my twin brother—making sure Hunter came home safe.

I haven't seen him for a year. I wonder what he looks like? He's probably changed. It sounds like Hunter's madly in love with this Eve girl. He's willing to die for her. How am I going to convince my brother to come home if he's obsessed with Eve? Hunter was always so stubborn, just like Daddy.

Gazing out into the black Millennium sky, the pulsating sea of shining white stars became blurry as I closed my weary eyes.

I don't remember falling asleep.

Chapter XV
Julia's Second Dreamtime

Rocking back and forth in her favorite chair, Momma's face came into focus. She sipped on a glass of white wine, reading a black book by candlelight. My mother always burned aromatic candles, the fat ones that made the house smell like fragrant roses. Immediately, I realized I had returned home, at the speed of thought, to experience my second Dreamtime.

Like my first experience, my astral journey across space and time felt euphoric, like a warm rush of fond memories on a cold, lonely night.

My mother did not sense my return—the return of my soul to my Earth body.

The air in the room vibrated with my thoughts.

Why couldn't she feel my positive, radiating energy?

The answer was simple. Obvious. She drank too much. Took too many meds. How could she be aware of anything spiritual when her mind wasn't right, not in tune with her inner self? In touch with the universe.

On the other side of the dark family room, in the shadows, Hunter lay motionless in his hospital bed. Beyond the bay window, a quarter moon drifted through an ocean of stars, waiting for the dawn to break on the horizon. The only sounds were the *tick—tick—tick* of the grandfather clock and the steady *beep—beep—beep* of monitors.

Reading by the dim light of the candle flame, my mother's shadowed face revealed mascara-stained tears running down her cheeks. Holding a white handkerchief to her mouth, she turned the pages of a black-covered book.

Sobbing, she put the book down on the table and looked into my eyes.

"I'm so sorry, Julia," she said, wiping the ash-grey tears from her cheeks.

I stared at the stack of black books setting on the table.

My diaries!

Momma had found my sacred journals. How did she know where to look? She was never supposed to find them, let alone, *read* them. No one should be allowed to read your secrets, especially your parents.

My mother's going to hate me, I thought. *Now that she knows how I really feel, she'll never forgive me.*

Every time Momma turned a page, I imagined the intimate details she had read, the vivid descriptions of how I *really* felt about her.

Page after page after page of my traumatic relationship with my mother. My most recent 2015 diary had a lot of stuff about Jeremy in it. Really personal things that Momma should never read.

Put those back where you found them, my thoughts screamed. *You have no right to take my sacred journals. Burn them, but don't read them.*

Lying helpless in my comatose body, I could do nothing but watch my mother sob as she read my diaries. The morning light revealed a heavy fog crawling through our backyard. The ocean hid behind the ghostly grey mist that drifted over our sea-cliff home.

Daddy wandered into the family room. His eyes looked tired, like he hadn't slept. His silver goatee had been overtaken by a stubbly beard.

"What are those?" my father asked, pointing at the stack of journals by the flickering candle.

Startled, she slammed my diary shut and said, "Nothing, just some old books I found."

My father snuck up behind her and grabbed the top diary off the table.

"Give me that!" my mother shouted, grasping for the black book.

Daddy turned his back and shuffled toward the bay window, flipping through the pages of my journal.

Oh no, I thought. *Now my father is learning my deepest secrets. Why don't they just publish my private stories in the local newspaper; or put all my journals on the Internet.*

Momma gathered the stack of diaries in her arms and ran out of the room, crying.

Holding my journal in the air, he shouted, "For God's sake, Gloria! You're not supposed to be reading these!"

He marched across the family room and set the book on the stand beside my bed.

Kissing my cheek, he said, "Good morning, sweetheart. Sorry about your journals. Your mother hasn't been herself."

My father kept telling his children how Momma wasn't herself. But, she *was* herself.

Where had he been living all these years?

Please stop making excuses for her, I thought.

Daddy checked the EEG equipment under my hospital bed, then walked over to Hunter and studied his medical charts.

My brother looked like an alien from outer space. That's because he wore the BCI control cap over his head. I wondered why I didn't have the head gear on. After all, it was *me* who could communicate in a coma, not my brother. It was *me* who was locked-in, not him.

My father turned on the television. A new, big screen had been mounted on the wall between our hospital beds.

The news reporter announced the date:

Monday, August 21, 2015

Daddy returned to my bed, grabbed my diary and marched out of the room, yelling, "Where are you, Gloria? We need to talk."

I stared at lifeless Hunter, knowing I would meet his active body, the one with a soul, later that day. Or night.

I mean, daynight.

You know what I mean—later on in Millennium time.

From out of nowhere, two strangers marched past the bay window.

Cloaked in thick fog, they wore camouflaged uniforms and carried military rifles.

It didn't take long for me to figure out why armed guards walked the perimeter of our estate.

All I had to do was listen to the news.

The reports, repeated over and over, sounded unbelievable, like something from a scary movie or a bad dream.

Bombings!

The Wainright Foundation offices in London had been bombed on August 5th.

Two blasts destroyed the research facilities, killing twelve people. Thirty innocent bystanders had been injured in the terrorist attacks.

On screen, Dr. Fletcher was being interviewed by Scotland Yard.

Hospitalized, wrapped in head bandages, he was the only staff member from the London office who had survived the bombings.

Oh my God, I thought. *Daddy's in grave danger.*

The world news got worse.

Kidnappings!

On August 6th, three Wainright Foundation doctors had been kidnapped from their homes.

When they showed the abducted men's photos, I was shocked to see the familiar faces of my father's closest colleagues:

Dr. Richardson. Dr. Dustin. Dr. Herrick.

The part of the story that terrified me the most was that the terrorists did not ask for money, they wanted to negotiate a trade. The three renowned scientists for Dr. Wayland Wainright!

For the first time I knew for certain, someone planned to kill my father.

Momma and my brothers and sisters were also in danger.

Our home wasn't safe anymore.

Lying there helpless, unable to defend myself, I thought:

Would I feel pain if a terrorist murdered me?

Would I witness my own death?

What if my Earth body was killed?

Would my Millennium body die too?

To make matters worse, Daddy's best friend, Professor Van Campbell, had left town on a world-wide mythology and folklore lecture. In Vienna, he collapsed at the podium, suffering a heart attack. Professor Johan survived, flown to a New York hospital after his surgery.

Because of our family's high security status, "house arrest", as Daddy called it, my father was prevented from visiting his life-long friend.

In the kitchen, my parents argued about my journals.

Daddy wanted to lock them in a safe until my return.

Momma said she would guard them, make sure no one read them.

Except *her*, of course.

Upstairs, Sebastian and Crystal cried while Ruby screamed at Emily and Grace. Zachary and Alexander teased Astrid and Pearl, chasing them down the stairs.

Complete chaos in the Wainright house.

Welcome home, Julia, I thought.

My mother screamed at Daddy that she was fed up with the constant surveillance by government officials and the military. She reminded him how she and children hadn't left the house in three months. They all felt like prisoners in their own home.

The news also reported world-wide disturbances caused by my father's research.

Social, political, and religious groups fought over the existence of Planet Millennium.

I watched the videos of mass demonstrations and protests and riots with mobs looting stores and buildings burning and civil unrest. It looked like the world had gone mad, split in two groups: either you believed in Millennium, or you didn't.

Believers.

Non-believers.

As Daddy used to say, "People will fight and argue over anything."

How would *you* react to the announcement that life existed on another planet? That an ancient sage in the Andromeda Galaxy taught our philosophers and prophets and poets and playwrights and authors and teachers. That people from Earth live on another planet, right now.

How would you feel if you heard that alien life forms existed somewhere else in the universe?

Would the news upset you, cause you to worry?

Or, would the announcement make you happy?

I spent my first night at home alone in my bedroom, wide awake.

Wondering where Jeremy might be.

Praying that he still loved me as much as I loved him.

Thinking about how I was going to bring Hunter home to my mother.

Hoping the world would believe my father's *Planet Millennium Report*.

Wishing I could communicate with my family.

Upset that my mother read my diaries. Violated my trust.

Worried that Momma would never forgive me for all the things I wrote about her.

Although living my second Dreamtime, I still had trouble grasping that my other body slept in a tower atop Doubting

Castle—located on the Open Road—in the kingdom of Pellagus—in the Upperworld—on a planet called Millennium—in the Andromeda Galaxy.

See what I mean.

It's a lot to get your head around!

Just as the morning sun peeked through my shutters, Momma entered my bedroom, kissed my cheek, and said, "Good morning, Julia."

She still loves me, I thought. *She hasn't read all my journals yet.*

She wheeled me and Hunter downstairs into the family room and then she hurried out the door into the next room.

Pots and pans rattled in the kitchen. The smell of eggs and sausage and oven-warmed cinnamon rolls made me hungry. The kind of hunger where you're full but you still want something sweet to eat.

While the family ate breakfast, Momma argued with Daddy over negative words I had never heard mentioned in our home:

Bankruptcy. Foreclosure.

She screamed at my father about how he had lost our oceanfront mansion, how he had spent his entire fortune on that "damned Planet Millennium project".

Lying there helpless, I tried to imagine some other girl moving into my bedroom.

Not having the ocean as my backyard.

Relocating to a strange, new town.

Moving scared me. Losing our house sounded frightening.

I know the thought of starting over devastated my mother.

She couldn't handle change.

The babies cried and the boys argued while the girls chattered among themselves as Daddy explained how he would not allow the house to go into foreclosure.

Not let the bank take away Momma's security.

That he believed his Millennium research would pay off someday.

How he would save the family from death and destruction.

"You're nothing but a dreamer!" she screamed.

My father pleaded his case with her, but Momma told him where to go.

In the middle of their marathon argument, the door bell rang.

Thank God, I thought. *At least they'll stop fighting and Momma will put on her happy face for the relatives, like nothing's wrong.*

It wasn't the in-laws who had come to visit.

A woman followed my father into the family room.

I had seen her before, but I couldn't remember where.

Dressed in a navy-blue dress with yellow polka-dots, the tall, thin woman with porcelain-white skin and shoulder-length red hair stared at me with her green eyes.

Wouldn't stop looking at me.

"Here they are, the twins," Daddy said. "This is Hunter. He's worn the BCI control cap for several weeks, but so far, we have not recorded any locked-in signals."

My father shuffled toward my brother, continuing to explain the BCI test results, but the woman ignored him and walked straight to my bed.

She held my hand and leaned over my body, whispering in my ear, "Hello, Julia. If you're in Dreamtime, I know you can hear me."

Her hypnotic emerald-green eyes looked straight through me as she smiled and kissed my cheek. Feeling her positive energy, a warm wave of pleasure surged through my body.

I also felt something touching my chest.

A Triamulet!

The medallion, dangling from a gold chain around the woman's neck, displayed a sparkling crystal mounted in the center of the gold triangle.

Why doesn't my Triamulet have a crystal? I thought, admiring her medallion.

"Darling," my father said to Momma, who had just entered the room, "this is Elizabeth Dow, the woman I told you about. She'll be staying with us for a week or so."

Of course! Stupid me! It was the Coma-X survivor who had been on television with Daddy. She had been to Millennium.

As a female, she had experienced Dreamtime.

The woman was 139 years old!

"Most kind of you and your lovely wife," she said, walking over to Momma and shaking her hand. "I hope you do not mind my intrusion. I shan't be a nuisance."

"I pray you can help my son and daughter," my mother said, doing her best to smile. "I'll get the guest room ready."

Her eyes looked bloodshot from crying and arguing.

Momma stumbled out of the room.

She had been drinking.

I could always tell.

At least Momma didn't call the woman "one of Daddy's crazy colleagues", or some other embarrassing statement.

"And that is Julia," my father said, pointing at my bed.

"Yes, we have already met," Elizabeth said, winking at me.

"Excuse me?" he asked.

Ignoring his question, she gestured toward Hunter. "You realize, of course, that you have the BCI gear attached to the wrong patient."

"As I told you over the phone, Gloria has demanded that Julia be left alone. But now that you're here, I know she'll change her mind. Once you talk to her, tell her your experience, she'll allow Julia to wear the headset."

"I believe I can be a positive influence on your wife, Dr. Wainright."

"Call me Wayland."

"Most kind of you, but Dr. Wainright is my preference. Business, you know."

Daddy blushed, grinned sheepishly, and said, "I'll have my daughter escort you to your room."

He yelled, "Ruby, I need your help."

My radical sister shuffled into the room wearing, what can only be described as, a vampire outfit—black lace on more black with dark-purple lipstick, a pierced eyebrow, and a silver nose ring. Her unkempt, magenta-red hair had been combed in seven different directions.

If I ever looked like that, Momma would call me every bad name she could think of and put me on restriction for the rest of my life. Maybe disown me.

When Ruby bent down to pick up Ms. Dow's travel bag, I spotted it.

A tattoo!

My sister wore an outrageous red, blue, and green-colored dragon crawling down her shoulder onto her arm.

Momma had lost control of her children.

Elizabeth followed Ruby out the French doors, with Daddy right behind them. I noticed he had his fingers crossed. I imagined he hoped that my mother would listen to the voice of reason—Ms. Dow.

I would have crossed my fingers too, if I could.

That evening, my keen sense of hearing allowed me to overhear the dinner conversation between Elizabeth and my family.

No doubt, when you're 139 years old, you learn to deal with all sorts of people in difficult situations.

Elizabeth had learned nature's secret—patience.

That's why she never mentioned Millennium or Dreamtime, or anything to do with the Wainright Foundation's research on Coma-X. Just small talk and women's stuff to make Momma comfortable.

She did, however, surprise my mother with her vivid stories of her childhood. Elizabeth's descriptions of the English countryside in 1888 sounded so real, so authentic, my mother seemed to enjoy them. Didn't argue or call anyone at the dinner table "crazy" or "insane".

My mother, instead of being critical, sat and listened.

Even the kids, captivated by the mysterious female guest, kept quiet and behaved themselves.

After dinner, Momma wheeled Hunter and me upstairs.

The expression on her face had changed.

She kept staring at me as tears rolled down her cheeks.

I sensed that Elizabeth had made a lasting impression on my mother.

The next morning, Daddy wheeled me and Hunter to the conservatory. Lying in my bed, I watched the fog layer burn off, allowing the morning sunshine to color the dark-gray ocean a navy blue. Hundreds of sea gulls rode the swirling winds while a pair of white pelicans flew over our domed roof made of glass.

After breakfast, Momma had loaded my brothers and sisters into the family van for church services—ten o'clock Mass.

Ruby drove. She had become my mother's new designated driver.

Elizabeth Dow, wearing a wide-brimmed straw hat and green summer dress, strolled through our backyard rose garden, down the brick pathway to sit on my favorite stone bench.

The natural retreat area, perched on the cliffs overlooking the ocean, was my childhood friend on all those starry nights when I couldn't sleep.

When I had to get away from the rest of my family.

I wondered what was going through Elizabeth's mind as she gazed out across the Pacific Ocean. She'd been to Millennium and seen landscapes that mere mortals can only dream of.

Did she miss the gyro planet or was she happier on Earth?

Did she share my father's obsessions, always dreaming of returning to Millennium?

The doorbell rang.

Could it be him? I thought. *Please, dear God, let it be Jeremy.*
My intuitions were correct.

I smelled vanilla-scented cologne.

Within moments, my father brought Jeremy to the side of my bed.

His hazel eyes sparkled against his olive skin as he looked at me, romantically. I felt really good about the way I looked. I was able to see myself in a wall mirror across the room. Momma had dressed me in a red satin top and curled my hair like I was going to church with her.

Smiling, he held my hand. Right in front of Daddy.

He held my hand without asking permission. And my father didn't look upset. Momma would have thrown a fit.

"Please, talk to her," Daddy said. "I'll be outside with our guest."

My father hurried out the conservatory door into the backyard and down the red brick path toward Elizabeth.

Jeremy looked so handsome. Had never seen him dressed up before. He wore a royal-blue shirt with a gray tweed jacket and black slacks. His wavy hair looked perfect combed back.

"Hello, Julia," he said, squeezing my hand. "I'm sorry that I only visit you on the weekends, but your mom doesn't like me over here. I'd come to see you every night if I could."

I loved his low voice.

"This is the first time I've been here when your mom wasn't standing over me listening to every word I say. Before she gets home, I need to tell you something."

His square jaw and straight white teeth gave him the look of a movie star.

"I don't know what to think of all this Millennium mess. I'm worried about your father being hurt, about what will happen to you. You need to know that I'm here for you. Just because your mother doesn't let me visit doesn't mean I don't want to be with you."

He's been the quarterback and captain of the football team, I thought. *Jeremy could have any girl he wants.*

*But he has chosen **me**, a girl in a coma, lying helpless in a hospital bed.*

He must really love me!

He told me all about school and his mother in Massachusetts and his dad's new girlfriend and his summer job busing tables in a restaurant on Cannery Row in Monterey. I liked to hear about his life, but I really loved when he told me how much he missed me.

Unable to carry on a conversation with the boy of my dreams drove me absolutely crazy.

Not crazy as in insane. Good crazy.

You know what I mean. That feeling where you are so frustrated you want to clench your fists and explode.

Scream.

Hit something.

"When you wake up, we are going on a date. Alone. Just the two of us. I don't care what your mom thinks. We are not kids anymore. We deserve to be together."

The conservatory door swung open, causing a gust of ocean air to blow my hair across my face.

Jeremy gently moved the hair off my face. His warm fingers gently brushed my cheek.

I felt a funny, weightless sensation in my stomach.

He squeezed my hand tightly as my father walked toward us. Elizabeth followed him into the room.

"This is Julia's boyfriend," Daddy said. "Jeremy, I want you to meet Elizabeth Dow."

"Hello, young man," she said.

Jeremy shook her hand and said, "Nice to meet you."

"Please visit Julia as often as possible," she said, matter-of-factly.

This woman doesn't know Momma very well.

Jeremy's lucky that he can see me once a week.

"Talk to her as much as you can," she said, pointing to me.

"Believe me, she can hear you."

Elizabeth knows I'm in Dreamtime, that I can hear and see and feel everything.

"I will talk to Gloria," my father said, "about him visiting more often. When the time is right, I'll get her to change her mind."

"Did I hear my name?"

Startled, everyone turned and looked at Momma standing in the doorway, her arms folded.

"What am I missing?" my mother asked, her eyebrows raised in defiant curiosity.

"Nothing, darling," Daddy said. "We were just discussing how important it is for all of us to talk to Julia."

"I talk to her all the time," Momma said, giving Jeremy a stare that would "freeze a polar bear", as my father would say.

Instead of lowering his eyes, Jeremy stared back at my mother, holding my hand in defiance.

Someone's standing up for me, I thought. *He's willing to fight for me. He's holding my hand in front of Momma. Don't let go.*

You could feel the tension build.

Negative thoughts filled the room, bouncing off the conservatory glass.

Astrid, Pearl, and Crystal ran into the room giggling and screaming for Daddy to hold them.

"Jeremy, say goodbye to Julia," my father said, picking up Crystal and Pearl into his arms.

Astrid cried, tugging on my father's pants leg.

Jeremy looked into my eyes, squeezed my hand, and said, "Bye, Julia. See you soon."

Daddy and Elizabeth escorted Jeremy out the conservatory door into the back yard. They carried on a conversation while they strolled down the brick path through the rose garden.

The boy of my dreams disappeared around the side of the house.

Momma had ruined another meeting with my boyfriend.

She'd gotten really good at that, wrecking my life every time I started feeling good about myself.

As the week unfolded, I overheard Elizabeth tell my mother bits and pieces of the Dreamtime experience.

Each day, a little more.

Surprisingly, my mother listened and did not criticize the woman who claimed to have visited another planet.

I believe it's a girl thing.

Females trust each other.

Momma sat at the dinner table, night after night, remaining silent as Elizabeth told her tales of Millennium and Metamorphosis and the Triamulet and Coma-X.

My mother didn't act belligerent when she heard Elizabeth's fantastic stories, especially the ones about Dreamtime.

Although my mother still drank her bottle of wine with dinner, I noticed she'd stop drinking after she ate dessert. Instead, she enjoyed a cup of hot lemon tea with Ms. Dow.

Our guest became a positive influence on our mother.

Monday morning, August 31st, would be remembered as the "if only" day by my father and his Wainright Foundation doctors and research team.

If only we would have done this experiment earlier.

If only the world could see *these* scientific results.

If only the *Planet Millennium Report* had published *this* undeniable evidence.

I knew something was going to be different that day because, after lunch, my grandparents came by the house with a van and a station wagon and picked up all my brothers and sisters.

Then, Dr. Shankar arrived, wearing his white medical jacket. He was the foundation's only top-level doctor who had not been kidnapped by terrorists or injured in a bombing.

Daddy set up two video cameras in the family room and wheeled my bed directly in front of the big screen mounted on the wall.

My mother sat by Hunter, rocking back and forth.

She drank tea with Ms. Dow.

No alcohol.

She had stopped taking all those different colored pills.

Earlier that day, Momma had finally agreed to allow the Brain Computer Interface equipment to be used on me.

Elizabeth stood by my bed and held my hand while Hari removed the control cap gear from Hunter's head. The doctor walked toward me with the electro-studded cap in his hands.

While Dr. Shankar set up the BCI system on the computer and my father prepared the head gear, Elizabeth said, "My intuition tells me Julia is in a state of Dreamtime."

She's right, I thought, *I am ready to communicate with you.*

When the computer software launched, the big-screen monitor turned blue with white letters and numbers. The symbols looked just like keys—letters within squares—positioned in the same rows as a keyboard.

At the top of the monitor, six words blinked off and on in large black fonts:

YES   NO   UNKNOWN   UNDECIDED   REPEAT   HELP

A rectangular box or column with a white background filled the right portion of the screen. At the top of the column, in bold black letters, it read:

"Mrs. Wainright," Dr. Shankar said, "because your son is not locked-in, his electroencephalography that measures electrical activity along the scalp has not allowed us to communicate with Hunter. We believe Julia *is* locked-in."

While Hari fitted the cap to my head, Daddy told my mother, "Dreamtime will allow us to measure the electrical signals from Julia's brain. Essentially, her thoughts."

Elizabeth reminded my mother that only females awaken in their Earth-coma bodies, not males. That is why Hunter cannot communicate.

"I trust you, Elizabeth," Momma said. "If Julia is awake, I need to talk to her, in private.

What's my mother going to say to me? I thought. *She's acted weird all this week, ever since she read my journals.*

The BCI control cap fit snugly on my head.

"Ready?" Hari asked.

Daddy nodded, *yes.*

When Dr. Shankar turned on the computer, I felt a tingling on my scalp.

Nothing uncomfortable.

After a few seconds, the sensation stopped.

"Julia," my father said, "I need you to look at the screen, at the top row of six simple words. We'll ask you some simple questions and we want you to answer either 'yes' or 'no' by focusing on the correct answer. Stare only at that one word."

I focused on the word, YES, anticipating my father's first question.

"Julia, can you hear me?"

The word YES illuminated, then NO.

I stared at the YES on the screen.

No one said anything.

How come it's not working, I thought, looking at the blank response box on the screen.

"Do not be alarmed," Dr. Shankar told my mother, "she needs to learn to think in a manner the system recognizes. Give her a few minutes, she will adjust and learn to think correctly."

While my mother asked Daddy what was wrong, Elizabeth pointed to the screen and asked, "How does this system work?"

"Simple," Hari said. "When the word she chooses lights up or illuminates, her brain alerts her that something is different about that word or letter. It works the same with the keyboard symbols. When a letter becomes brighter, her thoughts transmit that letter to the sensors.

"She will be able to type about ten words per minute by using the power of her thoughts. A bit slow, but it's better than no communication. With this system, she can eventually send an email or a tweet."

"By next year," Daddy said, "Dr. Shankar will have perfected a BCI cap that is able to access the speech area in the brain. In other words, paralyzed patients like Julia, who are conscious, locked-in, will be able to talk to us via a computer voice."

While everyone fixated on the screen, it dawned on me.

I reminded myself to stop looking to the right at the response box and concentrate on the YES word every time it became brighter.

Focus, Julia, focus, I kept telling myself.

Within seconds, my father shouted, "She's here! Julia's home!" as he ran to the screen pointing at the big black YES that had appeared in the response box.

"Oh my God!" Momma shouted. "She's been awake all this time. Julia's been watching me."

My mother sobbed hysterically and yelled, "Sweetheart, Mommy loves you."

While my father ran to my mother's side to calm her down, Elizabeth leaned over and kissed my cheek.

The Coma-X survivor whispered in my ear, "I know what you're experiencing, my dear. Never be afraid. Enjoy your experience. Each moment is special."

Daddy told Dr. Shankar to make sure the cameras were working and he cleared his throat so Ms. Dow would step back, away from my face. So I could see the screen.

The crystal in her Triamulet sparkled as she stood by my bed.

While my pathetic mother whimpered by Hunter's side, my father asked me a series of questions.

"Hello, sweetheart, I love you," Daddy said, his voice quivering.

I looked for the "I love you too" button, but the screen did not have such a perfect answer.

My father asked, "Are you happy we are communicating?"

YES

"Are you experiencing any pain?"

NO

"Then, you're comfortable here, in your Coma-X body?"

YES

"Please confirm, are you on Planet Millennium?"

YES

"Are you with Metamorphosis?"

NO

"Then, who are you with? Spell the name. Concentrate on each letter."

All I had to do was focus on one letter at a time on the keyboard. When the letter glowed brighter, my thoughts translated the illuminated letter to the response box.

One letter at a time, I spelled:

NYX

Dr. Shankar looked at my father, puzzled. "Who is that?" he asked.

"Nyx is a Utopian," Daddy replied. "She is on a list that Professor Van Campbell has documented. Johan memorized the Utopians' names from reading the *Magnum Opus* while aboard the *Skipbladnir.*"

He looked into my eyes and asked, "Are you safe?"

YES

"Ask her about Hunter," Momma said.

My father held up his hand, signaling for my mother to be quiet.

"Where are you now?" Daddy asked.

It was frustrating, I mean, challenging, to spell longer words. It seemed like it took a long time between letters. But when I looked up at the screen and saw the answer, I felt extremely accomplished.

DOUBTING CASTLE

My father stepped over to the Millennium map pinned to the wall.

Hand drawn by Professor Johan, the map displayed all the kingdoms and cities and rivers and mountains and the major geography of Millennium.

Daddy smiled at Dr. Shankar and said, "Here's the castle, on the Open Road next to the Utopian River Gorge."

Then, he stepped next to my bed and continued the questioning.

"Have you seen Hunter?"

NO

"Do you know if he's all right?"

YES

My mother stood and yelled, "He's alive. Hunter's going to be fine. He's coming home."

"Do you know where your brother is?" my father asked.

YES

"Where?"

ESCALOT

My father pointed to the map and said, "Here it is, on the Sea of Esteem."

Daddy measured with a ruler. "Hunter's four thousand miles from Time Island. What's he doing way out there?"

As quickly as I could, I spelled out:

EVE

Momma pointed to the screen. "Look. What's an E V E?"

199

Dr. Shankar replied, "I believe that is the name of your biblical first woman on Earth."

YES

"Is Hunter in love with Eve?" Daddy asked me, while he looked at my mother.

YES

Momma frowned and asked me, "Where does she come from? Is she a foreigner?"

PLANET EPIPHANY

My mother ran up and stared at the screen, raising her arms in the air.

She yelled, "What the hell does *that* mean? Is Hunter coming home? Wayland, who in the world lives on Epiphany?"

"Calm down, Gloria," Daddy said. "We have no idea what Planet Epiphany means. Maybe Julia's mistaken."

Wishing I was wrong, I should have lied and pretended I didn't know a thing.

I could have answered, UNKNOWN, but Daddy told me to never fib. Momma went over to Hunter and placed her head on his chest, hugging him tightly.

"Julia, thank you for your answers. Do you want to continue?"

YES

"We can take a break if you'd like?"

NO

"Okay. Besides the family, is there anyone you want to see?"

YES

"Spell the name on the keyboard."

JEREMY

Daddy looked over at my mother.

She started sobbing again. My answer had upset her.

My father did not rush over to comfort her.

Momma ran from the room, holding a handkerchief to her face.

Elizabeth Dow never let go of my hand while Daddy

continued the slow process of having me spell out the answers to his questions:

"Why did you leave?" he asked.

TO BRING HUNTER HOME

"What is your mode of transportation?"

A GRYPHON

Grinning, my father looked at Dr. Shankar and said. "I wish Johan were here."

He continued with, "Okay, Julia. Describe Nyx's appearance."

RABBITFISH

"Have you seen the *Magnum Opus*?

YES

"Have you read the book?

A FEW PAGES, MAYBE MORE LATER

Elizabeth asked, "Do you enjoy *Dreamtime*?"

UNDECIDED

After another hour of questioning, mostly about Planet Millennium, Dr. Shankar requested that Daddy stop the questioning.

"Please tell Hunter we miss him, that we love him very much. Tell him we hope to see him soon."

OK

"One more thing. Tell Hunter that I am truly sorry, that he can be an artist when he returns"

I WILL

"Promise me you'll be careful."

I PROMISE

"Anything else you would like to share with us?"

I MISS YOU!

My father leaned over my bed and kissed me on the forehead, whispering, "Please be safe, Julia. Take care of yourself on Millennium. Learn as much as you can."

Without warning, Dr. Shankar turned off the computer.

The screen went dead, and with it, my voice. I mean, my way of communicating.

Daddy pointed at the computer. "This BCI technology will save the Foundation. This can change everything."

Then, my father looked at me. "I need to take Julia on the Howard Blake show."

"Is that a wise idea, Dr. Wainright?" Elizabeth asked.

"My reputation is at stake," he replied.

"Your family's *lives* are at stake," she said, frowning. "Keep in mind, any additional publicity about Planet Millennium could get all your colleagues killed."

My father looked at me and said, "Let me think about this some more. I'll talk to Gloria, see what *she* thinks."

Ms. Dow smirked, telling him, "Good luck. I already know your wife's answer."

Elizabeth winked at me and said, "Why don't you wait for Julia to wake up. Ask her if she wants to share her experience. Let her make her own decisions, speak for herself."

He acted like he didn't hear her and said, "Maybe I can get Professor Van Campbell to come forward. He's out of the hospital now and feeling a lot better."

"Dr. Wainright, you and your family are in danger. Acting stubborn and foolhardy is not a good quality to have right now."

Daddy turned red, staring down the woman who had spent many months on Millennium. "Thank you for your help, Ms. Dow. I'll take your comments under consideration."

My father wheeled me and Hunter upstairs to our bedrooms, but Momma never came to see me.

Only Hunter. Her favorite child.

I did not have the BCI cap on, so communication with my mother would have been one way only—her doing all the talking. I felt that's what she wanted. To lecture me without me being able to respond. To yell at me.

While I lay in my coma, I concluded: she avoided me because she was either embarrassed, knowing that I saw her reading my diaries, or she hated me because she knew, that I knew, that she knew the things I had written about her were the truth.

The next morning, Daddy wheeled me down to the family room in front of the screen.

Dr. Shankar placed the BCI control cap on my head.

I was prepared to answer more questions, but my father and Dr. Shankar spent all morning editing the video and reviewing the computer information.

The activated screen displayed the Brain Computer Interface program, but for some reason, Hari did not turn on my headset.

While I lay there, I dreamed of Jeremy standing by my bed, holding my hand, and talking to me through the computer interface. I had practiced typing:

I LOVE YOU

Practiced it over and over again with only my thoughts.

Next, I spelled out:

WILL YOU MARRY ME?

But I decided that it was better for him to ask *me*.

What do you think?

Should a paralyzed girl, talking through a computer interface, propose marriage?

He would only say "yes" because he felt sorry for me.

I decided the proposal was a dumb idea.

What was I thinking?

Just as Daddy decided to activate my control cap, a loud banging at the front door made him put the headset down.

Homeland Security officials had arrived with federal agents.

More bad news.

Because of an assassination attempt, Dr. Shankar's family had to be transported to a safe location by federal agents.

I'll never forget the pale, worried expression on the doctor's face as he rushed out the door. I'd never seen him look like that.

Elizabeth left the house right after Hari.

"I'll be right back," Daddy yelled at my mother as he ran into the family room, turned off the computer and left the house, slamming the front door behind him.

While I lay in limbo, totally frustrated, Momma fed leftovers to all nine of her uncontrollable children.

When they finished eating, she demanded they go upstairs.

They nagged and complained it was a weekend night. They wanted to watch a movie on the big screen in the family room.

She screamed at them, "Get to your rooms and don't dare come down here until morning! Ruby, you stay here with me."

My two brothers carried Sebastian and Crystal while my five sisters scurried up the stairs, fighting and teasing each other, arguing over what game they were going to play.

Once the house quieted down, Momma told Ruby, "Come with me."

My mother wore her pink flannel night gown with a rhinestone-beaded rosary around her neck as she entered the family room.

Pointing to the computer, she said, "How do you turn this thing on?"

"Mother," my sister said, sarcastically, "like, when are you going to join the 21st century?"

Momma rolled her eyes and gave my sister that *don't-give-me-a-bad-time* glare.

Setting a full bottle of red wine on the night stand by my bed, my mother never made eye contact with me.

Ruby started the computer and found the desktop icon to get the Brain Computer Interface software running.

"What kind of program is this?" Ruby asked, moving the mouse from side to side as she watched the pointed cursor hover over YES and NO.

"Never mind," Momma said, "go put your brothers and sisters to bed like I asked."

Ruby dragged her feet out the door, complaining of how much work she had to do.

Believe me, little sister, I thought, *you haven't a clue of what real work is.*

Momma stood in the shadows in front of the picture bay window.

A full moon, larger and yellower than I had ever seen, hovered over the ocean.

She stood in the moon's silhouette, motionless, staring at me.

Standing in the dark, she wouldn't move.

Realizing that Ruby had launched the program correctly, I stared at the giant screen, focusing on the letters that would form the sentence that might break the spell of silence between Momma and me.

I spelled out:

CAN WE TALK?

My mother looked at the screen, nodded her head, *yes,* and stepped out of the shadows to the side of my bed.

Using a chrome cigar lighter, she lit a tall red candle and poured herself a full glass of Merlot.

Looking into my eyes, she said, "I don't know where to begin. I have so much to say."

Momma put her shaking hand on mine.

Sighing, she asked me, "Did you see me reading your journals?"

YES

"Do you still love me?"

YES

I wanted to answer, "Undecided", but that would have been untrue, a lie.

"I'm so sorry," she said, "I couldn't help from reading them. Are you mad at me?"

UNDECIDED

"I don't blame you."

My mother took two gulps of wine.

"I realized this week, after reading all the things that you wrote in your diaries, that I've been a horrible mother."

I couldn't believe my ears.

Her admitting that she'd been a bad parent after all these years of abuse.

At first I felt anger.

She always made me feel guilty.

Made me feel sorry for her.

But I loved her too much to remain upset.

"I want to change," she said. "Be a good parent for all my children. Especially you, after all I've done wrong."

Momma arched her eyebrows and stared into my eyes.

"Will you give me a second chance?"

YES

"Will you forgive me and come home if I treat you right?"

YES

"What's the first thing you want me to do?"

STOP DRINKING!

Momma glanced at her bottle of wine. "I will, as soon as you come home."

NO!

"What do you mean, no?"

STOP NOW!

My mother stared at me for what felt like eternity.

She took a deep breath and held up her glass like she was toasting an event.

Took a sip of red wine, closed her eyes, and swallowed.

She picked up her bottle from the night stand, holding it by its narrow glass neck.

"Julia, if I told you this was my last drink, can you and I start over?

YES

"Will you come home?"

YES

"I promise to stop drinking!" Momma shouted.

She turned, thrust her arm back, and threw her bottle of wine across the room—straight for the picture window.

Like a slow motion scene in a movie, I watched the bottle turn over and over in midair, spilling red wine as it sped toward the huge yellow moon.

When the red bottle struck the floor-to-ceiling picture window, it exploded, sending a shower of sparkling glass fragments cascading over the grand piano, sofa, and coffee table.

The tingling of a million particles of shattering glass bouncing across the hardwood floor rang in my ears.

A gust of cold ocean air swirled through the room and blew out the candle.

I lay in the dark, stunned by what I had witnessed.

Momma's silhouette stood silent against the full moon, its yellow reflection shimmering on the dark-grey ocean.

From the chaos came a feeling of calmness, like all the tension and anxiety of a lifetime had been tossed out the window.

With her hair blowing in the cold ocean wind, my mother took the rhinestone-beaded rosary from around her neck and fell to her knees.

She began to pray.

My final image on Earth was my mother kneeling, moving her trembling fingers from bead to bead, reciting, "Hail Mary, full of grace."

The moonlit room grew dark as my eyesight faded away.

My dream had ended as suddenly as it had begun.

I asked God if I could spend a few more minutes with my mother.

My request went unanswered.

Dreamtime had come to an end.

DAYNIGHT

OF THE

BOAR

Chapter XVI
Escalot

Awakened suddenly by the loud *knock—knock—knock* on the iron door, I sat up in bed, startled. Looking down at my Triamulet, I realized I had fallen asleep with my clothes on. A beam of yellow light poured through a crack in the wooden shutters while I wiped the sleep from my eyes. Across the room, red-orange embers smoldered in the dying flames of the fireplace. Knowing my soul had returned to my Millennium body, my thoughts turned to Momma.

Is she all right? Who's taking care of her? She'll catch a death of cold with the wind blowing through the broken window.

The creaking of the iron door interrupted me.

Nyx entered the bed chamber carrying a silver tray with two bowls of strawberries, a loaf of ambrosia, and pewter mugs filled with amrita.

"Good morning, Princess Julia," she said, smiling. "Time for breakfast; your gryphon awaits you."

While Nyx placed the tray on the wooden table, I jumped out of the yellow bed and opened the shutters. From the tower window, I could see all the way to the Utopian River Gorge. To the east, a sunrise of purple, orange, and yellow clouds hugged the distant mountains. Grey geese honked as they flew over the misty Palatine Forest. Strange and exotic growls, howls, shrieks and squeals echoed from within the primordial woods.

Remember when you went camping and sat around the campfire and you'd hear weird animal sounds coming from the dark woods? Wondered what creatures were making those scary noises? Or what they looked like?

All I knew was, I was glad we were *flying* and not hiking to Escalot. The light of the morning dawn revealed boarman soldiers moving about the central courtyard below. Erda stood on the connector bridge to the tower, waving to me while she held Ava's leather reins. Waving back, I took a deep breath of crisp air.

I sat with Nyx and ate my breakfast in silence.

"Is something on your mind?" she asked.

I shook my head, *no.*

The Utopian raised her eyebrows. "I feel your negative energy."

I sighed and said, "I'm worried about my mother."

Nyx reached across the table and patted my hand. "Please, enlighten me."

"Momma told me she's going to stop drinking, but I don't believe her."

"Has she lied to you in the past?"

"She's made a lot of promises, but my mother never kept them. She's so unhappy."

"Ah, unhappiness." Nyx sipped amrita from her pewter mug. "Do you feel there is some way to make your mother happy?"

"If Hunter came home, that would end her misery."

"And what, may I ask, would make *you*, Julia Wainright, happy?"

"If Momma would stop drinking and be good to me, let me be myself. Stop treating me like a servant."

"So, would you say your own happiness is based on how your mother feels about you? How she treats you?"

I thought about her question, struggling for an answer.

Somehow, answering "yes" seemed like the wrong reply.

While I finished my strawberries and ambrosia, I tried to figure out why I felt so confused.

"We must leave now," the Utopian said, standing. "Later today, I shall ask Metamorphosis to explain one of the Universal Truths."

"What truth?"

Nyx wiggled her whiskers and opened the iron door. "There is no way to happiness; happiness *is* the way."

Before I could think about her statement, she stepped to the window and yelled, "Erda, prepare the gryphon. We shall be down before you say 'Metamorphosis'."

I quickly strapped on my belt and sword, envisioning my reunion with Hunter. Following the Utopian down the spiral stone staircase, we marched out the arched door, past the pair of boarman soldier guards, and onto the connector bridge.

Erda greeted me while Nyx helped me mount the gryphon.

Ava raced down the stone bridge and leaped off over the iron railing, lifting us into the Millennium sky. Holding on to the leather saddle straps, my stomach rose into my throat as we became airborne.

Flapping her majestic wings, the gryphon flew over the castle walls.

Doubting Castle disappeared behind a grove of monkey puzzle trees.

Heading southeast, we soared over the Palatine Hills and down into a sea of green and gold grasslands teaming with herds of extraordinary animals.

Wildlife with multiple tusks and twisted horns and armored plates with spiked tails roamed over the rolling terrain, what Nyx called, Glittering Plains. Kangaroos with orange and black stripes jumped through the sea of swaying grass. Mammoths, giant ground sloths, and wombats rested in the shade of towering acacia trees that dotted the great plains. Flocks of flightless moas fled from saber-toothed cats and cave bears. White eagles with black heads circled high in the blue Millennium sky.

Nyx pointed ahead with her spear. "Escalot awaits us."

Only the breathtaking scenery with the tri-colored sky could get Momma and Jeremy and Elizabeth Dow and the Dreamtime experience off my mind.

Flying over the kingdom of Pellagus, Nyx pointed down to McDougal's Cave at Cardiff Hill. Farther south, we spotted the Cave of Montesino.

We turned inland and followed the Hebrus River for two hundred miles, flying over Phlegra, where, according to Nyx, the god Zeus overthrew a race of giants.

We gained altitude as the red sky crept over us, giving the landscape an eerie, crimson hue. The grasslands gave way to evergreen forests and rocky hills with pointed pinnacles.

Ava glided past Vulture Peak, the tallest point in the Griddhraj Parvat Hills.

Soaring down out of the steep slopes, we entered a vast rift valley between the River of Grief and the River of Pleasure. Nyx told me that if one eats the fruit growing along the river banks, that the person begins reverse aging and dies as an infant.

Realizing that the places we had flown over had been documented in human mythology by previous visitors to Millennium, I asked about the fairy tale lands that Daddy and Professor Johan had described.

Nyx explained that the majority of the fairy tale kingdoms and castles and story-book characters existed to the far north, in the Kingdom of the Pot of Gold, where the Grimm brothers, Jacob and Wilhelm, had explored during *their* visit.

I guess we won't be seeing Cinderella's or Sleeping Beauty's Castle, or Red Riding Hood's cabin, or Snow White's cottage on this trip, I thought.

We followed the River of Pleasure for another three hundred miles. For the entire flight, I practiced my speech—my plea to Hunter. How I would talk him into coming home with me.

Tried to imagine what he looked like; I hadn't seen him in more than a year.

Erda pointed ahead, shouting, "Aye, there she be, the Open Road."

The gnome pulled down on the gryphon's reins and Ava dove toward a yellow cobblestone roadway.

The Open Road.

We followed the Great Way, as Nyx called it, while she explained how the famous road, a major trade route, looped around the entire Pellagus peninsula, past Never-Never Land and the Lost Boy's House at the southern end, then up the eastern coast past Black Hill Cove, Argo Bay, Hermopolis, and Kallipolis.

As the sky filled with billowy white clouds, the sage announced, "Escalot Castle ahead."

The gryphon squawked, flapping her black wings faster and faster.

The Open Road wound its way down the steep foothills, through ancient forests of twisted oaks and willows.

Beyond the treetops, Escalot perched precariously on the weathered cliffs of the great Sea of Esteem. Looking like a medieval fortress, stone towers emerged from the four corners of the walled city. A central dome with a copper roof rose from the castle's interior.

Hunter's in there, I thought. *I'll see my brother soon.*

Erda yelled, "Hang on," as Ava swooped down and landed at the gated entrance.

A wooden draw bridge crossed a muddy moat filled with horned crocodiles. Beyond the bridge stood the towering timber gates of the coastal city.

I asked Nyx why we didn't fly into Escalot, over the stone walls.

She pointed up at a tower.

Guards, clad in armor, stood with long bows pointed at us.

"The archers would shoot us out of the sky," Nyx replied.

The massive gates creaked open and we entered the castle city by foot.

Escalot, bustling with activity, looked like a medieval town that I once read about in my *King Arthur* and *Robin Hood* novels.

Nyx told me the seaside metropolis was a major trade center located on the Open Road. Escalot reminded me of Carmel By-The-Sea, because the city had been built on ocean cliffs.

We traversed the narrow cobblestone streets lined with two-story buildings—homes and storefronts and stables and taverns. Everywhere I looked, bizarre creatures roamed the streets or tended the windowed storefronts.

Dwarves and elves and boggarts and brownies and earth faeries carried on conversations and bartered on the street corners. Eight-legged horses and spotted oxen with spiral horns and giant wombats pulled creaking carts and wagons filled with wood, coal, and sacks of grain.

A giant and swamp elve sat in front of a tavern playing chess with a half-orc and forest dwarve. The odd-looking foursome drew *Gametasia* cards from a deck, moved their chess pieces, and exchanged treasure coins.

Actually, they fought and argued, then, they paid each other for a captured red queen.

If only I had my camera to photograph all the unearthly two-legged creatures sporting horns, or four arms, or wings, or tails, or feathers and fur.

No humans in sight.

We turned down a labyrinth of narrow cobblestone streets until we reached the far side of Escalot, to a row of rustic buildings standing next to the outer stone wall.

Nyx stopped in front of a two-story-tall white plastered inn with a brown thatched roof.

The wooden sign above the door read:

CROSSED HARPOONS INN

Two crisscrossed harpoons formed an **X**.

Erda tended to the gryphon while Nyx led me through the rustic inn's front door.

The noisy tavern fell silent as my eyes adjusted to the dark, smoky room.

Nyx escorted me to a wooden booth by the fireplace.

Sitting in the shadowed light, I found myself surrounded by a cast of humanoid characters with fur and scales and tusks and claws and antennae.

Every eye in the place focused on me, the only human being in the room.

Nyx ordered two mugs of mango juice from the cyclops waitress—a one-eyed giant with orange hair.

"Stay here," Nyx said, "I must find Metamorphosis."

Watching the Utopian climb the stairs, I grabbed the handle of my sword and tried to act normal.

Unafraid.

Within moments, the bizarre patrons ignored me, going back to their loud conversations and ale drinking and card games and gambling.

Through the haze, the cyclops brought two pewter mugs to the table.

She held out her huge hand.

"Ya owe me two red scruples an' a white frugle, dearie."

"I have no money," I said, shrugging my shoulders.

"Ya strange humans never got no treasure coins on ya," she yelled, frowning with her one bushy orange eyebrow.

She rolled her green eye, lumbered away, and then screamed up the stairs, "Nyx, ya owe me fer them drinks!"

Sitting by the blazing fire, I held the frosty mug with one hand and my sword handle with my other hand.

Waiting impatiently for my brother, I kept a watchful eye on the crowd of unearthly characters while I sipped on the sour mango juice.

Nyx pranced down the tavern stairs. Her furry white legs and fish tail made her easy to identify. She was followed by a man wearing a purple tunic, leather vest and a braided head band with a gold Triangulum against his forehead. He had a white beard that hung to his belt buckle.

That's Metamorphosis, I thought. *He looks just like the illustrations that Hunter drew at home, the ones Momma would rip off my wall and throw in the waste paper basket by my bed.*

Following the bearded man, another person with wavy black hair and a fair complexion came into view.

A human being.

Hunter!

Behind Metamorphosis, my brother strutted down the stairs in his medieval attire—a red puffy-sleeved tunic with a black vest and brown breeches with knee-high leather boots. A sword swung by his side. He wore a jewel-studded knife on his belt. A gold Triamulet showed through the leather laces of his v-neck tunic.

Unable to contain myself, I jumped up and ran toward him.

He looked strong and healthy, but different. No longer had the look of a teenage boy from Carmel High School.

The moment he saw me, he smiled and ran past Metamorphosis and Nyx into my outstretched arms.

Hunter hugged me tightly. We both had tears in our eyes as we laughed and kissed each other's cheeks.

He had grown taller since I last saw him.

"What in God's name are you doing here?" he asked. His smile had turned to concern.

"I came to find *you*," I replied. "Bring you home."

Before Hunter could respond, Metamorphosis interrupted us, saying, "Come my children, let us move to a quiet location."

My brother told Metamorphosis, "This is my twin sister, Julia."

"Ah, another Wainright on a mission," the sage said, extending his hand toward me. "Your father must be proud of his two oldest children."

I looked at Hunter. We both grinned.

"No, Daddy's not real happy with Hunter right now, or me,"

I said. "Momma's *really* upset."

I shook Metamorphosis's hand. A tingling sensation shot up my arm.

These Utopians are electrified with positive energy, I thought.

Hunter hugged me again and we followed Metamorphosis and Nyx up the creaking stairs, down a narrow hallway, and into a rustic room with oil lamps lining the walls.

A blazing fire popped and crackled in the floor-to-ceiling rock fireplace.

Hunter looked me up and down. "If I didn't know any better, I'd say Mom dressed us."

We both laughed.

It dawned on me for the first time that my twin brother and I wore similar clothes with matching colors.

Just like in third grade!

"This will do nicely," Metamorphosis said, gesturing, *sit down.*

The four of us sat at a wooden table in front of the rock fireplace—Metamorphosis at one end, Nyx at the other, and Hunter across from me.

I couldn't take my eyes off my brother. He looked so mature as the warm fire shadowed his square jaw and high cheek bones.

The cyclops waitress brought us four mugs of mango juice. She collected twelve coins, eight red scruples and four white frugles, from Metamorphosis before she rumbled out the door, slamming it shut.

"Now, what brings you to Millennium, young lady?" the Sage of the Ages asked me.

Pointing at Hunter, I replied, "I'm here to bring him home. Momma is really sick and Hunter needs to return before she gets worse. Our house has gone into foreclosure, the terrorists have bombed the foundation's headquarters and kidnapped all the doctors."

My voice cracked, holding back my tears. "Daddy's life is in danger. The terrorists are trying to kill him."

"What are you talking about?" Hunter asked, frowning at me.

The sage held his hand up, preventing Hunter from speaking.

"Calm down, young lady," Metamorphosis said. "Let us focus on the events here and now, *before* we deal with Planet Earth."

"Relax, Princess Julia," Nyx said. "Take a deep breath."

Glancing into Hunter's blue eyes, I sighed deeply and nodded with a *I'll-try-to-calm-down* look.

Metamorphosis asked, "How was your galactic trip to Time Island?"

Oh no, I thought, *he wants to make small talk. My family's lives are in danger and he's asking me about my trip.*

"Fine," I replied. "But, can't we talk about more important things than Time Island?"

"Of course," the sage replied, gesturing toward my brother. "Perhaps we should allow Hunter to share his experiences on Millennium before you demand his decision to return home with you."

I stared at Hunter and said, "Sorry. I'm in a hurry to get back, before it's too late."

"First of all, it is never too late for anything," Metamorphosis said. "I say this because all things happen in perfect order. There is nowhere to go. Nowhere because we are now here. They are one in the same word. Therefore, let us enjoy this moment in time together, right now."

The sage grinned, saying, "*This* perfect moment together is all there is."

He moved his white beard off his lap with one hand and held his mug with the other, while his third and fourth hands rested calmly on the oak table.

Everything he said went right over my head. I heard his words of wisdom, but it was impossible to focus, or "live in the moment", as he put it.

Excited to talk to my brother, I was obsessed with a plan of how to bring Hunter home to Momma.

"I'm sorry things are such a disaster back home." Hunter said, "I couldn't help them, even if I returned tomorrow. Dad has to solve his own problems. So does Mom."

Hunter had a different look in his eyes, one I had never seen before.

"Believe me, I think about Mom all the time," Hunter said. "But, I've made the highest choice. What I mean is, I must stay here to rescue Eve, my true love."

While the blazing fire warmed us, Hunter explained how he had met Eve of Epiphany aboard the *Skipbladnir*.

That the girl from another planet was the most beautiful girl he had ever seen.

That he had fallen madly in love with her.

That Metamorphosis had taken him and Eve on a journey to visit the first Great Treasure, Anthera, the Eternal Rose.

But they never made it that far.

When my brother told me how he had traveled through the Forest Primeval and fought Hocus and his pirate crew, ventured into the Underworld to defeat Vulcan and the dungeon trolls, and then killed a monstrous Grizzsect at the Battle of Doubting Junction; he sounded like he was reading a fantastic adventure story straight from a science fiction book or fantasy novel.

However, his stories were true, not fiction.

Hunter acted more mature than I expected.

His face beamed with confidence. His voice sounded so calm as he described how Ex, the Dark Master, had captured Eve and taken her captive on an Extractor ship, the *Walrus*.

He matter-of-factly announced how he would soon rescue her.

"Metamorphosis has taught me the Universal Truths," Hunter said. "I'm so much wiser now. I've discovered what's important in life. I know who I really am."

Listening to Hunter, I felt sick to my stomach.

Reality struck me as I studied the truthful look in my brother's crystal-blue eyes.

I had failed.

Hunter was not coming home with me.

"Are you coming back with me, or not?" I asked.

I don't know why I questioned him. I already knew the answer.

"Sorry, Julia," he replied. "I'm not sure if I'm *ever* coming home."

Stunned, I reached across the table and grabbed my brother's hand.

"Oh, Hunter. Don't say that. It will break Momma's heart. We all miss you so much. Daddy told me that you can be an artist, anything you want to be. Just come home. He will not interfere with your career."

Tears filled my eyes. The weight of the world, *both* my worlds, came down upon my shoulders.

"I have to go, Julia," Hunter said. "I'm wasting time sitting here. The longer I wait, the farther away I am from Eve."

For some unknown reason I didn't break down and cry.

That's what Momma would have done.

Hunter stood. I knew our talk had ended in failure.

Instead of begging and pleading with my brother, I stood and stepped around the table.

We hugged, tightly.

"Are you going to stay here?" he asked me.

"No, I've got to get back home. There is nothing for me here."

"*Everything* is here," Hunter said. "Come with us. Metamorphosis can teach you things you've never dreamed of. You will visit places you can only imagine in your dreams."

I arched my eyebrows. "I can't, Hunter. I've got to go home. Momma and Daddy and the children need me."

He shook his head back and forth. "Always taking care of everyone but yourself."

Hunter kissed my cheek and said, "I'm going to get my backpack. Talk to Metamorphosis. He'll help you feel better."

My brother hurried out the door, holding the handle of his sword.

Stunned, I brought my hands to my face, trying not to cry.

Nyx stood and hugged me, tightly. Her warm, soft fur felt comforting. "Please, Princess Julia, have a seat and I'll get you a cup of hot tea."

Emotionally exhausted, I sat at the table while she hurried out of the room, shutting the door behind her.

Metamorphosis and I sat together, silently.

Gazing at the flickering flames, I tried to figure out how I could change Hunter's mind.

The sage walked to the fireplace and threw two logs onto the red-hot embers. Instantly, the wood burst into flames, giving new life to the dying fire.

"My dear Julia," Metamorphosis said, "what troubles you so deeply that you would travel across the universe to bring your brother back home?"

Unable to answer, I stared at the Sage of the Ages as he stood by the fire.

His sparkling turquoise-blue eyes stared right through me, like he could read my mind.

The sage sat back down at the table.

"I understand your reluctance to speak with me," he said. "After all, we just met."

"I am *not* deeply troubled," I said. "I know what I'm doing."

Touching my hand, he responded. "Of course you do. Perhaps if we talk, I can help you discover the answers you seek."

I felt his positive energy as he smiled at me. I nodded, believing that I could trust the sage. He squeezed my hand and said, "Tell me, what is on your mind, Julia Wainright."

Chapter XVII
Metamorphosis

Metamorphosis removed a gold-handled scepter from his leather belt and held it in his lower right hand. The crystal ball at the end of the wand glowed with a violet-blue light. His long flowing beard became fluorescent white in the radiating glow of the crystal.

"Let us bathe in the positive rays of *Joyease*," he said.

The sage removed his square spectacles and placed them in his vest pocket. He stretched his butterfly-like wings, moving them gently back and forth. They looked translucent in the radiating blue light. Like colorful mosaics.

Have you ever seen stained-glass windows in a church when the early morning light shines through the multi-colored panes? Well, that's what his wings looked like.

Daddy bought me a kaleidoscope for my birthday when I was little. Still have it. Look through one of those tubes and you'll know what I mean by mosaic.

The sage took a sip of mango juice and said, "Please, tell me what concerns you. Perhaps I may ease your mind."

Upset with Hunter, and not in the mood to talk to a person I barely knew, I replied, "Nothing can ease my mind right now."

He wiped his white moustache with a purple napkin and said, "Tell me about your mother, the one who cannot live without Hunter."

"I've already told Nyx about her."

"Please, enlighten *me*."

Although his four arms and pair of wings distracted me, his facial expressions, especially his smile, calmed me down.

Trust him, I thought. *This is the great Sage of the Ages that Daddy has always wanted to spend time with. Go ahead, Julia, talk to him.*

I did.

"Momma has been miserable ever since Hunter left home."

"And you believe that Hunter's return shall bring your mother happiness?" he asked.

"I know that for a fact."

"I see." The sage laid his purple napkin on the table. "What if I told you that nothing, no thing, can make you, or your mother, or anyone else, happy."

"I wouldn't believe you."

"There is no way to happiness; happiness *is* the way."

"Nyx has already told me that."

"Excellent. Then, may I offer you some additional wisdom that may change your thoughts, allow you to expand your mind?"

"Can your wisdom help my relationship with my mother, make it better?"

"Of course. However, I am most concerned with the relationship you have with your *self*, not with her."

"I'm fine. I need to know how I can change Momma, make her a better person."

"You cannot change your mother, she is responsible for her *own* self. This is why our focus must be on *you*, not your mother."

"All right. I'm listening." I motioned with my hand, *go ahead.*

The sage said, "Another Universal Truth that shall enlighten you is, 'Now is all there is; live in the moment.'"

"I heard Professor Johan say that to Daddy. Did he learn that from you?"

"Many humans have taken my wisdom back to Earth."

"You mean, all those famous people whose names are engraved on Time Island?" I asked.

Metamorphosis shook his head, *yes*. "We are slightly off the subject. If you decide to stay for a bit longer, I shall discuss the Earth visitors."

Shrugging my shoulders, I said, "Sorry, I get off track sometimes."

The sage took another sip of juice. "As I was saying, there is no time but this time, this moment. There is nothing else to think about but now. The past and the future are merely illusions within your mind. They exist because you create them in your imagination. You daydream of the past and future, but they do not exist outside the now."

Biting my lip, I tried to comprehend the sage's message.

"Nothing exists outside this present moment, Julia. The choice is yours, either seize the moment, or focus your thoughts somewhere else and suffer the consequences."

"I am *not* suffering," I said, frowning at Metamorphosis.

"I say this because suffering seems to be a human condition. Instead of living in the present moment, you humans choose to live in the past, or you spend your time dreaming of some wonderful future. Your lives are spent anxiously waiting for that right time for something special to happen, some *thing* that will supposedly bring you permanent happiness."

I raised my index finger. "Like, Momma driving us all crazy waiting for Hunter's return?"

He smiled, accentuating the smooth wrinkles on his ancient face that gave the sage such a distinguished look. "Then, as your mother shall discover, you never obtain happiness when the future finally *does* arrive.

"Why?" I asked. "Tell me the answer again."

"Simple. Because happiness is only available right here, right now, in this moment. You shall know the magic feeling of living in the moment when you stop worrying about past things and future events, when you stop being attached to outcomes."

"I'm still confused. What has outcomes got to do with being happy, or my mother?"

"Stop and think. You continually worry about the future."

"You mean, like getting back home as soon as possible?"

"That is an excellent example. Another one is your mother spending all her time anticipating Hunter's return, believing that one event in the future shall bring her permanent happiness. You actually believe that when your mother finally gets her oldest son back home, that you too, shall *also* experience joy and contentment."

The sage's words made me think about how my mother's unpredictable moods affected how I felt about myself. I realized that when she acted moody and unhappy, I took on her problems and tried to make her feel better.

"You humans spend all of your time dreaming about your future, or, even worse, thinking negative thoughts about your past. Living in the past. I suggest you learn to live in the moment and free yourself from the chase. Stop striving for more and searching for something better. You already have everything you need to be completely happy, right here, right now. So does your mother, if she so chooses."

The sage patted me on the hand. "Hunter's return shall never bring permanent happiness to your family."

The door swung open and Nyx entered the room.

She set a wooden cup in front of me.

"Here you are," she said, "some elixir tea to make you feel better."

As she turned and walked out the door, Metamorphosis told her, "Please ask Hunter to bring my backpack and bed roll."

I took a sip of warm tea and said, "I'm starting to understand what you're saying, but I still want to help my mother feel better."

"What if I told you that the greatest happiness comes from self-love, discovering and nurturing your self, not from the love of others?"

I frowned at Metamorphosis. "I'd say you were wrong."

Raising his bushy white eyebrows, he said, "Keep in mind, I

do not speak of egotistical love, where all you ever think about is yourself and you care about no one else. I speak of *true* self-love, where you learn to act without a sense of self. Where you give without consideration, without expecting anything in return. When you act with compassion. Truly care about others."

"So, how does this apply to my mother and me?"

After I said it, I thought about all the times Momma treated me mean and then bought me an expensive gift to make up for her cruel behavior.

All I wanted was her love, not her gift of guilt.

There was always a price to pay when my mother gave us her *sorry-I-treated-you-bad* presents.

The sage wiped his white moustache with his purple napkin. "Be patient with your mother, forgive her behavior and focus on your own self growth. The harder you try to win her heart, the more resistance you shall create for yourself. Do not seek the favor of your mother. Stop worrying about her feelings for you. No longer be concerned about her opinions of you. Do not allow her behavior to affect your life."

I smirked. "That's going to be difficult to do."

"Time shall make you the wiser. Allow truth to always be your guide, your inner strength. Seek the highest truth. When you learn to love yourself unconditionally, your relationship with your mother changes instantly. You shall see her in a new light. You shall love her even more than you do now. Because you know how to love your self."

"Promise? That sounds too good to be true."

"My words come from the Source. I speak only of love. Do you feel my love, my positive energy?"

"Now that you say it that way, I do."

As strange as it sounds, I felt Metamorphosis's loving energy, his aura, radiating from his body.

"My point is, nothing can make your mother happy. Not Hunter's return. Not constant attention from you. Not priceless gifts. Not all the money in the universe. Nothing. No thing."

I closed my eyes, thinking of all the times I tried to please Momma and how I always failed miserably.

"Be happy with who you are, Julia Wainright. You already have the priceless gift of helping others. You possess a forgiving nature, the ability to forgive others. When you learn who you *really* are, to love yourself and nurture your inner being, your soul, that which sits in the center and knows, you shall live in eternal bliss."

"But, I feel like a failure," I said. "I made the wrong decision coming here."

"Nonsense. Your quest to bring Hunter home has not ended in failure. All things happen in perfect order. There are no accidents in the universe. Believe me, there is a divine reason why you are here, sitting with me, at this exact moment in time."

"I want to believe you."

"Believing is Seeing," the sage said. "When you discover who you are, Julia, you shall See the truth. The Light."

The door opened and Hunter walked in with Nyx.

My brother said, "Here's your stuff, Metamorphosis," setting a leather backpack on the floor.

The sage patted my hand, "Julia, you have noble work to perform on Earth. People desperately need your positive energy and your unconditional love."

Thanking Metamorphosis, I couldn't take my eyes off Hunter as he stepped toward me.

I jumped up and ran into his arms.

We hugged and he said, "I did a drawing for you."

He opened the flap to a red leather satchel hung over his shoulder. He pulled out a piece of parchment paper and handed it to me. I stared at the illustration. Hunter had drawn *me* standing in my Millennium outfit, holding my sword. I looked like a comic book heroine. A superhero.

"You always asked me to draw fantasy characters for you," he said. "This time, the fantasy is real."

Tears ran down my cheeks. "I wish you'd come home with me. I'm going to really miss you."

Hunter squeezed me tightly and said, "Please tell everyone they are always in my thoughts. Give them my love. I hope to see you again, Julia. Be safe."

With tears in his eyes, he kissed my cheek, slung his leather backpack over his shoulder and hurried out the door, down the hallway.

Gone.

My brother has left me, I thought. *I don't think I'm ever going to see him again.*

If he doesn't come home, the family will have to stare at his useless, comatose body for years to come. Decades.

His brothers and sisters won't ever get to know the Hunter I grew up with.

How am I going to tell Momma?

She'll go crazy.

Looking down at my Triamulet, I wished I had never seen the gold medallion.

I wished my father had never visited Planet Millennium. I wished Hunter and I were kids again, sitting on Daddy's lap in his library, laughing and giggling while he read fairy tales to us.

Nyx patted me on the shoulder as she told Metamorphosis, "I shall take good care of Princess Julia."

Metamorphosis slipped on his robe, smiled, and hugged me with all four arms. "Be good to yourself, young lady."

I wiped the tears from my eyes as the Sage of the Ages closed the door behind him.

Staring at the smoldering fire, I thought, *Let's get out of here, now. I need to get home. I've seen enough of Millennium to last me a lifetime.*

"We shall stay here tonight," Nyx announced, opening the door. "Your room awaits you."

Her words shocked me.

I felt so lost.

So alone.

Millions of light years from Earth and I had to wait another night to get back home.

"I want to leave now!" I shouted.

"Princess Julia, calm down," Nyx said. "The black sky has arrived. It is too dangerous to fly. We shall get an early start in the morning and have you back to Time Island tomorrow, Daynight of the Jaguar."

I hung my head as Nyx escorted me down the stairs, past the crowded tavern, and into a narrow corridor. I had lost all track of time as I followed the sage, trying to make sense of my journey.

Maybe a good night's sleep is what I really need, I thought. *But Dreamtime will take me back to Earth in my paralyzed body. I want to wake up, get out of bed, and hug my family.*

I talked myself into staying up so I wouldn't experience Dreamtime: *Just stay up all night long. You don't need sleep, you're a teenager. Stay awake, Julia!*

Stopping in front of my room, she gave me a brass key and told me, "I'll be next door. If you need anything, knock on the wall."

The kind sage offered to bring me dinner but I refused to eat.

I was too upset to be hungry.

"Please, lock the door and do not leave," she said. "Get a good night's rest, we have a long flight ahead of us."

Locking the door behind me, I stood in dim light.

The drab, musty-smelling room had two oil lamps hung on the wall and a burning black candle setting on the night stand next to the tarnished brass bed.

No fireplace.

Across the room, a porcelain wash basin and white towel set on a dressing table.

The oval mirror mounted above the table beckoned me.

The oak floor planks squeaked with every step I took as I shuffled across the room, stepping over a round throw rug embroidered with two crossed harpoons that formed an **X**.

I opened the red velvet curtains to the only window in the room.

Iron bars greeted me.

At first, the black metal barrier upset me, but I realized that no one could break into my room.

You know, one of those weird creatures from the tavern.

I felt safe.

Rubbing the sleeve of my white chemise against the foggy glass to look through the window pane, the empty courtyard revealed a two-story plastered-stone wall standing stark white against the pitch-black sky.

A gloomy grey fog crawled over the wall, drifting in from the Sea of Esteem. Three moons hovered above Escalot, illuminating the misty landscape with a ghostly blue haze.

Closing the red curtains, I stepped to the wash basin and stared at myself in the oval mirror.

Self-critical, I told myself how bad I looked.

No makeup.

Red eyes from crying.

Tangled hair.

Ugly.

I wasn't feeling very good about myself.

Found a pearl-handled brush in the dresser drawer and combed my black hair.

Staring at my reflection, my thoughts turned to Earth.

You'll be home tomorrow. You're going to wake up and your world will have changed forever.

The advice Metamorphosis gave you sounded really good.

You need to take better care of myself.

Wonder if Momma has stopped drinking?

After washing my face, I sat on the edge of the bed, drying my cheeks with the towel.

Chilled, I crawled under the beige wool blanket, leaving the oil lamps burning.

Holding the handle of my sword in one hand and my Triamulet in the other, I focused on the flickering candle flame next to my bed, trying to get Hunter off my mind.

Staring at the gold medallion, I recalled how Nyx had explained that the Triamulets are only visible to the person wearing the medallion, or to Utopians, or to Extractors. My Triamulet, like all the medallions, were invisible to all others.

She also reminded me how the Extractors were obsessed with my capture so they could remove my Triamulet. So I could not return to Earth. So they could drain my essence and possess my soul forever.

I told myself to stop worrying. That I'd be home soon.

Although I promised myself I would stay awake that evening, my eyes grew weary as I listened to the muffled sounds of the tavern's drunkards and gamblers and braggarts and, as my mother would have called them, "party animals."

Emotionally and physically exhausted, I closed my eyes.

I do remember shutting my eyes.

I don't remember falling asleep.

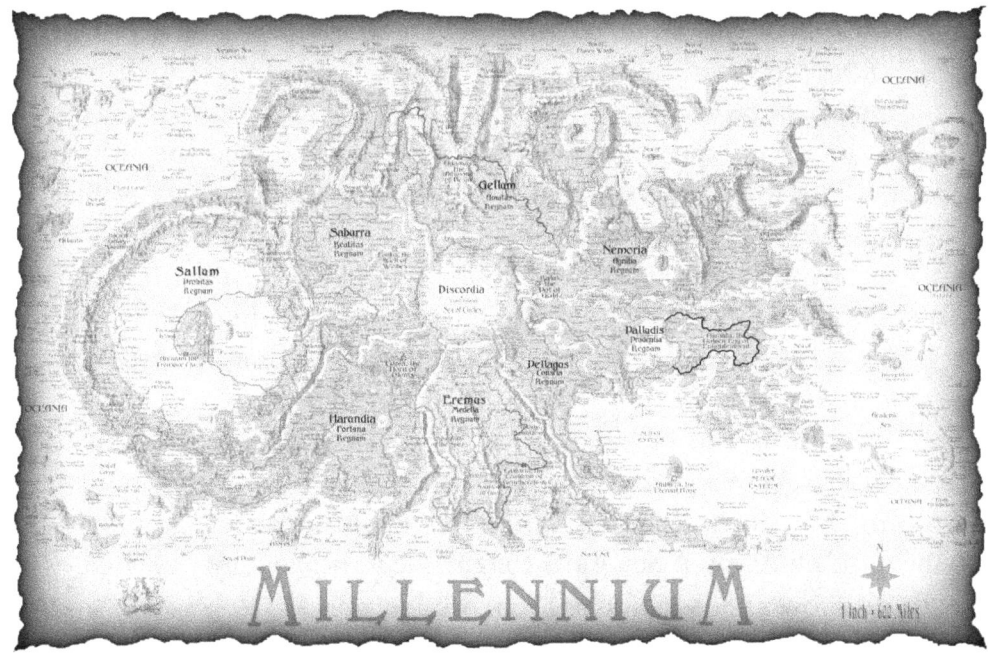

Chapter XVIII
Julia's Third Dreamtime

ELCOME HOME JULIA, painted in big red letters on a white banner pinned to the ceiling, came into focus as I gathered my senses. When I could not move my body, I knew immediately that I had fallen asleep in my room at the Crossed Harpoons Inn.

My third Dreamtime had begun.

Cursing myself for not staying awake, I wished I could have arrived home and surprised Momma by sitting up in bed and hugging her and telling my family how much I missed them. Instead, I had returned to Earth in my comatose body.

Calm down, I told myself, *remember what Metamorphosis said, "Enjoy the moment. All things happen at the right and perfect time." There's a reason you're here, Julia.*

Think positive.

Jeremy is going to visit you.

Balloons and party streamers and confetti adorned the family room. A "Happy Birthday" banner had been hung in front of the new picture bay window.

Across the room from me, propped up in his hospital bed, emotionless Hunter wore a green party hat on his head.

My immediate thought was, *Hunter would be really upset if he saw how goofy his other face looks right now.*

The setting sun hovered above the surface of the restless ocean. The glowing orange ball peeked through the grey clouds rolling over the horizon. Thousands of white caps blew across the dark-blue water. Sea gulls fought the wind as they flew in circles above the jagged cliffs.

Carmel By-The-Sea had been blessed with another breathtaking sunset.

The children laughed and giggled in the kitchen.

While my brothers and sisters listened, Momma sang a familiar song:

> "Twinkle, twinkle, little stars,
>
> How I wonder where you *two* are,
>
> Up above the world so high,
>
> Like *two* diamonds in the sky,
>
> Twinkle, twinkle, little stars,
>
> How I wonder where you *two* are."

She sang that nursery rhyme to me when I was little.

The new version was clever, where she revised the lyrics in honor of Hunter and me.

I hadn't heard Momma sing in years. She always had an angelic voice.

Besides the party streamers and balloons, the wall opposite my bed had been covered with five huge posters—hand-painted messages from my brothers and sisters.

They read:

WE MISS YOUR SMILE
ALEXANDER AND ZACHARY

BRING HUNTER HOME WITH YOU
Emily and Grace

LUV U
crystal and sebastian

COME BACK SOON
Astrid and Pearl

CAN I BORROW YOUR CAR
HA HA HA
RUBY YOUR FAVORITE SISTER

Smiling inside, I realized how much they loved and missed me. Positive brain chemicals rushed through my body. A euphoria overwhelmed my senses.

As Nyx told me, "Happy thoughts release positive brain chemicals that result in bliss."

Such a simple formula for a happy life.

Happy thoughts.

Positive chemicals.

Bliss. And so on and so on, forever and ever.

I know what you're thinking.

Too good to be true.

Ever since I began thinking positive thoughts, affirmations, my life has changed.

Think about it. It makes sense.

According to Nyx, "Sad thoughts release negative chemicals that result in depression."

That's my mother's problem. Depression from sad thoughts. Negative thinking.

When I get home, wake up, I'm going to share my discovery with Momma. She can really use some bliss in her life.

My reflection in a mirror on the opposite wall revealed a BCI control cap on my head. A blue ribbon had been pinned to the side of the headset. Momma had dressed me in a matching blue satin top.

Surprisingly, I wore red lipstick and blush.

My straight hair had been curled at the ends.

Momma had dolled me up for the birthday party.

Imagine waking up in the morning and your mother has put your makeup on for you! That's what it felt like when I saw myself in the reflection.

The big screen displayed a message in bold black letters:

WELCOME HOME JULIA!

TYPE A MESSAGE.

THE COMPUTER IS ON.

LOVE,

MOM AND DAD

Immediately, I concentrated on the letter I, then A, then M, then H, then O, then M, then E.

I looked at the white response box in the right portion of the screen.

The black letters read:

I AM HOME

Excited out of my mind, I continued to communicate using my BCI cap, typing a message for my family to read, hoping someone would come over to view the screen.

HELLO

TALK TO ME

HAPPY BIRTHDAY TO WHO?

Feeling comfortable with spelling words on the computer interface, I stopped typing and lay there, waiting for my family to discover I had awakened.

I mean, in my coma, awake.

You know what I mean. Conscious. Locked-in. Aware of my surroundings.

Smelling the delicious aroma of a home-cooked meal, I knew my mother had served Daddy's favorite meatloaf with mashed potatoes and mushroom gravy.

Listening to Momma entertain the children, I noticed something sounded different about her conversation with them.

What I mean is, my brothers and sisters seemed calm.

They listened without interrupting.

My mother never raised her voice.

Ruby never screamed.

No one cried, or nagged, or pouted.

Daddy entered the family room holding Sebastian in his arms. My father had lost weight. His hair had turned silver-white. He had grown a full beard, a look I had never seen before.

Crystal and Pearl, their clothes covered in food stains, followed their father to the white sofa. He plopped the girls onto his lap and recited a poem he often told Hunter and me.

In his story-telling voice, Daddy recited:

"A wise old owl sat in an oak,

The more he heard, the less he spoke;

The less he spoke, the more he heard;

Why aren't we all like that wise old bird?"

While the children giggled and asked Daddy about the wise old owl, he told them he had a better story and grabbed a leather-bound book from the coffee table.

Opening the *Brothers Grimm Fairy Tales*, he read the story of *Rumpelstiltskin*.

"Once there was a miller who was poor. But he had a beautiful daughter. Now it happened that he had to go and speak to the king, and in order to make himself appear important, he said to him, 'I have a daughter who can spin straw into gold.'"

Before my father read the next line, Momma yelled, "Wayland, please give the babies to Ruby so she can take them upstairs and get them ready for bed."

Ruby shuffled into the room wearing earphones and snapping her fingers to a song no one but she could hear. I swear she had the same black-on-black vampire outfit and voodoo hairdo she wore the last time I saw her.

She glanced over at me and stuck her tongue out, like she somehow sensed I had returned.

My father gave the girls to my rebellious sister and she chased them up the stairs.

Daddy hurried to the television and turned on the news, obsessed with the latest reports.

Can you blame him? He had been the top story on so many of the reports.

When I saw the date on the bottom of the screen, October 5th, I knew the family had celebrated Momma's birthday.

I watched Daddy watching the nightly news. He looked so upset, running his fingers through his white, scruffy beard.

Rioting still occurred in many countries. However, many of the demonstrations that focused on the existence of alien life forms and Planet Millennium had been peaceful. Non-violent.

The featured story showed government officials negotiating the return of the three Wainright Foundation hostages. They kept showing photos of the kidnapped doctors, Daddy's best friends.

So far, the negotiations had failed.

Ironically, armed guards stood outside our picture bay window as I watched the news.

The soldiers wore night-vision helmets as part of their routine patrol of our estate.

All of the sudden, my father screamed, "When I find out who leaked the video to the media, heads are going to roll!"

No wonder he acted so upset.

His oldest daughter's face covered the screen.

Me.

I looked terrible, lying there in a coma for the whole world to see. I immediately recognized the video as the one Daddy had taken of me during my last Dreamtime.

The ten-minute video of my BCI communication had gone viral on the Internet, over a billion hits in thirty days. My story had become the number-one topic on social media sites world-wide. People enjoyed debating the possibility of life on another planet, that humans could travel to a distant world. And return.

Professor Van Campbell's face appeared on the television screen. My father smiled and clapped his hands, reacting to a positive news story.

The prior weekend, the professor hosted a successful benefit event, "Save the Wainright Foundation". The proceeds went to resurrect my father's research projects, as well as our home.

Thank God, we don't have to move, I thought. *I won't wake up in a strange house when I return home during the holidays.*

My calculations had my return trip from Millennium to Earth happening in forty to sixty Earth days, that is, if everything went as planned, I should arrive home around Thanksgiving.

Nothing should go wrong, I told myself.

All we had to do is fly a gryphon from Escalot to Time Island. Simple enough. Right?

The meteorologist announced, "A fast-moving storm will hit the northern California coast after midnight."

"Darling," my mother yelled from the kitchen, "can you check on Julia and Hunter for me?"

"Will do," Daddy yelled back.

Turning off the television, my father walked to Hunter's bed to check the monitor readings and write down data on a metal clipboard.

As he wandered toward me, I saw the fatigue in his tired eyes.

He read the monitors under my bed.

When he went to grab the clipboard hanging on the foot rail, he glanced up at the big screen.

Immediately, he turned and grabbed my hand, leaned over and kissed my cheek.

"Hello, my precious angel," he said. "I'm glad you're safe."

With tears in his eyes, he looked up at the screen and mumbled, "Are you coming home?"

Concentrating on the top row of one-word responses, my mind typed:

YES

He patted my hand. "I have a surprise for you," he said, smiling. "Wait here."

Sometimes, Daddy is funny.

Of course I had to wait there.

I was paralyzed!

Momma came running into the room, holding her hands to her face.

Daddy stood in the doorway, keeping Alexander, Zachary, Emily, Grace, and Astrid from entering the family room.

My mother rushed up to me with tears streaming down her face.

She touched my cheek with her warm, soft hand.

"I have so much to say to you," she said. "Can you hear me?"

She looked up at the screen.

YES

Smiling, she wiped her eyes with a white handkerchief.

"I put your journals back where they belong. No one will find them, I promise."

She stared at the screen, waiting for my answer. I wasn't

sure how to respond, still upset with her for reading my private diaries.

So, I decided not to answer.

Momma took a deep breath and looked into my eyes.

Her voice trembled. "Are you coming home?"

UNDECIDED

I surprised myself answering that way, knowing I planned to return. Shame on me for trying to upset her.

"I understand," Momma said, half-grinning and squeezing my hand. "I have good news. I've quit drinking. I stopped the night I promised you I would."

THANK GOD

After I typed my response, I thought of all the times I dreamed of her being sober. Being kind to me. Compassionate. And loving.

"I want to start over when you return. Begin a new relationship. I've hired a housekeeper. I won't make you do the chores anymore. I've also hired a nurse to care for Hunter."

She looked at the screen.

REPEAT

Held her hand over her heart and said, "I'm sorry for treating you like a servant. I can raise the children without your help. As a mother, I know how horrible I've been. Please forgive me. Come home, Julia. Give me another chance."

I BELIEVE YOU

Momma leaned against the bed and placed her head on my chest, hugging me tightly. She closed her eyes and cried.

"You've made me the happiest woman on Earth," she said, sobbing.

I wanted to say more to my mother but she just lay there and continued to cry for joy.

Daddy pointed, motioning for the children to go upstairs, telling them, "Stop complaining. You can all talk to Julia tomorrow."

He hurried over and helped my mother to her feet.

"Gloria," my father said, "please go upstairs and get ready for bed. I'll move Julia to her bedroom and set up the laptop. You can talk to her before you go to sleep."

"But, what if she leaves us again?" she asked, wiping the tears from her eyes.

"Don't worry," he replied, "Dreamtime lasts at least one week. You'll have plenty of time to spend with Julia."

Ruby came down and helped Momma up the stairs.

My father looked into my eyes and asked, "Where are you now? I mean, what location on Millennium?"

ESCALOT

"Where are you sleeping?"

CROSSED HARPOONS INN

"Are you still with Nyx the Utopian?"

YES

AND METAMORPHOSIS

Before I could type Hunter's name, Daddy said, "That's fabulous. You are with the greatest sage in the universe. Learn all you can from him. Memorize everything he tells you."

METAMORPHOSIS GONE

"What do you mean?"

TOOK HUNTER TO FIND EVE

"You saw Hunter?"

YES

"Is he coming home?"

I didn't want to tell Daddy about my brother's decision to remain on Millennium. I wanted to tell the family in person when I got home. So I could explain everything to Momma.

HUNTER OKAY

"What does that mean?"

TALK TO YOU WHEN I GET HOME

HUNTER SAFE

He arched his eyebrows. "I can tell by the sound in your voice, I mean, the way your answering, that Hunter's not coming home."

NOT SURE

The truth was too painful to place on the screen. And, I didn't want Momma to read it.

My father threw his arms in the air and said, "Okay, we'll talk when you return."

THANK YOU

"Be ready for your mother to ask a lot of questions about Hunter." Daddy squeezed my hand. "I'm going to wheel you upstairs now. We have a big day ahead of us tomorrow. I'm going to have Dr. Shankar, Professor Van Campbell, and Elizabeth Dow come visit you. We need to ask you some important questions while you're still on Millennium. Would that be okay?"

No, I thought, *that's not okay. I needed to see my boyfriend.*

Upset, I concentrated on spelling one word:

HELP

Daddy placed his hand on the side of my face and asked, "What's wrong, sweetheart?"

NEED TO SEE JEREMY
NOW

My intuition told me that Jeremy had come to visit me as often as he could.

That he loved me with all his heart.

I was right!

"Don't worry," Daddy replied. "I'll make sure he comes to see you tomorrow. Your mother's been letting him visit you three nights a week and on weekends. Don't tell her I said this, but I think she's beginning to like Jeremy."

HAPPY TO HEAR

The reason I had decided to return home was to be with Jeremy. We had experienced such a weird, away-from-each-other relationship since we fell in love back in the summer of 2014.

Daddy wheeled me into the elevator and upstairs to my bedroom.

He switched on the night light next to my empty canopied bed that waited for my other body's return.

Sorry. I said that wrong.

Not my other body's return, the return of my soul to my Coma-X body. Earth body.

After attaching the laptop computer to my headgear, he opened the shutters and cracked the window open, allowing the cool ocean air to enter my lungs.

Dark clouds had blown in from the Pacific and it started to sprinkle. Within seconds, the autumn wind blew rain drops against my window. I loved the pitter patter of rain hitting our tile roof.

The crashing of waves at high tide and the smell of the salt air made me happy with my decision to return home, with or without Hunter.

My father clicked the BCI icon on the computer screen.

The laptop set on an elevated, portable stand next to my bed.

He asked me to say something.

I think he meant to say, "Type something."

I did.

I LOVE YOU

Smiling, he told me he loved me too.

Daddy hurried out the door and down the hallway. With my sensitive hearing, I heard his footsteps scurry down the stairs. His library door slammed shut.

From the quietness that followed came, "Meow."

Maddie pranced into my bedroom and jumped onto the peach-colored bedspread covering my lower body.

She stepped across my stomach and sniffed my lips. Her whiskers tickled my cheeks and nose.

I wanted to itch my face. The curious cat licked my chin with her rough tongue.

At the same time, a soft, slobbering tongue licked my hand. Pooh had managed to sneak upstairs to welcome me home.

"Out of here, both of you," Momma yelled, clapping her hands. The cat jumped off the bed and followed the golden retriever out of the room.

My mother shut the door.

"Sorry," she said, "your father left it open."

OKAY

She hurried to the side of my bed.

As soon as she read my message on the blue screen, she smiled and said, "I need to finish our earlier conversation. I promise not to cry this time."

I'M LISTENING

She took a deep breath and said, "I've made a lot of mistakes. With the help of my therapist, I know I can change. My biggest problem was that I never believed your father's stories about Millennium. Now that I can trust him, know that he's not insane, I can focus on becoming a better wife for him and a better mother for my children."

Momma held my hand. "Am I making sense?"

MORE THAN YOU'LL EVER KNOW

She nodded, acknowledging my sincerity.

"So, you forgive me for all the bad things I've done?"

FORGIVEN

"I've apologized to Jeremy and his father. I'm getting to like that boy. He told me last week that he's gotten a scholarship to play football. He seems like a good kid."

I was dying to type that he's not a kid anymore. He's on his way to college, just like me. But, I let it go. She still wanted to protect me from the entire world, and I wasn't back home yet.

So, I typed:

HE LIKES YOU TOO

My mother smiled.

"I feel so much better now that I'm sober. I forgot what it felt like to be me. We are going to have so much fun together when you return."

CAN'T WAIT

I really looked forward to having a relationship with my mother. I had learned that it is never too late to change.

While Momma brushed my hair, she went on and on about how she had talked to the high school principal at Carmel High and I would be able to graduate with just a few more hours of class time and some final testing.

She bragged how well the kids were doing with the tutor.

How I shouldn't worry about all the Wainright Foundation problems, as she put it, that the twenty-four-hour security would eventually be lifted once the world realized that Daddy was right, that Planet Millennium really *did* exist.

That the hostages should be released soon.

That we would *not* lose our home to foreclosure.

That our lives would soon return to normal.

"I mean by normal," she said, "that I'll be a good mother and won't drink anymore."

GREAT NEWS!

Impressed with my mother's new attitude, her new positive outlook on life, I prepared to type how I had truly forgiven her when the door opened and Daddy walked in.

"Hari's coming tomorrow morning, Darling. Your parents and your sisters called, they want to talk to Julia, at least say hello. Sounds like we're going to have a lot of visitors this week. Right now, you need to come to bed and get some rest; it's been a really emotional day."

Momma stared into my eyes. "Do you want me to stay by your side so we can talk?"

Torn between Daddy's concern for her health and my own need to talk to my mother, I decided to let her get some rest.

SEE YOU TOMORROW

"Okay, sweetheart," she said, "We'll talk in the morning."

She kissed my cheek and whispered, "I love you."

I LOVE YOU TOO

My father put his arm around her, then he led her out the door and down the hallway.

Within a few minutes he returned to tell me, "Love you. Good night."

He blew me a kiss and closed the door.

Within seconds, the door swung open and Daddy hurried into my room saying, "I forgot to turn the computer off."

NO! LEAVE IT ON

He pointed to the screen, "If I leave the computer on, would you like to record some of your experiences on Millennium?"

YES

"Okay. Your wish is my command."

He patted my hand. Before he closed the door, he waved and said, "I'll check on you later Julia. Have fun on the computer."

With the screen in front of me, I actually looked forward to a night of typing my Millennium story. Ease the boredom of lying there with only my thoughts.

Without warning, I heard a *tap—tap—tap* on my bedroom window.

Someone stood outside my window!

The person wiped the rain drops from the glass and stared into my bedroom.

A face came into view.

Jeremy!

The boy of my dreams stood outside my room, on the roof, in the pouring rain.

He looked through the water-spotted glass, smiling and waving at me.

How did he know I was locked-in?

Within seconds he had climbed through the window and stood at my bed.

Shaking off the rain and cold, he removed his gloves, leather jacket, and his black baseball cap.

His tennis shoes squeaked on the hardwood floor as he walked cautiously across the room.

Put his ear to the door, listening.

Hurrying back to my bed, he whispered, "Hello, Julia. I thought you'd like some company."

YES

Jeremy ignored the laptop screen.

He stared directly at me with his round hazel eyes.

"Your father called me earlier. He said I could come over tomorrow and talk to you. But I couldn't wait. I had to see you tonight. For the past month, your parents have pointed to a screen above your bed and told me how you communicate using the keyboard."

He pointed behind him. "Wait. I left it open. It's cold in here."

Tiptoeing across the room, he closed the window and hurried back.

Jeremy froze in his tracks, staring at the computer screen displaying keyboard symbols.

"Is this thing working?" he asked, pointing at the laptop.

YES DUMMY

Completely frustrated, I couldn't help but type a sarcastic statement. Shame on me.

His jaw dropped and he looked at me with his hand over his mouth.

Speaking in a low tone of voice, he whispered, "I see you haven't lost your dry sense of humor."

He grabbed my hand and squeezed so hard it would have hurt under normal circumstances.

"I'm not sure what to say," he said, blushing. "Can you tell me where you are?"

He held up his hand. "No, tell me when you're coming home."

He looked at the screen.

SOON

"When?"

HOLIDAYS

"By Christmas?"

YES

"Great!" He smiled with those dreamy dimples. "I really miss you."

I MISS YOU TOO

I was dying to say "I love you", but I wanted him to tell me first. I needed to see his sweet lips say the words.

"I've watched your Internet video a hundred times," he said, "and I still can't believe you're on another planet."

IT IS TRUE

Jeremy nodded his head in acknowledgment after reading the screen. "Tell me about Millennium."

Before I answered, he leaned over me and rolled the laptop stand around the opposite side of the bed. So he could see my face and not have to turn his head around to read the screen.

Using the power of my thoughts, I typed:

THE PLANET IS BEAUTIFUL

BUT WEIRD

"Like a science fiction movie?"

YES

"Why did you go there?"

TO FIND HUNTER

"That's what your dad told me. Have you found your brother?"

YES

"What happened? Is he okay?"

HE WILL NOT COME HOME

"Why not? Is something wrong with him?"

HAS FALLEN IN LOVE

"With a human?"

NO

GIRL FROM PLANET EPIPHANY

HER NAME IS EVE

"Have you met her?"

NO

EX HAS CAPTURED HER

"Ex?" he asked. "Who's that?"

I realized the conversation had gone in the wrong direction. I could have spent hours describing Millennium and Hunter and Metamorphosis and Eve and the Extractors and, you know, all the stuff a teenage boy would love to hear.

Worried my parents would find Jeremy in my room, I became anxious. I wanted to talk about us. Our love.

So, I typed:

STOP

"What's wrong?

MILLENNIUM LATER

TALK ABOUT US!

He nodded, *yes*, squeezed my hand, and asked, "Do you miss me?"

MORE THAN LIFE ITSELF

"You're on my mind every moment of every day. I can't stop thinking of you."

MAKES ME HAPPY

"I never thought I could love a girl in a coma, but you proved me wrong. I mean, not knowing if you're ever going to wake up has been harder to deal with than I ever imagined. What I'm trying to say is, I discovered that I am willing to wait for you, no matter how long it takes."

He leaned over and looked into my eyes.

Closer to my face than he had ever been, I felt his positive energy.

His eyes twinkled in the amber lamp light.

"I need to ask you a question."

He closed his eyes and swallowed.

"If I kissed you right now, would you be upset with me?"

I thought about it for a moment as he opened his eyes.

Even though I couldn't kiss him back, I had waited for this moment for more than a year.

No, longer than that.

Ever since I could remember, I dreamed of being kissed by a boy.

I responded:

PLEASE KISS ME

Jeremy moved his eyes to look at the screen.

His face took on a glow I had not seen before. He had such a passionate look in his eyes.

"I love you," he said, moving closer.

His eyes shut while he moved his mouth toward mine.

His sweet breath felt warm and moist against my face.

In slow motion, I watched his beautiful face move closer.

Closer.

My entire body became hot as he moved nearer to my face.

The air between us became electrified.

The closer he got, the hotter I felt.

Although trapped in a paralyzed body, I burned with desire.

Jeremy tilted his head to the right and closed his eyes.

Our lips touched.

I saw a flash of light when his mouth pressed against mine.

His kiss was beyond anything I had ever imagined.

The feel of his soft lips sent a shock wave through my body.

Time stood still.

A sensation I had dreamed of—the breathless wonder of the first kiss—burned deep inside my body. I felt like Sleeping Beauty being kissed by the prince.

My head spun when he pulled his lips away.

Opening his eyes, he whispered, "You smell wonderful."

He touched the side of my face, keeping his soft hand against my cheek.

"I love you, Julia Wainright."

As I stared at his beautiful face, my vision became blurry.

At first, I thought the blissful dizziness came from the enchanted kiss, but I realized that my Dreamtime was coming to an end.

I tried to type, so I could share my loving feelings with him, but the screen looked blurry.

Cursing everyone I could think of, I cried inside as his face turned to dark-grey, to an unrecognizable silhouette.

Yearning for another kiss, I watched helplessly as the outline of Jeremy's handsome face continued to fade away.

Fade away.

DAYNIGHT
OF THE
JAGUAR

Chapter XIX
The Extractors

Blurry images of Jeremy's face and body remained in front of me as I tried to figure out what had happened to my eyesight. Was I still on Earth or had I returned to Millennium? Unlike my first two Dreamtime awakenings, I never saw a flash of white light or felt a warm glow in my soul.

Instead, a foul, rancid odor alerted me that something horrible had gone wrong.

A hard, sharp object rubbed up and down my left cheek, irritating me as I tried to focus my eyes.

"Jeremy?" I asked. "Is that you?"

The sound of my own voice startled me.

I realized immediately I had returned to Millennium.

The darkened face came into focus.

Captain Kraken!

Two sinister black eyes with vertical pupils glared at me. Green scales covered the hideous face that hovered over my body.

Kraken stroked my cheek with his black, curved fingernail—claw. I tried to scream, but he covered my mouth with his rough, scaly hand.

The reptilian eyes of the Extractor glared at me while his slimy drool dripped onto my chest, wetting my white chemise.

His hot, putrid breath made me gag.

I held my breath.

The area rug in the middle of the room had been pulled back, exposing a trap door in the wooden floor.

Wicked, high-pitched giggles and whispers came from the

opening. They sounded like voices from the fantasy movies Hunter and I loved to watch.

Like cockroaches crawling from a bath tub's drain, three hobgoblin pirates emerged from the door in the floor.

Kraken's crew of disfigured buccaneers stood three feet tall with dark hairy faces and beady red eyes. Their pointed noses and sharp teeth gave them a menacing look.

The pirates wore black breeches, royal-blue waistcoats, and tricorn pirate hats. Their knee-high boots clicked on the wood planks. Brown drool dripped from their pointed chins as they spit wads of tobacco on the floor.

The hobgoblins stood by my bed holding daggers, dirks, and cutlasses in their hairy little hands.

Captain Kraken cackled and slid my sword from its sheath, handing *Galatine* to one of the snickering pirates. He sneered and pulled a red scarf from his leather belt.

Before I could scream for Nyx, the cruel captain gagged my mouth, tying the scarf behind my head.

He signaled his pirate crew to climb down the ladder, through the door in the floor.

I felt the Extractor's incredible strength as he lifted me over his shoulder, holding my ankles while he climbed down the ladder.

Face down, I heard the trap door shut above us.

For the first time, it hit me.

Oh my God, I thought, *I'm supposed to return to Earth in the morning. This can't be happening. Momma's expecting me home.*

Gagged and unable to yell for help, anger overtook my fear.

I hit Kraken on his back as hard as I could with my fists.

Hit him again.

His rough scales hurt my hands.

A third time. Punched him with all my might.

He hissed, but the monstrous Extractor never said a word. I knew he could speak because he had screamed at me when he attacked Ava, our gryphon, while we flew over Discordia.

I pulled on the green tentacles that ran down his neck and spine. Like the arms of an octopus, they coiled tightly around my wrists, making it impossible for me to move my arms.

The blackness turned to yellow fire light as we reached the bottom of the ladder.

Two pirates carried flaming torches.

Kraken's tentacles released my hands as he put me down.

The three hobgoblins surrounded me, hissing and poking me with their bony fingers. One pirate held my sword in the air; its blade cast a shadow on the rock wall.

We stood in a damp, moss-covered tunnel.

Kraken spit a glob of green seaweed phlegm onto the rock wall and said, "Earthlin', I don't want no trouble. Folla' me an' you'll not be hurt."

The Extractor grabbed a torch from one of the pirates and marched down the eerie tunnel.

While the pirates waddled behind me, I followed the captain's torch light into the musty-smelling underground passage.

In the shadows, black cave rats squealed, jumping from rock to rock. Their eyes glowed red in the fire light. Swarms of brown cockroaches the size of cell phones scurried over the green, moss-covered walls. Above me, yellow-headed bats with purple fur chirped as they rustled nervously on the rock ceiling.

Freaked out by the tunnel's wildlife, I tripped and almost fell several times trying to keep up with Kraken.

The pirates giggled when I stumbled.

One of them kicked my leg to hurry me along. I looked over my shoulder and gave them all a dirty look.

Since I stood twice as tall as the creepy little creatures, I knew I could defend myself when the time came. My years of martial arts lessons would be put to the test.

It was Kraken I worried about. I felt defenseless against the monstrous Extractor known as The Intimidator.

Ahead, daylight appeared in the tunnel.

We turned a corner and my eyes adjusted to the morning light. Sightseeing was the last thing on my mind, but I couldn't help but admire the awesome scene in front of me.

We stood in a cave-like grotto facing the Sea of Esteem.

Crystal-blue water washed up onto the rocky ledge of the grotto. A natural rock archway, some fifty yards away, looked like an entrance, a passageway, to and from the sea-side cave. Beyond the arched-bridge opening, the lagoon revealed a coral reef that formed a barrier, protecting the grotto from the crashing waves of the restless sea.

I would learn later I had been taken to Goblin Grotto. It's on the Millennium map.

A wooden skiff, tied to a mooring on the rock outcropping, bobbed up and down in the gentle waves.

Beyond the reef, a hundred yards off shore, a lone ship with black sails had set anchor.

A Millennium sunrise colored the horizon a deep pink, yellow, purple, and orange.

The spectacular panorama was ruined by the sudden appearance of two beastmen pirates lumbering down a rock path toward us. The grotesque beasts, standing ten feet tall, grunted and waved when they saw Captain Kraken and the hobgoblins.

I would have run but there was nowhere to go. With the pirates behind me, my only option would have been to dive into the water.

Kraken can easily out swim me, I told myself. *Be patient, stay alert. Your chance to escape will come.*

Kraken rushed over to me, grabbed my arm, and forced me to stand next to the grotto wall facing a circular fire pit built into the stone floor of the grotto.

A blazing fire with orange and yellow flames swayed back and forth to the rhythm of the sea breeze.

The beastmen, wearing tattered breeches with belt buckles made with horned skulls, lumbered over and grabbed my arms. One beastman stood on each side of me, snarling and staring at me with their crazed, blood-shot eyes. The vice-like grip of their five-fingered hands hurt my arms.

I panicked, knowing I had lost my chance to escape.

Closing my eyes, I visualized my home.

My bedroom. My books.

My family.

Jeremy.

Without warning, a swooshing noise, like a giant bird landing, echoed off the rock walls of Goblin Grotto.

When I opened my eyes, Captain Kraken ordered his pirate crew to stand at attention.

The captain, nicknamed The Intimidator, stuck out his chest and strutted across the cave, pointing at me with his curved black nails.

He yelled, "Here's the Earthlin'. Over here, Master Ex."

That must be the Invisible Villain, I thought. *Now I'm in deep trouble.*

I couldn't see him, but I felt Ex make his way toward me.

A foul odor, different from the disgusting smells of the beastmen and hobgoblins and Kraken, overwhelmed me.

"Welcome ta *my* planet, Julia," Ex said.

The low, reverberating voice came from six feet in front of me.

"How do you know my name?" I asked the voice with no visible body.

"I know all things," Ex replied.

"I doubt that."

"Ah, we got ourselves a spirited Earthlin', full of defiance."

"I've done nothing to harm you. Let me go."

"Freedom is hard ta find in my part of the world," Ex said. "I'm willin' ta set ya free, but I ask one small favor."

"What's that?"

"Tell me whar that pesky brother of yers is. Might he be with that pathetic sage with the mangy white beard?"

I frowned, saying, "I don't know where Hunter is."

"Well then, we'll jus' have ta keep ya here 'till ya get yer memory back," he said.

"You'll have a long wait," I responded, sneering in the direction of the evil voice.

"Jus' so me crew doesn't have ta wait *too* long, tell me whar Hunter Wainright is, or I'll burn yer pretty little face."

The beastman to my right let go of my arm, bent over, and picked up a glowing, red-hot poker from the blazing fire. He held it up for all to see, and jammed it back into the flames. A flurry of orange sparks flew into the grotto air.

The hobgoblins clapped their hairy hands, hissing and showing their sharp yellow teeth.

"That's not fair!" I screamed. "I've done nothing to harm you, or your friends. Let me go."

"I'm fair as they come," Ex shouted, "as long as ya keep an open mind."

The hobgoblins laughed in their high-pitched voices.

"Silence!" Ex shouted. "Ta show my fairness an' generosity, I'll give ya a chance ta gain yer freedom. If ya can solve a simple riddle, I'll let ya go."

"What if I can't guess the riddle?"

"Then, my alien visitor, ya'll end up with a face that only a mother could love."

"Okay, go ahead."

I'm pretty good with riddles, I thought. *I can guess the answer.*

"The Riddle of the Sphinx is an easy one, Earthlin'. It is, 'What walks on four legs in the mornin', on two legs at noon, and on three legs in the evenin'?'"

There's thousands of choices, I thought. *What animal has two legs, and then grows a third leg? This question's not fair. The four-legged thing must be a weird Millennium creatures.*

"I need yer answer, now," Ex yelled. "Ya either know it, or ya don't."

"It's got to be one of the creatures here on Millennium. I

haven't been here that long. Your riddle isn't fair."

"When I tell ya the answer, ya'll know I'm righteous."

I turned red with frustration, searching my memory for a possible answer. Trying to remember any weird animals I'd seen in Daddy's library books.

"Well?" Ex asked in a deep, sinister voice.

"I don't know. I give up. What has all those weird legs?"

"*You* do, my pretty."

"Me?"

The voice with no body laughed wickedly and said, "Humans crawl on all fours as a baby, walk on two legs as an adult, and walk with a cane in old age."

I blushed. "A human, of course."

Kicking the beastmen in the shins with the heel of my boot, I yelled, "I've done nothing to hurt you. Let me go home."

My lips quivered, imagining my fate.

"I'll give ya another chance ta earn yer freedom," Ex said, "I've heard how smart ya aliens are. I got a riddle that, an Earthlin' like you, should easily solve."

I nodded, *okay.*

What choice did I have?

"There are two sisters. One gives birth ta the other an' she, in turn, gives birth ta the first. Who are they?"

Come on Julia, think. You're on Millennium, so it's got to be two goddesses who are sisters. All those mythology books you've read, you should know this one. Focus. Who are the two goddesses?

"Yer time is up," Ex said, his deep, haunting voice three feet from me. "Who might the sisters be?"

"They are Hera and Gaea. Wait, maybe Freya and Hel. Or, they could be Ishtar and Inanna."

"Ahhh, brilliant answers, but wrong." Ex chuckled. "Captain Kraken, tell the Earthlin' the answer."

"Day an' night!" the captain screamed, sneering.

His black iguana eyes gleamed in the morning light while

259

he spit another glob of green seaweed phlegm onto the rocks of Goblin Grotto.

"Now, ain't that answer 'bout as Earthly as ya can get?" Ex asked, laughing.

The hobgoblins laughed with the Dark Master.

"Quiet, ya fools!" he shouted.

The disfigured pirates hissed and groaned. Hanging their heads in resentment, tobacco-stained brown drool dripped down the front of their waistcoats and breeches.

Ex yelled, "Even though ya proved yer human stupidity, here's me final offer. Forget yer stubborn brother. Join me, become an Extractor. I'm offerin' ya yer last chance ta pledge yer allegiance ta me."

I stared defiantly in Ex's direction and shook my head, *no.*

"Ya have chosen poorly!" Ex screamed. "Ya'll soon regret yer decision!"

Unexpectedly, I felt the gold chain around my neck being lifted up and over my head.

Someone help me, I thought, *Ex is taking my Triamulet.*

"Give that back!" I screamed. "You have no right to take my necklace!"

My thoughts ran wild:

Pray Julia, pray. Dear God, I knew I should have turned back when I had the chance. He's got my Triamulet, now I'm never going to get home. I'll be good, don't let them torture me. I feel like I've died and gone to hell. If I ever get out of this, I'm going straight to Time Island, go to sleep and get back home. Please God, help me. I'll be good, I promise.

The gold chain and medallion floated through the air and remained motionless six feet off the ground. Ex had placed the Triamulet around his own neck.

The Dark Master screamed, "'Tis time ta rearrange yer young, flawless face ta somethin' more appropriate, in case ya decide ta become an Extractor."

The beastman grabbed the glowing iron poker from the

blazing fire and raised it slowly toward me.

"Hold 'er tight," Ex yelled. "After we burn 'er pretty little face, we'll take 'er ta the ship. Kraken needs a first mate."

With a cruel look in his wild, blood-shot eyes, the sadistic beastman held the red-hot poker six inches from my face.

I felt the radiating heat waves from the glowing tip and smelled the smoldering stench of old burnt flesh rise from the poker.

This maniac is really going to burn my face, I thought. *God, please, don't let him hurt me.*

Helpless, I closed my eyes and held my breath, praying for my life.

Within an inch of my face, the heat from the hot poker became unbearable.

I prepared to scream in agony.

During extreme fear, everything slows down. A strange silence overtakes your mind.

Instead of closing my eyes, I kept staring at the glowing red metal that headed straight for my face. I wanted to blow out the tip, like I would a candle flame.

About to scream at the sadistic monster to please stop, I heard a *swoosh* and a loud *thud.*

The sickening sound of ripping flesh.

I looked up at the beastman pirate.

A silver-tipped arrow, dripping with blood, had impaled the monster's neck.

The beastman dropped the iron poker and grabbed the shaft of the quivering arrow, gasping for air. Dark-red blood gushed from his neck.

Choking, the monster fell to his knees, writhing in pain.

The other beastman gripped my upper arm and drew his saber, waving the shining blade high in the air.

Above us, two boarman soldiers, wearing pig-face basinet helmets, dropped their long bows and charged down the rock path. Their shining suits of scale armor rattled as they grabbed their iron maces and spiked flails hanging from their metal belts.

Hunter and Nyx ran down the path behind the soldiers. She leaped from the rocks to the cave floor, holding her spear above her head. My brother drew his sword and shouted, "Julia! Stand ready!"

"Put the girl on the boat!" Ex shouted.

Two screaming pirates charged the boarman soldiers as they crossed the grotto.

Metamorphosis flew down from above, hovering like a giant butterfly.

The Sage of the Ages really can fly, I thought.

Kraken attacked Nyx.

The Extractor swung his saber at the Utopian, who reflected his powerful blows with her spear.

The sound of clanging metal echoed off the cave walls and down the tunnel.

Metamorphosis swooped down with his scepter drawn and bonked Kraken on the back of his reptilian head.

The captain stumbled and backed up, looking for his second attacker while he swung his saber at Nyx.

Like a slow motion movie, Hunter sprinted straight at the beastman gripping my arm with his black fingernails. It hurt so bad I wanted to scream, but I clenched my jaw, refusing to let the beastman know I was in pain.

My brother jumped high in the air and kicked the slow-moving monster in the face.

The stunned beast released his grip on my arm as Hunter landed on his feet.

The growling beastman swung his muscular arm and knocked my brother to the ground.

Grunting, the monster raised his saber above his horned head and swung the glistening blade down at Hunter.

Holding my breath, I watched my brother lying helpless on his back, holding his sword up to defend himself.

Sparks flew as the beastman's saber struck *Aroundight*, Hunter's sword, knocking the weapon out of his hand.

I knew the monster would kill my brother if I didn't do something.

Feeling a rush of energy, I jumped high in the air, kicking the beastman in the ribs.

Screaming, "Geeehaaahp!" I smashed my boot into the monster's side.

He groaned, grabbed his ribs and looked over his shoulder at me.

I motioned with my hands, *come get me*, and jumped onto a flat boulder.

The fire pit laid directly behind me.

No place to escape, I positioned myself in a martial arts stance. "Stand ready", as Hunter called it.

The snarling beastman lumbered straight for me, swinging his gleaming saber above his bald head.

Beyond frightened and high on adrenaline, I told myself, *You can do it, Julia. Kick the beastman's butt!*

As I leaped at the monster, Hunter jumped on the beastman's back and clung to his neck.

I karate-kicked the beastman's face with the heel of my boot. Landing on my feet, I looked up to see blood gush from the monster's nose.

The stunned beast reached back to grab my brother.

Hunter pulled the knife from his belt and slit the beastman's throat.

The beastman pirate stared in my eyes with a look of disbelief as he dropped his saber. He grabbed his bloody neck with both hands while Hunter jumped down to the grotto floor.

The moaning monster stumbled forward, lost his footing, and tumbled into the fire pit, head first.

A geyser of roaring red flames, sparks, and black ash exploded into the grotto air while the burning beastman screamed in agony.

"Arrrggghhh!"

The smell of burnt flesh made me sick.

"Kill the Earthlings!" Ex shouted.

The hobgoblin pirate who had stolen my sword charged toward me, screaming and showing me his sharp yellow teeth.

Shouting, "Give me my sword back, you little creep!" I pushed Hunter out of the way and ran straight at the hobgoblin.

Launching myself through the air, I karate-kicked the pirate in the chest.

At that moment, I felt so powerful.

So independent.

Dazed by the blow to his chest, the pirate stumbled backward, trying to catch his breath.

I leaped and spun full circle in midair, striking him on the side of the head with my boot.

My sword flew out of his hand and hit the grotto wall as he dropped to the rock floor, his face cut and bleeding.

The wounded hobgoblin crawled away toward the water, leaving a trail of blood.

I ran and picked up *Galatine* while Hunter picked up his sword. That moment will remain etched in my memory forever.

There I stood with my twin brother on another planet, dressed in medieval clothing, holding swords in our hands, fighting hobgoblins and beastmen and Extractors.

Full of rage, I ran to the crawling pirate and stood over him in victory, raising my sword above my head.

The hobgoblin held his stubby arms up and squealed for mercy. "Pleeease, sparrre me life, matey."

Go ahead, Julia, I thought. *Kill him. Kill the pirate!*

I held *Galatine* above my head, shaking.

Seeing the terror in the pirate's eyes, hearing his pathetic voice, I hesitated.

I can't do it, I thought. *I can't kill him.*

Lowering my sword, I pointed the blade in the pirate's face, shouting, "Tell Ex I want my Triamulet back, or he's next!"

The bleeding pirate scrambled to his feet, scurried across Goblin Grotto, and jumped off the rock ledge into the water.

Hunter ran up and grabbed my arm. "Great job, Julia. You put that pirate in a world of hurt."

Holding the sword with my trembling hands, I scanned the grotto for Ex and my Triamulet.

Looking for my medallion dangling in midair, I yelled to Hunter, "I should have killed that pirate."

"No. You did the right thing," my brother yelled.

Across the grotto, the armored boarman soldiers battled with their mace and flail, driving the pair of pirates back toward the water.

Swinging a spiked iron ball on the end of a chain, the grunting boarman struck the hobgoblin pirate on the side of his unprotected head with the lethal flail.

Blood splattered onto the buccaneer's waistcoat as he crumpled to the ground, dead.

When the last standing pirate saw the crushed skull of his ship mate, he turned and leaped off the rock ledge into the lagoon.

Across the grotto, Kraken the Intimidator, angrier than ever, swung his saber at Nyx while he cursed both Utopians.

Metamorphosis remained just out of reach, harassing the frustrated captain from above.

The confused bully shouted, "Help us, Master! The girl's getting away!"

"Destroy the sage's wand!" Ex screamed, standing on the opposite side of Goblin Grotto.

"Ya no-good coward! Take care of Metamorphosis yer self!" Kraken shouted.

The frustrated captain swung his saber one last time at Nyx before he turned and leaped off the ledge, diving into the waves below the grotto.

Hearing the location of the Invisible Villain's voice and seeing the Triamulet float through the air, Metamorphosis pointed his scepter, *Joyease*, at the moving medallion. Holding the gold wand above his head, Metamorphosis flew toward Ex. The crystal ball on the end of his scepter glowed with pulsating ultra-violet waves. The astral glow from *Joyease* exposed a mysterious shape moving toward the water.

Shielding my eyes from the glare, Ex's shape had been exposed.

A ghostly shadow with a glowing, violet-blue outline revealed a two-legged humanoid creature with fiery-white eyes covered with lizard-like skin. He wore a feathered cloak on his body. On his head, wings protruded from the sides of a dog-skin helmet.

"Morphman, ya'll regret this!" Ex screamed, growling and pointing with his dagger-like fingernails at the Utopian.

The now-visible Extractor vaulted high into the air and flew through the archway, soaring into the blue Millennium sky.

Amazed at how fast Ex flew away, I watched my medallion disappear above the Sea of Esteem.

Hunter came over and hugged me.

"Are you okay?" he asked, holding my shoulders and looking into my eyes.

"My Triamulet," I said, breathing heavily. "How am I...going to get home?"

"Don't worry, Metamorphosis will have an answer."

Hunter grabbed my hand and put his arm around me, leading me across the grotto to Nyx and the Sage of the Ages.

Just as I began to feel safe, Captain Kraken exploded from the water, pointing his saber at us.

Riding Tyrannus, he shouted, "See ya soon, Metamorphosis. Ya got lucky this time! When we meet again, I'll have yer head on the end of me saber!"

The boarman soldiers, standing guard at the entrance to Goblin Grotto, raised their bows, pulled, and released in unison.

One arrow missed Captain Kraken's head by inches.

The second arrow struck Tyrannus, impaling his tail fluke. The flying sea monster let out a loud chirping sound, like a giant dolphin in distress, as he flew through the archway and over the two bleeding pirates rowing the skiff.

We watched Tyrannus dive into the sea next to the *Jolly Roger,* Kraken's vessel. The motley crew pulled anchor as the defeated captain climbed up a rope ladder on the port side of his infamous pirate ship.

Nyx asked me, "Princess Julia, are you all right?"

I nodded*, yes.*

"My, young lady," Metamorphosis said, "you certainly know how to defend yourself."

"Thank our mom," Hunter told the sage.

Knowing he meant the martial arts lessons we took together as children, I thought of home.

I'm never going to get home without my Triamulet. We have to find Ex. That could take weeks, or months. My parents might die of old age by the time I get back.

"Julia, do you still want to go home?" my brother asked.

"After this experience, more than ever," I replied, staring at the dead beastman lying in a pool of blood.

"Then, you shall," Metamorphosis said, patting my shoulder.

With tears of frustration in my eyes, I asked, "How? Nyx told me to never lose my Triamulet, or I could not return home. It's gone. Ex has it."

The sages looked at each other and grinned.

"Nyx wanted to make sure you knew the importance of the sacred medallion," Metamorphosis said. "However, I have something superior to the one you lost to Ex."

Metamorphosis reached into his leather vest and pulled out a Triamulet with a sparkling crystal in the middle.

"That's like the one Elizabeth Dow has," I said, staring at the medallion.

"Ah, Elizabeth," Nyx said. "She stayed quite a long time. We treasured our moments together. We hope to see her again."

"What do you mean, *again,*" I asked. "Isn't a Triamulet good for one trip only. That's what you told me. That's what my father's Millennium report says. One time only."

"This sacred Crystal Triamulet allows intergalactic travel an unlimited number of times," Metamorphosis said, placing the gold chain with the sacred medallion around my neck.

I stared at the gold triangle on my chest and said, "You mean, I can return to Millennium whenever I want?"

"Anytime you choose, Princess Julia," Nyx said, smiling.

"Only a few humans have taken advantage of the eternal power of the Crystal Triamulet," Metamorphosis said.

"Who was the last one to do that?" I asked, thinking it might be Elizabeth Dow.

"Hunter, *you* tell her," Metamorphosis said.

"William Shakespeare. He visited here, first as Francis Bacon. Then, he showed up the second time as Shakespeare the playwright."

"Willie was one of our favorite Earthlings," Metamorphosis said. "He loved to sit by a fire and have philosophical discussions. Unfortunately, like all humans, he acted impatient, in a hurry to get back home. He said he had a lot of writing to do, so he decided to leave."

"Speaking of leaving, I'd love to stay and talk more," Hunter said, "but we have to go."

"To find Eve?" I asked.

Hunter nodded, *yes.*

Metamorphosis said, "The Open Road awaits us, my son."

Nyx whistled and pointed at the sea cliffs above us.

Within seconds, Ava the gryphon soared down and landed on the grotto floor.

Erda waved to us from her saddle.

Hunter hugged me tightly. "Please give my love to Mom and Dad and Ruby and Alexander and Zachary and Emily and Grace and Astrid and Pearl and Crystal and Sebastian and Pooh. Tell them how much I miss them."

He looked out across the Sea of Esteem. "I don't know how long it will take me to find Eve."

"Think positive, Hunter," I said. "All things happen in perfect order."

My brother and Metamorphosis looked at each other and smiled.

The sage said, "Your wise sister has discovered a Universal Truth, one of the Secrets of the Universe."

Hunter hugged me again and kissed my cheek.

He pointed to the gryphon. "This time, do you think you can make it home safely?"

I burst into tears. Not knowing when I would see Hunter again, if ever, I could not control my emotions.

"I'll be careful," I said, sobbing and hugging him tighter and longer than I ever had.

"Come, Princess Julia," Nyx said. "Our ride awaits us."

I turned and hugged Metamorphosis. The sage held me with two arms, patted my shoulder with one hand, and held the side of my face with the other hand.

He lowered his bearded chin and looked over the top of his spectacles. "I wish you all the joy that a person can wish."

I wiped the tears from my eyes, turned, and hugged my twin brother one last time.

"I love you, Hunter."

"I love you too, Julia."

The Sage of the Ages pointed to Ava. "The gryphon of legend awaits you, young lady. Godspeed."

Nyx took my hand and led me across the grotto. I gazed out through the rock archway at Kraken's fleeing ship. The black sails faded over the horizon, into the fiery-red sky.

Torn between sadness and happiness, I mounted the gryphon. Happy that I would be returning home.

Sad because I might never see Hunter again.

"Aye, 'tis a good day ta fly," Erda said, pulling her goggles and leather cap over her braided red hair.

Ava ran, leaped off the grotto's ledge and flew through the archway.

Holding onto the saddle straps, I looked back at Hunter.

Standing next to Metamorphosis, my brother waved and raised his sword.

The blade gleamed in the two daystars of Millennium.

I waved back.

Taking a deep breath, I bid my twin brother farewell in my mind.

What I mean is, I knew that Momma had changed, so at that very moment, I stopped feeling guilty that I couldn't bring Hunter home.

I let that feeling go.

As Metamorphosis would say, "I stopped thinking like that".

The flight of the gryphon from Escalot to Time Island turned out to be the longest trip of my life, both time-wise and emotionally.

Nyx commanded Erda to fly straight through.

No stops.

No landings.

The gryphon master had packed ambrosia and extra water bags on her saddle.

If you've ever been on a long trip, you know the frustration of wanting to get where you're going. I've been known to be impatient on family vacations.

During our flight, Nyx taught me that a good traveler has no fixed plans and is not intent on arriving. Once that wisdom sunk in and I realized there was nothing I could do about getting to Time Island any faster, I settled in and enjoyed the flight of the gryphon.

Morph's philosophy about living in the moment, that there is only now, this moment, really helped me enjoy the final journey of my Millennium adventure.

With Hunter on my mind, I remained silent during our trip over Pellagus, over the Hills of Cleito and the Gates of Dawn, past Phoenix Hill, then northwest, up the Utopian River Gorge.

I witnessed the passing of a red and black sky before we reached the crater's rim.

When Ava soared down into the great crater, I said a silent prayer, knowing we had reached the halfway point to Time Island.

As we descended, Nyx pointed out Lupercal Cave, located along the narrow East Crater Trail that hugged the vertical granite cliffs, one hundred miles above the Sea of Circles.

Under a beautiful blue atmosphere, hang gliders crafted from dodo feathers and dragon leather dotted the sky.

Friendly pixies, boggarts, brownies, knockers, gnomes, and cave faeries waved to us as they rode upward on the rising warm air of the crater thermals.

A towering green waterfall spilled from the heavens to the abyss.

"That is Emerald Falls," Nyx said, explaining that the great Acheron, one of the Underworld's major subterranean rivers, flowed 3000 miles under the kingdom of Pellagus before emptying down the cliffs of Discordia.

The fluorescent-green water erupted from the southeast wall and plummeted fifty-five miles to the bottom of the crater.

Only fifty miles to go, I thought, with a sigh of relief.

Erda pointed to Celestial City.

Built on sheer granite walls, the pointed towers and cathedral arches of the majestic cliff metropolis could be seen from the crater's rim.

While I watched the coming of the red sky above me, I realized that I had witnessed the passing of a blue sky, and a red sky, and a blue sky, and a black sky, and a blue sky, and now, a second red sky.

More than a daynight had come and gone. That meant at least seventy days had passed me by on Earth since my last

Dreamtime. I asked Nyx how long I'd been on Millennium.

The sage replied, "You have been here for five daynights. Actually, six calendar daynights, from the 14th of Aries to the 19th of Aries, Year of the Dragon, 9001 A.E.."

She told me I could look at a Millennium calendar when we arrived at the ship.

All I cared about was I had been gone for seven to eight months.

Erda must have sensed my anxiety. She looked at her pocket watch, what she called a weary wheel, and shouted, "Aye, we best be puttin' spurs ta the nags!"

She yelled, "Hang on, Princess Julia," yanking down hard on the leather reins.

As the gryphon pulled in her black wings and went into an aerial dive, the gnome screamed, "Yahoo-hoooo-eeeee!"

And what a dive.

Straight down!

With my stomach in my throat, I held on tightly as Ava fell out of the sky.

Soaring at top speed, I enjoyed the most exhilarating ride of my life.

After a spiraling free fall, the smiling gnome with a front tooth missing turned and pointed down at the swirling fog.

Through the grey mist, I spotted the *Skipbladnir* below us, sailing the Sea of Circles.

The gryphon master pulled up on the reins, making Ava level off for a landing.

We circled and glided down to land on the wooden deck of the ancient ship.

Thank you, God, I thought, *I'm almost home.*

Sitting on the gryphon, I gazed up at the streaking white tails of comets and shooting stars disappearing beyond the rim of the crater as the Andromeda constellations carved their sparkling formations into the fiery-red sky.

Alfrigga greeted us as we dismounted the gryphon.

I shook Erda's tiny hand, thanking her for getting us safely aboard the *Skipbladnir*.

The gryphon master pulled up on the leather reins and Ava raced across the deck, leaped over the ship's brass railing, and soared high into the crimson atmosphere.

Nyx and I walked up the forecastle steps while the crew of half-orcs manned the deck. The cadence call bellowed from the bowels of the ship.

"Rrrooowww! Rrrooowww! Rrrooowww!"

The low reverberations of a medieval horn sounded from the crow's nest above us.

I looked up and Balder waved to me from the top of the main mast.

Standing on the forecastle deck, I asked Nyx, "How far are we from Time Island?"

"Behold the sacred place of galactic entry" she said, pointing beyond the ship's prow.

Rising from the Sea of Circles, the shard-like obelisk stood stark against the grey mist.

We're here, I thought. *Here already!*

On the deck below us, Captain Gog clanged the ship's bell, shouting, "Ya. Prepare ta droppin' der anchor!"

Nyx put her hand on my shoulder and said, "I must speak to the captain about preparing the skiff."

She placed her warm hand on my cheek. "Julia, I request that you take time to reflect on your Millennium journey. Carefully consider your decision to return to Earth."

The Utopian sage turned and walked down the forecastle steps to greet Captain Gog.

They disappeared below deck.

DAYNIGHT OF THE RAVEN

Chapter XX
Time Island

Here I stand on the deck of the *Skipbladnir,* under a red Millennium sky, staring out across the Sea of Circles at Time Island. Now that you know how I ended up here, on this ship at this exact moment in time, what would you do if you were me? Would you remain here, on Millennium, or would you return home, to Earth?

Since you know me really well by now, I imagine you have figured out what my decision is.

As I told you at the very beginning, my thoughts are clear and purposeful. More than any other time in my life, I know what I'm doing.

I've made the right choice.

Taking a deep breath of Millennium air, I see Nyx walking up the forecastle stairs, returning from her meeting with Captain Gog.

Here she comes, expecting my answer.

"Have you made your final decision?" the sage asks, standing at the top of the steps.

Staring confidently at Nyx, I point to Time Island.

No words are necessary.

Nodding in approval, the Utopian signals the captain to prepare the skiff.

We make our way down the stairs and across the deck to the ship's railing, where I bid farewell to Alfrigga and Balder.

Nyx and I follow Gog down a rope ladder.

We jump into the wooden boat.

The captain grabs the wooden oars with his huge hands and rows toward Time Island. We cut through the choppy waves, heading toward the black obelisk.

The cool sea spray hits my face.

I've never felt this alive. So free.

No regrets about leaving Millennium.

Home beckons me.

Arriving at the island, Captain Gog ties a rope to a mooring.

Timing the waves perfectly, Nyx and I jump onto the volcanic rock.

While the captain waits in the skiff, I follow the Utopian up the rope ladder onto the smooth rock surface of Time Island.

Nyx and I stand in the center of the sacred platform.

She touches my shoulder and tells me, "You have made the highest choice, Princess Julia."

Raising my eyebrows, I ask, "Metamorphosis talked about making the highest choice. What exactly does that mean? How do I really know when I've made the right decision?"

"Allow me to enlighten you," Nyx says, wiggling her whiskers.

"Making the highest choice is about opposites. These opposites create the great primal paradox."

"Paradox?" I ask.

Nyx's blue-green eyes sparkle as she says, "True words appear paradoxical. When confronted with a choice, that choice always involves opposites."

"Do you mean right or wrong? Good and evil?"

"Exactly. I offer you the answer to your dilemma. When faced with a choice or question involving two opposites, always choose the natural path, the truth. And if you are not certain, always err on the side of compassion. Love."

"How do I do that?"

"Rather than being forceful, be humble. Rather than grasping, let go. Rather than being rigid, be flexible. Rather than taking action, take no action. Be patient and do nothing."

"That's it? The best action is non action?"

"Yes. I suggest you live the elusive paradox. Whatever you have been conditioned to believe, I ask you to consider the exact opposite view. When you think another person is wrong and do not agree with them, hold your tongue and be silent. Never argue again."

"That's the answer to solving all my problems?"

"There are no problems, only solutions. I suggest you embrace every problem as an opportunity for growth."

"I think I understand."

"Begin looking for the opposites in everything. Stop choosing one over the other. This shall keep you from being upset and arguing and worrying about whether you are right or wrong."

"I'll try the primal paradox when I get home."

Nyx grins. "I shall share my favorite paradox with you. 'Fulfill the needs of others and your own needs shall be fulfilled. Rather than putting yourself first, put yourself last, and you shall end up ahead.'"

"I like that one."

"I thought you would. This is because your purpose on Earth is to help others. Based on this highest of all choices, your life shall be blessed with endless bliss and contentment. As Metamorphosis reminds us, 'The greatest virtue is to act without a sense of self. The greatest kindness is to give without consideration.'"

"Now I understand how to make the highest choice."

"Wonderful," says Nyx, smiling. "Anything else on your mind?"

"I'm going to be a sage like you someday."

"We all need a purpose in life. Your choice is a wise and noble one."

"When I return home, is it really possible for me to make a difference, change the world?"

"All things are possible."

"Anything?"

"Just imagine all the possible possibilities. Your desire to change your world is but one choice, one, of the endless choices. Change your thoughts and the world changes with you. Miracles happen every moment in the universe. When you return home, be in the awe of the miracles around you. When you stop and observe, when you live in the moment, you shall see the miracles."

Contemplating her words, I grab my Crystal Triamulet hanging from the gold chain around my neck and ask, "What must I do to get home?"

"Simply lie here, close your eyes, and go to sleep. You shall awaken on Earth."

"Will you stay here with me?"

"I shall wait with Gog in the skiff."

"What happens to *this* body when my soul returns to Earth?"

"We take your Millennium body on the *Skipbladnir* to the sacred Place of Emergence, a cave leading to the Underworld. Your body remains there in a perfect, ageless condition, awaiting the return of your soul."

"What if I never come back here?"

"Your Millennium body dies when your Earth body perishes. Only your soul survives."

"And if I decide to return here sometime in the future?"

"Then, your Earth body dies when your Millennium body perishes."

"That means I would be in a coma for decades on Earth!"

"Exactly. This is why many Earthlings leave early. They do not want to return home and find their parents and brothers and sisters and friends long gone. Dead."

"When you take this Millennium body to the cave in the Underworld, is my father's body there?"

"Yes, as is Professor Van Campbell's, and all the other Earth visitors."

Rubbing my Triamulet between my fingers, I contemplate the sage's explanation of being in two bodies on two planets, one alive and one in a coma. I try to imagine *this* body lying next to my father's body in a cave in the Underworld.

Nyx looks up into the starry red sky and breathes deeply, holding her arms up to the heavens. A sea of twinkling stars surround her head like a glowing halo.

She brings her hands down on my shoulders and gazes into my eyes.

I gaze back into her tranquil face as she says, "Earth awaits you. When you return home, I know you shall live the wisdom that Metamorphosis and I have taught you. I see in your eyes that you hear the silent music in my words, the music of the cosmos.

"Practice the Universal Truths and your life shall be turned inside out and upside down. You shall not recognize your former life, your previous way of thinking, for you shall have discovered the Great Way, the path to happiness. Follow it, and you shall successfully navigate the storms of time and space."

I sigh and say, "I've lived through enough storms. I just want to be happy."

"Listen carefully and expand your mind, Princess Julia. When you return home to your family, embrace love as your mantra. Remain at peace with yourself and do not allow the dark forces, the Extractors on Earth, to affect you in any way, shape or form.

"Remember, you have no enemies; I speak of those who suffer from the ego-driven *Emotional Virus,* the *Dark Essence.* Forgive them; they are not aware of their illness. They have yet to travel the Open Road and walk the highest path, the Great Way. We are all one. What we do to others, we do to ourselves."

Nyx holds up a quieting hand, reminding me that silence is my friend.

"When you return to Earth, become a great teacher. With calm words and actions, with confident humility, speak grandly so that others feel your love and wisdom, so they follow you on the high road, the path to happiness.

"When you return, do not complain or make excuses for yourself or your government. Change the way things are. Make a difference by seeking the supreme truth."

"I will. I promise."

The sage smiles, seeing the contentment in my eyes.

I feel so peaceful right now.

Like no one can harm me.

So invincible.

She says, "Morph's teachings are easy to understand and easy to practice; yet so few in this universe understand, and so few are able to practice. Those who know him are rare indeed."

The Utopian places her hand on her chest, over her heart. "I wish you all the happiness in the universe."

Tears run down my cheeks.

I can't stop crying as I gaze at her beautiful face and say, "I love you, Nyx."

She places her furry fist on her chest and taps her heart.

"I shall always be here with you. All ways, and for all time."

I hug the sage, tightly.

"Have a safe journey home, Princess Julia. You shall feel my positive energy all the way across the universe."

She smiles, turns away, and walks across the black rock.

Nyx the Utopian waves and climbs down the rope ladder, disappearing over the edge of the obelisk.

Taking a deep, relaxing breath, I lie down on the sacred rock, running my hands over the smooth surface, knowing my name will be chiseled in the black granite after I leave.

After my spirit leaves my Millennium body.

Julia Wainright's name will be next to Wayland M. Wainright, along with all the other famous Earth visitors who have been to Planet Millennium.

Staring into the crimson atmosphere, the white heavenly bodies dance on the vast stage of the cosmos. Through the drifting patches of ghostly fog, a silver mist encircles Time Island, caressing her body while she stands proud and tall, welcoming the endless waves from her friend, the Sea of Circles.

This all seems like a mystical dream.

I remember Nyx telling me, "You remind me of a girl who dreams she is a beautiful butterfly, and when she awakens, she wonders if she is now a butterfly dreaming she is a beautiful girl."

Whispering, "Goodbye, Millennium," I close my eyes.

My thoughts are only of my family.

Of my Jeremy.

Of my home.

Hunter

Chapter XXI
Mother Earth

Traveling the astral highway at the speed of thought, I'm going home, back to Earth. Feeling weightless, a warm illumination overtakes my body, radiating and absorbing itself within my spirit, my soul. The glowing light inside me shines across the vast universe. A fantastic white light flashes and then pulsates within my mind. The light has *become* me as I travel through space and time.

Across the cosmos at the speed of thought.

As the light carries my formless spirit through another dimension, I accelerate from slow motion to a lightning-fast warp speed.

Everything is happening at once; yet, all things remain the same.

Time stands still as my invisible self, my non-being, rockets through the endless matrix of thought energy.

A timeless void overwhelms me, a magical place with no earth and no sky.

No physical boundaries.

The experience is real, nothing like a dream.

The warm afterglow in my soul feels ageless. It lasts but a moment in time and yet, it transcends an entire lifetime.

I feel the end of my astral journey when the uplifting, inner white light dims within me.

The warm illumination disappears and my body becomes heavy again.

My bright world goes dark.

I know exactly what has happened.

I have arrived.

My spirit has entered my Earth body.

I wake up.

Open my eyes.

The big screen above my hospital bed has a message typed in large black letters:

MERRY CHRISTMAS, JULIA.
WELCOME HOME!

The smell of a freshly cut pine and burning logs on the fire bring back fond childhood memories.

Opening presents.

Momma laughing with Daddy while they decorate the tree.

Hunter and I waking up early and sneaking downstairs to see what Santa brought us.

My family sits in the dining room eating.

The chatter and laughter and rattling of silverware on my mother's prized china makes me grin. The smell of turkey with dressing and smoked ham with candied yams makes my mouth water.

Lifting my hand to my face, I *know* I'm no longer in a coma.

Not paralyzed anymore.

Sitting up, I discover that Hunter and I are the only ones in the room.

Seeing my reflection in the mirror on the opposite wall, Momma has me all dolled up for the holidays.

Lipstick.

Makeup.

My hair curled.

My nails polished.

One good thing about being in a coma, you can't chew your nails!

A ten-foot-tall green tree stands next to the fireplace.

Twinkling white lights with purple garland, gold ornaments, and silver tinsel adorn the branches.

The crackling fire gives the room a warm glow.

God, I love being home for Christmas.

Outside, the final rays of sunshine hide behind the grey and yellow clouds. The dark-blue ocean looks angry, covered in white caps. The cypress trees and Monterey pines on the cliffs behind our home bend and twist to the rhythm of the swirling winds. Sycamore leaves blow against our picture bay window.

My brother, expressionless, lies in bed across the room from me. I have this lasting image of him wearing his medieval clothing, waving his noble sword as he stands next to Metamorphosis.

Surprisingly, Hunter and I no longer have tubes and wires attached to our bodies.

Daddy and his doctors finally figured out that I do not need a feeding tube and all the other contraptions they hooked to my body the past seven months. As Elizabeth Dow told my mother, "Coma-X is unique."

My BCI cap hangs next to my bed, unplugged. That means they expect me to wake up. I won't disappoint them.

My fashion-minded mother has dressed me in a red satin top and bottom, "Like the exquisite evening wear that movie stars prance around in," as she would say.

I reach down and grab my Crystal Triamulet.

The gold medallion and necklace has materialized. The sacred amulet made the galactic journey home with me.

The video cameras are running, so I hold up the golden charm and smile.

Just in case my video goes viral on the Internet again.

Just kidding.

It better not!

Pulling the sheets back, I sit on the edge of my hospital bed. Wiggling my toes, I look down to make sure they all work. I swear, my body does not feel like I've been lying in bed for almost eight months.

Stepping down onto the hardwood floor, I feel so alive and energized, like a child again. I know I sound giddy, but I can't help it.

I'm nervous to see my family, especially Momma.

I pray she is sober. Hope she's kept her promise to stop drinking.

Walking into the dining room, I announce, "Hi everybody, I'm home."

What else am I supposed to say?

Everyone stops and stares at me.

I wish I had a camera.

In shock, their mouths open and their eyes stare in amazement.

Momma drops her silverware and screams, putting her hands over her mouth.

All my sisters scream. Except for Ruby, who just smirks and gives me a thumbs up.

I smile and shrug my shoulders, like nothing has ever happened.

Daddy jumps out of his chair and runs to me, hugging me tightly.

While I squeeze him, my family rushes over to hug and kiss me.

Except Momma.

She sits there with her hands over her face, crying her eyes out.

I'm surprised to see Elizabeth Dow at the table.

And there sits Professor Johan and Dr. Shankar, shaking each other's hands.

"Don't they have homes? It's Christmas Eve!" as Momma once said.

Pooh wags his tail while he licks my feet. Maddie rubs her furry body and tail against my leg.

Complete chaos at the Wainright house.

I love it.

Welcome home!

My brothers and sisters bombard me with questions. I can't get a word in.

Baby Sebastian pulls on my pants leg. I pick him up and hold him in my arms. He grabs my Crystal Triamulet and tries to put it in his mouth.

"No, sweetheart," I say. "We don't want to swallow the crystal."

"A crystal?" Daddy asks. "You're wearing a Triamulet with a crystal!"

I nod, *yes.*

My father can't take his eyes off the sparkling gem.

"Isn't it beautiful," I say, taking the medallion out of Sebastian's hand and dropping it down my satin top.

Elizabeth comes over and gives me a special hug.

By *special* I mean, she and I have an out-of-this-world connection:

Dreamtime.

I stare at Momma's place setting.

No wine bottles on the table. No vodka. No whiskey.

No pill bottles.

My mother is sober. That changes everything.

After Professor Johan hugs me and Dr. Shankar shakes my hand, my mother asks everyone to leave the room.

"Go gather round the tree," she says. "We'll open one gift tonight."

Daddy points to the family room. "Come on, kids. Your mother wants to welcome Julia home."

The children laugh and giggle, running past me toward the Christmas tree. Our three guests follow Daddy out of the dining room.

"Are we opening gifts early," I ask Momma.

"It can't hurt to open one present the night before

Christmas," she says, rushing toward me with tears in her eyes.

She runs into my arms. "You really *have* come home. I knew you would. I'm so sorry, sweetheart."

I raise her chin with my hand. "Momma, we don't need to talk about my journals anymore. I forgive you."

Before she answers, I place my index finger on her lips.

"There is no need to apologize. I don't live in the past anymore. Everything that's happened before this moment no longer matters. All is forgiven."

My mother smiles. "All right. But I still need to tell you how sorry I am. That's the last time you'll hear it from me, I promise."

"I accept your apology."

"That makes me so happy, Julia."

"I know what a great mother you can be."

"I can't turn back the clock. I'll make sure your brothers and sisters never go through what you did, that they get the best of me. Even Ruby!"

We both laugh, holding hands.

Momma looks through the doorway into the family room. Hunter lies in his hospital bed with a red Santa cap on his head.

"Is he coming home?" she asks.

"I wish I could tell you 'yes', but I don't know. Maybe not."

"I've been thinking about this Eve girl, the one he's in love with." She places her hand over her heart. "It's not about Eve, or love. It's about Hunter's relationship with his father. How they would fight and argue all the time. Your father blames himself for Hunter's unwillingness to come home."

"It's not Daddy," I say, squeezing her hands. "It really *is* love. Hunter thinks of nothing but Eve. I saw the look in his eyes."

"So, my son *is* happy?"

"He's the happiest I've ever seen him."

"I can live with that. It's just that I miss him so much."

"He told me to tell you he misses you very much. He sends his love."

Momma closes her eyes. "I feel his presence in this house. I don't mean his comatose body, I mean his spirit."

"You are feeling his thought waves, his positive energy. I have learned that thoughts travel all the way across the universe. I know he thinks of you all the time."

"Thank you, I needed to hear that. Welcome home, Julia Rose."

My mother hugs me again, tightly.

"Can I get you something to eat?" she asks.

"It's really weird, but after a 200-million-light-years-from-home journey across the universe, I'm not hungry right now."

Momma laughs and smiles. "You haven't lost your sense of humor, young lady."

Grinning, I say, "I've been told I can be witty at times."

Rolling her eyes, she says, "Oh, how I remember some of the clever things you said as a young girl."

She points to the twice-as-long-as-normal dinner table.

"Look at this mess. That's what I get for having so many children."

Laughing, I ask, "Do you want me to help you with the dishes?"

"Don't worry, the whole family does them now. Or, I have the housekeeper to help me."

Momma throws her hands in the air. "Let's not talk about housework, let's go open presents. I got you something. I had this feeling you'd be home for Christmas."

Pointing to the red phone on the kitchen wall, I announce, "I need to call Jeremy."

"Can you wait until we open presents?" she asks. "You can wait another hour. Spend some time with your family. Please?"

Giving in, I say, "Okay, Momma. One hour."

I want to tell her, "No", but I remind myself, *another hour can't hurt.*

Dying to see Jeremy. Can't wait for my second kiss.

But this time, I'll be the one to kiss *him* on the lips.

Glancing at the kitchen wall clock, I notice it's almost ten o'clock.

No problem.

Plenty of time. Jeremy will stay up late tonight, it's Christmas Eve.

My mother tugs the sleeve to my satin top. "Would you like to change into something else?"

"Not right now. I'll change before I see Jeremy."

We walk arm in arm into the family room, my thoughts spinning.

My relationship with my mother has changed forever.

All we need is for Hunter to come home and we can be a family again.

Don't hold your breath, Julia. He might be gone for years.

Or, worse yet, Momma might never see him again.

God, there I go again with negative thoughts.

Stop!

Stop thinking like that, Julia Wainright.

There is nothing I can do about my brother.

At least we have his Coma-X body at home.

Okay, maybe it's not his better half, but it's better than nothing. Right?

As long as his Earth body is breathing we know he's alive on Millennium.

My mother and I sit together on the white sofa next to the Christmas tree.

Everyone gawks at me. Even the dog and cat.

Elizabeth won't quit staring at me. Our eyes lock and we smile. We share a confident, *I-know-what-you-know* grin.

She's wearing her Crystal Triamulet on the outside of her black cashmere sweater. I wonder if she and I are the only ones on Earth wearing the special medallions that hold such awesome power.

Daddy hands out one gift at a time.

He looks great. Trim and fit.

His clean-shaven face reminds me of the father I grew up with.

My brothers and sisters rip through the wrappings and ribbons, laughing and screaming.

Momma jumps up, retrieves a gold-paper-wrapped present from under the tree.

She hands me the gift.

I can't believe I'm sitting here with my family opening presents.

It seems like just a few hours ago I battled hobgoblin pirates and beastmen and Extractors.

Actually, it *was* just a moment ago in time.

The gold-foil paper and red ribbon takes me a moment to unwrap.

Opening the box, I stare at a black leather book.

What's this?

A classic novel?

The embossed, gold-leafed title reads:

JULIA'S JOURNAL
2016

Holding back my tears, I hug Momma and notice a different, subtle fragrance about her.

Her perfume is new. Just like her new attitude.

"I have a lot to write about," I tell her, holding up the book. "All positive!"

Momma smiles. "Nothing but good things will go in your diary from now on."

My brothers and sisters run up to my mother to hug and thank her for their gifts.

As I observe her laugh and enjoy her children, I realize that Momma has found her own happiness and didn't need my help.

Thank you for your wisdom, Metamorphosis.

After all the confusion of gift opening, Daddy walks over to Momma and me to announce he has to drive to the airport to pick up a guest, that he is running late, that he will be back before midnight. Without hugging any of us kids or saying goodbye, he puts on his overcoat and rushes out the front door.

Momma tells me that he told her earlier that he had to pick up a visitor at the airport, a Coma-X survivor who is flying in from Australia. He told her that the person would be staying at our home for a few days.

"Don't worry," she says, "he'll be right back. Security guards stay with your father at all times."

Hmmm. Christmas Eve is an odd time to pick someone up from the airport. Who's this person from Australia?

My thoughts turn to Jeremy. Just as I begin to ask my mother about using the phone to call him, Professor Johan comes over and sits next to me.

Grinning, he says, "Dr. Shankar wants to examine your Crystal Triamulet."

I hold my hand against my chest, wanting to say, *no.*

My intuition tells me to *never* take off the medallion.

Never.

"I don't know, Professor," I say. "Can we talk about this in the morning?"

"Hari is leaving this evening," the professor says. "He just needs it for a short while, maybe twenty minutes. He needs to measure the medallion, weigh it, and take some photos."

Just for a few minutes, I tell myself. *Don't be difficult. They'll bring it right back.*

Elizabeth Dow comes over to tell me, "Don't worry Julia. They examined my medallion and I got it right back."

Pulling the gold chain up and over my head, I place the Triamulet in Professor Johan's hand.

The crystal sparkles in the twinkling lights.

"Okay," I say, "but please bring it back as soon as you're finished. I promised myself I would never take it off."

The professor smiles and motions to Dr. Shankar, *come with me.*

The two of them walk out of the room, down the corridor toward the library.

As I watch my precious medallion leave the room, I feel anxious, like something isn't quite right. Like when I would lend my books to Ruby and she never returned them.

Feeling confused, I think, *Julia, you're home now. Relax, enjoy your family. Your Triamulet is in good hands. When you get it back, guard it with your life.*

"Okay, kids," Momma yells, "time for bed. Santa is coming. You don't want him to see you tonight. Take your gifts upstairs."

Emily, Grace, and Astrid come running over to me and shout, "We don't want to go to bed. We want to visit Julia!"

"You'll have plenty of time to see your sister in the morning," Momma said. "Now get to bed, girls. Santa's reindeer are on their way."

My brothers and sisters hug and kiss me before they run up the stairs to their bedrooms.

Holiday music plays on my father's stereo. Every year, he and my mother put on those old scratchy records on his turntable. Can you believe that? He still has vinyl albums, what he calls "licorice pizzas". They are as old as my grandparents.

Now that I've been to Millennium, I realize my grandparents aren't so old after all.

"Silent Night" plays as Elizabeth, Momma, and I sit by the warm fireplace.

The wind whips leaves and twigs against the picture bay window while yuletide logs pop and crackle in the blazing fire.

I kneel down and pick up the torn wrappings and ribbons littering the floor.

"Julia," my mother says, "the housekeeper's coming in the morning. Leave that."

Dropping the crinkled paper, I sit back on the sofa.

"How about some herbal tea?" Momma asks.

Elizabeth nods and my mother hurries toward the kitchen, wearing her plaid holiday apron.

She turns and says, "I have so many questions I want to ask you."

I nod at my mother as Elizabeth asks, "How are you, young lady?"

"Fine," I tell Ms. Dow. "A bit bewildered, but feeling great."

"Please, call me Elizabeth."

"Thank you for helping my mother through all her problems. Without you, she would never have let me wear the BCI cap. I overheard the advice you gave her while I was in my coma. You had such a calming effect on her."

"Your mother just needed someone to believe in, a woman she trusted."

"She believes in you, I can tell."

The tea kettle whistles on the kitchen stove while Momma sings, "Hark the Herald Angels Sing".

"Are you staying here, at our house?" I ask.

"Your father requested that I be here when you awakened. We figured you'd be here around Thanksgiving, but when you didn't wake up, he asked me to stay until you did."

"I had some serious delays on my return trip. I almost didn't make it home."

She raises her eyebrows. "I can only imagine. Is that how you ended up with a Crystal Triamulet?"

"Ex stole my original gold medallion."

Before she could respond, I ask, "How did you lose *your* first Triamulet?"

"Hocus stole mine."

"I know who he is! He's the Extractor that Hunter fought in the Forest Primeval."

"Quite right. They call him the Show-Off Braggart. And believe me, I know how he got his name. He would not stop bragging about himself and all the imaginary adventures he has been on. So full of himself, he really loved to hear himself talk!"

I laugh. "He must have that *Virus,* the *Dark Essence* that Nyx explained to me. The emotional disease that inflates people's egos and makes them believe they are better than everyone else."

"Quite right. All the Extractors suffer from the *Virus.* It is highly contagious."

"How did you escape Hocus?"

"The sea snake captain and his crew of pirates were defeated by Metamorphosis and Pendragon the Utopian. They rescued me from the *Manzet.*"

"A ship?"

"Yes. My rescue took place on the Sargasso Sea, in the kingdom of Sallum, on the Daynight of the Dragon."

Elizabeth holds up her hand. "I want to hear about your adventure. I'm afraid mine is old news around here. Tell me about Ex."

Just as I begin to explain my battle with Ex and the Extractors, my mother prances into the room and announces, "Sugar cookies and lemon tea. Doesn't that sound delicious?"

"Yes, Momma," I say, grinning at Elizabeth.

"We'll talk later, dearie," she says, as my mother places a silver tray on the coffee table.

"I need to call Jeremy," I say. "Now!"

"All right," Momma replies, "I'll go get my cell phone."

Cell phone? My mother has really come of age, I think. *She probably has her own computer by now!*

Taking a bite of sugar cookie, I close my eyes to savor the sweet taste while I listen to Nat King Cole sing, "The Christmas Song".

Daddy's favorite holiday song.

Home, sweet, home, I think. *Safe and secure with my family.*

My thoughts are interrupted by the sound of hurried footsteps running down the marble corridor toward the family room.

Opening my eyes, I sense something has happened.

Dr. Shankar runs into the room shouting, "You father just

pushed Josef and me out of the library and locked the door!"

But Daddy's gone to the airport, I think. *What is he doing back home?*

"Where's my Triamulet?" I ask.

Hari points to the corridor. "In the library."

Momma and I jump up, spilling the tray of tea and cookies. Her white china tea pot shatters on the hardwood floor.

"We need the key to the library!" Hari shouts. "Hurry!"

"I'll get it," my mother yells, running up the stairs.

Elizabeth shuffles toward the library in her red high heels.

Sprinting past her, I race down the west corridor to Professor Johan, who stands at the library entrance, banging on the doors and begging my father, "Open up, Wayland! Please, let me in!

"Where is my Crystal Triamulet?" I ask.

The professor points to the library. "With your father."

I push him out of the way and bang on the mahogany doors.

"Daddy, it's me. Let me in. Now!"

Placing my ear to the door, I think, *What's going on? What's he doing in there?*

"I have the key!" Momma shouts as she and Elizabeth run toward me.

Behind them, Dr. Shankar stands at the end of the corridor telling Ruby to keep the children upstairs.

The howling wind whips pine tree twigs and leaves against the glass of the west corridor windows.

My mother, breathing heavily, fumbles with the chrome key.

Grabbing her shaking hand, I yell, "Give it to me."

Jamming the key into the lock, I turn the brass knobs and push the library doors open.

The room is dark, except for the twinkling bulbs on the Christmas tree and the aquarium lights.

Momma turns on the light switch.

I can't believe my eyes.

The cabinet!

Below the aquarium, the louver doors stand wide open.

Running across the room, I slide on my knees on the marble floor and stick my head into the open cabinet. The doors on the other side, the same ones Hunter and I snuck through so many times as children, are wide open.

Oh my God. The garage door is open!

The freezing wind blows in my face as I climb through the cabinet and into the twelve-car garage. Daddy's auto court.

"Julia, where are you going?" Momma yells.

My heart races, looking for my father.

I collapse to my knees. His favorite black sports car is gone.

The freezing wind blows my hair in my face while I stare down our winding driveway that leads to the front entrance of our estate.

Running back to the cabinet, I scream, "Daddy's gone! He has my Triamulet! Call security! Don't let him through the gates!"

Guided by the outdoor lights, I run down the red-brick driveway.

My legs feel heavy. I could run much faster on Millennium.

Gusts of cold ocean wind cut through my thin satin outfit.

Numb, I can't feel a thing.

On my left, two agents run toward me. They have their pistols drawn.

I sprint as fast as I can.

Faster, Julia. Run faster!

Reaching the bend at the driveway entrance, my heart sinks.

Two guards stand by the front iron gates.

No sports car.

No Daddy.

I stop and gasp for air, watching my hot breath turn into steamy vapor. The freezing air hurts my lungs as the windstorm whips my hair across my face.

The two agents catch up to me and ask me what I'm doing outside?

Breathless, I point to the guards standing at the entry gates and yell, "Find out…if my father…has left the grounds."

While one of the agents calls on her phone, Hari and the professor come running up.

"Calm down, Julia," Professor Johan yells over the sound of the howling winds.

He takes off his jacket and wraps it over my shoulders. "You're barefooted. Let's get you inside."

"Ms. Wainright," the agent yells, "approximately ten minutes ago, our surveillance team followed your father out the gate."

"They have to stop him!" I shout. "Make him come back home!"

"Settle down, young lady," the female agent yells. "What's this all about?"

Professor Johan tells her, "Please call us and let us know where Dr. Wainright is. Have him contact us as soon as he stops his car. Don't let him out of your sight."

"That's our job," the agent responds, "to never let him out of our sight."

"Just have Wayland call us as soon as possible." Dr. Shankar yells, frowning.

The two agents nod and head toward the entry gate.

Professor Johan and Hari escort me back to the house.

My feet are freezing as I open the front door and hurry into the family room.

I stand next to the fire, shivering.

After Momma cleans up the spilled cookies and the broken tea pot mess, she sits on the sofa, staring at me with a blank look on her face.

"Daddy took a ride in his sports car," I say, my voice quivering. "The agents are following him. They'll have him call us when he stops."

Hari and Professor Johan return to the library.

Elizabeth, sitting next to my mother on the sofa, looks at me with a frown on her face. She senses, like I do, that Daddy's planning to do something news worthy.

But what?

My mother refuses to cry. Biting her lip, she stares at the fire, her face expressionless.

The grandfather clock chimes at midnight.

12:00 a.m..

Twelve gongs drown out the holiday music.

Elizabeth tells my mother and me, "Merry Christmas."

Momma stands, marches across the room and turns off the holiday music by screeching the needle across the vinyl record.

Elizabeth and I jump from the loud noise.

"It's Christmas, for God's sake," Momma says. "What is Wayland thinking?"

She mopes to the bay window and stares at the trees whipping back and forth. A yellow, three-quarter moon hides behind fast moving clouds.

"What am I going to tell the children if their father's not here in the morning?"

"Don't worry," I say, "he's on his way home at this very minute."

I know better. But what else am I going to say?

My mother returns to the sofa and we three women sit in silence, staring at the decorations on the tree and the thirteen red stockings hung from the fireplace mantle.

I hold the cordless phone. The agents will call me any minute now. My mind is on Jeremy. I still haven't called him. I'm too upset right now. What would I say to him?

"Hello, my love," I mumble to myself, "I'm home and, oh, by the way, turn on the news. That's my father being chased by federal agents down Highway One!"

I'll phone him in the morning. When things have settled down. When Jeremy hears about my father, he'll know the Wainrights really *are* crazy!

The magic crystal in Elizabeth's gold Triamulet sparkles with the reflection of the twinkle lights.

I touch my chest, knowing that *my* medallion is missing.

Like a foolish little girl, I've lost track of my most prized possession.

1:00 a.m..

As the grandfather clock chimes and gongs once, the telephone rings.

"Hello," I answer.

It's the agent who followed Daddy.

Asks me if I'm Mrs. Wainright.

I tell him, "Yes", just in case the news is negative. Don't want my mother getting more upset than she already is.

"Go ahead," I say, trying to remain calm while I stare at Momma's face.

The agent tells me:

Dr. Wainright has outrun the federal agents in his Aston Martin sports car.

Turned off his lights and lost them somewhere on the Seventeen Mile Drive.

His car is so fast it out ran the Paparazzi motorcycles.

They think he headed north, they are not sure.

They will call me back with an update.

Daddy has my Triamulet, I think. *What's he going to do with it?*

"Call me as soon as you know something," I say, my voice quivering.

My mother knows by the look on my face that something is wrong.

"They're not sure where Daddy is," I announce.

"Your father is scaring me to death," she replies.

Elizabeth grabs her hand. "Calm down, Gloria. Your husband has been through a lot this past year. I'm sure he just needs to get away and think for a while."

I hope she knows my father better than I do. I think he's planning something with the news media. He's so obsessed with clearing his name and proving that Millennium exists.

2:00 a.m..

No one talks.

We listen to the *beep—beep—beep—beep* of Hunter's monitoring equipment.

What is there to say?

It feels like that day Daddy returned from the hospital. We all remember that horrible day the evil spirits stole the happiness from our home. The only other sounds have been the two chimes from the grandfather clock and the crackling fire and the winter wind blowing her stormy breath against our home.

Professor Johan and Dr. Shankar return from the library. While Hari stands by the fire, the professor hands me a yellow piece of paper.

"Your father left this on his desk," he says.

The hand-written note from Daddy reads:

Be back as soon as possible...

I show the note to my mother.

"Good news," I say. "He'll be home soon."

"Your father can really mess up the holidays," she says, getting up off the sofa and placing another log on the fire.

Professor Johan and Dr. Shankar stand across the room viewing the video cameras, scribbling notes on their yellow pads. The professor says, "We have the Triamulet materializing around Julia's neck as she's waking up. Wayland will be pleased that we have captured the event on film."

Elizabeth sits on the piano stool by the picture bay window, staring at the reflection of the yellow moon on top of the restless ocean waves. The winter gale blows leaves and pine needles against the glass.

Below our home, the pounding surf crashes into the rocky shore.

3:00 a.m..

Three gongs of the grandfather clock and no word from my father.

Upstairs, the children giggle.

Remember how it was impossible to sleep on Christmas Eve? Hunter and I would sit at the top of the stairs, waiting for Santa Claus to come down the chimney.

The phone rings. I swallow and answer.

"Mrs. Wainright?"

"Yes. Go ahead."

"We have some bad news."

I close my eyes and listen, my fingers crossed. Praying.

"We have located your husband's black Aston Martin parked at a lookout point on Highway One, near Big Sur. We observed him in a prone position in the vehicle. At first we thought he was sleeping or passed out from drinking too much. Dr. Wainright was unconscious. He has been diagnosed as being in some sort of a coma, according to the paramedics."

"Was he wearing a gold necklace with a medallion?" I ask.

"No ma'am," he replies.

What am I going to tell Momma? I think. *The truth, Julia. Remember what Daddy taught you. Always tell the truth.*

In shock, I put the phone down and announce, "Daddy's in the hospital."

My mother stands and puts her hand over her mouth.

Ms. Dow jumps up and puts her arm around Momma.

"A car accident?" Elizabeth asks.

"No," I answer.

"Did he drink too much?" Professor Johan asks.

I shake my head, *no.*

The professor sits in Momma's rocking chair, leans forward, and buries his face in his hands.

"What then?" my mother asks.

I walk over with my arms extended to hug my mother.

She pushes me back and holds my shoulders.

"Tell me, Julia, what has happened to your father?"

Tears run down my face.

Momma looks straight into my eyes and asks, "A coma?"

Staring back, I can't answer her.

"He's in another coma, isn't he!"

Momma knows.

Elizabeth knows.

Professor Johan and Dr. Shankar know.

Our father has left his family again for Millennium.

My mother places her warm hand on the side of my face and asks, "Can you take care of the children? I am going to the hospital to be with your father."

Kissing her cheek, I say, "Of course, Momma. I'll take care of everything. I've had lots of practice."

Holding back her emotions, she says, "When I bring your father home, do you mind if he uses your bed for a few days?"

Staring at my enamel-pink home on wheels, I try to imagine Daddy lying there next to Hunter.

Momma bursts into tears and runs up the stairs. I hear the children crying.

Needing to clear my head, I go to Hunter and stand by his bed. Holding his hand, I wonder how my brother will react when he meets his father on Millennium.

I think about how Daddy will awaken in that cave in the Underworld, the Place of Emergence.

He'll see my Millennium body lying next to him.

This all seems so impossible.

Professor Johan and Hari talk on their cell phones, making arrangements to drive my mother to the hospital.

Elizabeth walks over and stands across the bed from me, holding Hunter's other hand.

She says, "All things happen in perfect order. There are no accidents in the universe."

I look at my twin brother, then I gaze into Elizabeth's green eyes.

We smile, as if we know each other's thoughts.

She and I have been taught the Secrets of the Universe. We share the female energy, the feminine mystique.

"Events unfold at the right and perfect time," she says. "Your father has decided to settle his affairs with Hunter. Who knows, they might *both* be home in a few weeks."

Positive thinking.

But the truth is, they may *never* come home.

While Elizabeth feels Hunter's forehead with the back of her hand, I can't take my eyes off her sparkling crystal.

Her gold medallion beckons to me.

My thoughts are clear and purposeful.

I have made my decision.

I will borrow her Crystal Triamulet.

Just for a few days.

If she refuses, I'll *borrow* the necklace when she's asleep.

I'm sure she'll understand.

You understand, don't you?

So I can go get Daddy, bring him home.

Nyx

Metamorphosis

Cernunnos

Pendragon

Bodvar

Barbus

Captain
Kraken

307

"I wish you all the joy that you can wish."

—Metamorphosis, Sage of the Ages

www.ingramcontent.com/pod-product-compliance
Lightning Source LLC
Chambersburg PA
CBHW071250170626
46809CB00001B/152